This Book Belongs To

· CLIENT ·
PRIVILEGE

William G. Tapply

Delacorte
Press

The trademark Delacorte Press® is registered in the U.S.
Patent and Trademark Office.

Designed by Christine Swirnoff

Manufactured in the United States of America

Quality Printing and Binding by:
Berryville Graphics
P.O. Box 272
Berryville, VA 22611 U.S.A.

For Bud Sheridan

Acknowledgments

The author is grateful for the wise, tolerant, and informed counsel provided by the Middlesex County A.D.A.'s, especially Jane Rabe, who showed me around, answered my naive questions, and introduced me to her colleagues. Errors or distortions here are mine, not theirs. Rick Boyer helped me get the story straight, as usual. Jackie Farber and Jed Mattes were more patient with me than I deserved.

"Still his quality is not wisdom, but prudence. The lawyer's truth is not truth, but consistency, or a consistent expediency."

HENRY DAVID THOREAU
"On the Duty of Civil Disobedience"

· ONE ·

THE JUDGE'S YOUNG CLERK made a fist, extended one knuckle, and rapped twice on the veneer panel of the door. He paused, then pushed it open. He stuck his head into the room.

"Mr. Coyne, Your Honor?" he said.

I heard no reply, but the clerk withdrew his head and nodded to me. "Go ahead in, sir," he said.

The Honorable Chester Y. Popowski was seated behind a big desk in the corner of the large square room. The Superior Court judge's chambers little resembled those created for television. There was some cheap wood paneling on the walls and fading maroon wall-to-wall carpeting on the floor. A glass-fronted bookcase held some thick legal tomes. The judge had fewer volumes than I had in my law office. No flagstands flanked the desk. No oil portraits hung on the walls. No rich leather furniture. It was a big room, and it looked as if its occupant had a short lease, which was true. Massachusetts Superior Court judges rotate among the various jurisdictions in the state. Pops' tenure in Middlesex County was one year, of which he had already served seven months.

His robe hung on a coatrack beside him. His solid blue tie was loosened at his throat. He wore bright yellow suspenders. A newspaper was spread over the top of his desk, serving the dual function of tablecloth and reading matter. Pops held a cardboard container in one hand and a white plastic spoon in the other. He was looking up at me over a pair of half glasses perched low on his nose. His thick thatch of snow-white hair looked like a wig. Laugh lines crinkled at the corners of his eyes and he was giving me his famous smile. Pops had a face that inspired faith. It was a wise face, an honest face, a confident face.

Those qualities in that face were enhanced, not contradicted, by the thin white scar on his left cheekbone. It was perhaps two inches long, and it angled from just below the outside corner of his eye toward the corner of his mouth. It was barely noticeable in the winter, but after Pops had spent some time in the sun that scar seemed to glow proudly like a battle wound.

Which, in fact, is what it was. I was with him when he got it. It was back in our law school days in New Haven. Racial tension ran high in that city, as it did in many American cities in those days, although those of us who spent our time in an ivory tower tended to perceive it as an abstraction. On that particular evening, Pops, Charlie McDevitt, and I had emerged from a cheap restaurant in a marginal part of town. We had lingered after eating, debating fine points of due process and pending Supreme Court decisions, as we usually did. Charlie and I had lubricated the conversation with several shots of Old Grand-dad apiece, while Pops, typically, had sipped on a single glass of draft beer.

We carried the debate into the empty streets and continued it as we meandered toward Pops' car, which was parked a few blocks away. Suddenly Pops yelled, "Hey! Cut it out!" and darted away from us. He ran across the street, where we could see some sort of fight in progress.

Pops piled into the middle of it. By the time Charlie and I had gathered our wits around us and followed Pops, two of the men had fled and Pops was kneeling on the chest of the remaining one. He was pounding the man's face with his fists, mumbling "son of a bitch" and "dirty bastards," and Charlie and I had to drag him off. As soon as we did, that man stumbled away, too, and the three of us were left alone on the sidewalk. Then we noticed the flap of skin lying open on Pops' cheek.

He explained what had happened: he had seen two white men taking turns kicking a black teenager, who was curled fetally on the sidewalk. He had done what anybody would do, he said. He had gone to the rescue. One of the white guys had a knife, that's all.

That was the only time I have ever seen Pops hit anybody. The only time, in fact, I have ever seen him lose control. I believe he might have killed that man with his fists had we not pulled him off.

The scar remained as a kind of symbol of Pops' concept of justice. His face, somehow, would have been incomplete without it.

That scar and that hair and that altogether distinguished face gave Judge Popowski, unlike virtually all the other judges in the Commonwealth, instant recognizability among television viewers and other casual political observers. Pops looked like a judge. His appearance was an asset, and while he took no credit for it, he was grateful for it. He knew it gave him an advantage.

In the case of Judge Popowski, though, unlike the cases of most people, the face actually revealed the man. I knew that the Honorable Chester Y.

Popowski was, in fact, distinguished, wise, honest, and confident. Honorable, even.

He waved the plastic spoon at me and jerked his head at a chair across the desk.

"Take a load off, Brady," he mumbled.

I sat in one of the half-dozen orange upholstered chairs that were scattered in an imperfect semicircle in front of Pops' desk. The chair was shaped like a pair of hands trying to collect water from a spring. The back stopped below my shoulder blades. My chronic lumbar ache began almost instantly.

He gestured at the doorway. "Bright young man. My clerk. Name of Robert. *Law Review* last year. You wouldn't like him."

"Why not? He seemed pleasant."

Pops spooned a mouthful of white stuff into his mouth. "Harvard boy," he said.

I shrugged. "Makes no difference to me. Some of my best friends went to Harvard."

"So happy Groundhog Day," he said.

"You too."

"My favorite holiday," he said. "Never thought it was right to sit in session on Groundhog Day. You figure the little bugger's gonna see his shadow today?"

"Punxsutawney Phil? No way. It's been raining all day."

"Sun's probably shining down there in Pennsylvania, scare him back into his hole for six weeks. God, I hate New England winters."

"Me too," he said. "Well, hey. Congratulations, Pops."

He spooned another glob of white gunk from the container into his mouth and rolled his eyes in distaste. "Thanks. You heard."

I gave him a frown. "Had to read about it in Norma Nathan's column. You'd think, your own lawyer . . ."

He waved his hand. "It only just happened, Brady. I think old Norma knew before I did."

"Well, Federal District Court. That's nice."

He nodded. "What I been waiting for. Assuming I pass muster with the Bureau and the Judiciary Committee and the full Senate."

"No reason why you shouldn't."

"Provided our esteemed senior senator, who submitted my name, hasn't pissed off too many of his colleagues, which he probably has, and assuming that he has, that his colleagues don't decide to use me as some kind of lever to sock it to him. Which they probably will." He shrugged. "You want some coffee?"

I shook my head. "All you ever have is instant. I can't stand instant."

"I stopped drinking the stuff, myself," he said. "Goes right through me. As it is I gotta take about three piss recesses a morning. Damn prostate. I go to this urologist at Mass General, he pokes his finger up there and massages the thing. Most uncomfortable sensation you can imagine. He tells me my problem is I'm not getting it regular. I tell him, hell, Doc, I get it regular. Once a month, like clockwork."

I smiled. "So how is Marilee?"

He took another mouthful. "In Sarasota right now, working on her tan. Her face is getting to look like an old penny loafer. I tell her she's gonna get skin cancer, never mind ugly." He shrugged. "You eaten?"

I shook my head. "This is my lunch hour. You summoned me."

He held the cardboard container to me. "Want some of this?"

"What is it?"

"Cottage cheese with little pieces of pineapple in it. I also got a Baggie with carrot sticks and celery. Nice glass of Belmont Springs water. Power lunch."

"I'll pass." I reached into my shirt pocket and took out a pack of Winstons. "Mind if I smoke?"

He shrugged. "Go ahead."

"I mean, there's signs all over the place, corridors, men's room, elevators, no smoking in this building. Hell, what I understand, you can't smoke in the entire city of Cambridge these days."

Pops waved his hand around the room. "No signs in here. Judge's chambers, you can smoke. I'm the law in here."

I lit a cigarette.

"Happy Candlemas Day, too," he said.

"Huh?"

"February the second. It's been Candlemas Day in England since something like the fifth century. You know what Candlemas Day is?"

"No. I suspect I'm going to find out."

He waved his spoon. "I'll spare you the details. Ancient Christian celebration. The blessing of the candles. Properly blessed candles presumably warded off bad fortune. Folks burned blessed candles when somebody got sick, or during a storm, or whatever. Upshot of it is, there's this myth that goes along with Candlemas Day, which is the same day that we celebrate Groundhog Day, which probably explains our heathen faith in the little brown critter reacting to his own shadow. There's a rhyme. Want to hear it?"

I puffed on my cigarette and smiled. "Oh, please."

He grinned. "Goes like this. 'If Candlemas be fair and bright, / Come,

Winter, have another flight; / If Candlemas brings clouds and rain, / Go, Winter, and come not again.' "

I had been Chester Popowski's lawyer for about fifteen years. Even judges need lawyers. Pops had been a classmate of mine at Yale Law. He was several years older than I. He ran around with Charlie McDevitt and me for a while in New Haven. Charlie and I used to hold open house most weekends at our big old rented Victorian by the water, and Pops usually showed up. But he always seemed a little self-conscious about what Charlie and I considered fun. Pops had served two stints in Vietnam between college and law school. He managed to make me feel deprived by not having been to war. In the presence of Chet Popowski, I felt immature and trivial. Pops had always seemed serious and straitlaced. Uptight, Charlie used to call him. After he met Marilee, Pops came to the bacchanalia Charlie and I sponsored with less frequency and, it seemed to me, even greater discomfort.

After law school Pops became an assistant district attorney for Middlesex County, in East Cambridge, Massachusetts, just across the Charles River from my office in Copley Square. He had come back from Indochina with that great shock of prematurely white hair. Photogenic as hell on his tall, athletic frame. And Pops had a beautiful voice and beautiful teeth and a penchant for winning tough cases. Governor Sargent soon appointed him to the District Court bench, and a few years later he was elevated to Superior Court.

Now he had been nominated for Federal District Court, and I assumed he wanted to discuss it with me.

I looked around for someplace to drop the ash from my cigarette, and Pops produced a glass ashtray from a drawer in his desk. "You want to talk about the appointment?" I said "That why you summoned me?"

He dropped the cardboard container and the plastic spoon into the wastebasket beside his desk, pulled a handkerchief from his hip pocket and wiped his hands and mouth, and shook his head. "Wanted to show you something," he said.

He gathered up the sections of newspaper that had served as his tablecloth and dropped them onto the floor. Tucked into the blotter on the desk was a folded piece of paper. He unfolded it and handed it to me.

It was an eight-and-a-half-by-eleven piece of white paper. Twenty-pound bond. I felt the tiny serrations along the edges with my fingertips. Computer paper. Printed on it in dot matrix was this message:

I KNOW ABOUT KAREN LAVOIE.

There was no signature, no date, nothing else on the piece of paper.

I looked at Pops. "What's this?" I said.

He shrugged. "Came in the mail three days ago."

"Who sent it?"

"I've got no idea."

"Who the hell is Karen Lavoie?"

His eyes wandered to the bank of tall narrow windows in his corner room that looked out over the squat flat buildings and chimneys of East Cambridge ten stories below. The Bunker Hill Monument poked up in the distance. Beyond that arched the Tobin Bridge. Sooty smoke and steam rose straight up from the stacks and chimneys into the sullen gray February overcast. Pops didn't speak for several moments. Finally his eyes swung back to mine. "It's nothing to worry about."

I stared at him. "Bullshit," I said.

"I'm not exactly—shit, okay, so I'm worried. Hell, I want this appointment. Something wrong with that?"

"So who's Karen Lavoie, Pops?"

"Now don't get huffy, Brady. Believe me. I know the FBI and all Teddy's enemies are going to do their damnedest to dig up dirt on me. This does not intimidate me. I've promptly paid every parking ticket I ever got. All those times in New Haven, I never put my lips around a stick of cannabis. I spent four celibate years in Southeast Asia. There's nothing in my bank accounts I haven't got records of. The only people I owe money to are bankers. I've never set foot in a gay bar. My judicial record is, as far as I can see, impeccable. I have managed to avoid pissing off women and blacks and gays. I've sent bad guys up for long stretches. I've never visited a shrink. I know all about the things that screw up appointments. I've been in this racket a long time. Should I be worried?"

I cocked my head and looked at him. Then I tapped the single sheet of paper with the dot-matrix message on it.

"Evidently," I said.

He gazed down at the top of his desk and smiled. When he looked back up at me, he was no longer smiling. He removed his reading glasses and pinched the bridge of his nose. "This is politics," he said. "This is big-time politics, now. A federal seat. I want it very badly. I've been aiming toward this. I wouldn't mind, five, ten years from now, maybe they think of old Chester Y. Popowski when one of the nine old men kicks off, either. Be a nice move for some future president, putting a second-generation Pole into the Supreme Court. Best job in the world for a lawyer, Supreme Court

Justice. Be pretty nice. A Pole in the Vatican, a Pole on the Court. So, yeah, I'm worried. It's my nature to worry. I worry about all kinds of stuff. Phyllis gets an F on a French test, I worry she's gonna get kicked out of Mount Holyoke. Patty goes to the movies with that Tommy kid, the linebacker with that souped up Datsun that's shaped like a torpedo whose tires squeal around the corner, I worry I'm gonna get a phone call from the cops some night. I worry about bombs when Marilee flies to Sarasota. I worry I screwed up and they nail me on appeals. I worry about cholesterol. I worry I don't get enough fiber. I worry Marilee's gonna find a lump in her breast. I worry about her nightly headaches. It's why I gotta eat cottage cheese and yogurt and have my prostate massaged. Because I worry. It's also why I'm a good judge. Worrying keeps you sharp. Look for bad stuff. Head it off. So, yeah, you could say I'm worried. I'm always worried."

"So I repeat. Who the hell is Karen Lavoie? What is this all about, Pops? Come on. This is me, your lawyer here."

"Okay, just listen for a minute," he said, holding up his hand. "I got a phone call this morning while I was sitting in the kitchen eating a slice of dry toast and worrying about why the oil burner wouldn't shut off. Fella who sent me this cryptic message." He tapped the dot-matrix words on the computer paper. "Wanted to have a conversation."

"Did you?"

"Of course not."

"What'd he want to talk about?"

He put his finger on the piece of paper. "Her."

"Karen Lavoie."

He nodded.

"And?"

"And I told him he could shove it."

"Naturally," I said.

"He wanted to meet me in a bar, for crissake."

"But you're not going."

"He said he'd be there waiting for me. I told him he could wait six weeks for all I cared, see if the groundhog's prediction turned out to be accurate. He laughed. He said he'd be there, waiting, and if I knew what was good for me I'd be there. Then he hung up on me."

"You think that's a good idea, Pops?"

"What?"

"Standing him up?"

"What else could I do? Last thing I need is to be seen in some bar being hassled and threatened by some sleazebag who wants to muck around in my past. Christ, everybody in the city knows me."

I nodded. "You're probably right. On the other hand . . ."

"I know," he said. "Not going suggests certain problems, too."

I leaned back and smiled at him. "Pops, why'd you want to see me?"

He shrugged. "You're my lawyer. I can tell you anything. Our relationship is privileged. You give me good advice. You're my friend. I've got this little problem here."

"Look," I said. "I've got an idea. Suppose I go."

"What are you saying, Brady?"

"I'll go to the bar. I'll listen to the guy."

He shook his head. "I can't ask you to do that."

"You didn't. I offered."

"That's not what lawyers are for."

I shrugged. "It's what friends are for, Pops."

Pops reached across the desk and put his hand on my wrist. "If you could just find out what his agenda is . . ."

"The guy didn't introduce himself?"

"No."

"Didn't say what he wanted?"

"Just to talk."

"When?"

"Tonight. Nine o'clock."

"Where?"

"Skeeter's."

"And this guy insisted on a face-to-face meeting?"

"Yes."

"You figure blackmail, huh?"

He nodded.

"I won't be party to blackmail, you know," I said.

"Believe me, I have no intention of paying him a cent. I have no reason to."

"Okay. I'll go. But you've got to tell me all about this Karen Lavoie."

He peered at me for a minute. His eyes wandered away, then swung back to meet mine. "Karen . . ." he began. Then he stopped.

I arched my eyebrows. He nodded slowly.

"Oh," I said.

"Yeah."

"I'm disillusioned," I said.

"Come off it, Brady. This isn't easy."

"Sorry. What happened?"

He shrugged. "It was a long time ago. It happened. I'm not proud of it. But it's got nothing to do with anything."

"Hey, Pops—"

"Honest, Brady. Leave it there, okay?"

"Like hell."

He sighed. "Do I have to spell it out?"

"Any reason you shouldn't?"

He shook his head slowly back and forth. "No, not really. Mainly, it's embarrassing. A fucking cliché. What do they call it nowadays—the Jennifer Complex? She was young, I wasn't. What can I say? It lasted, oh, a month, maybe, before I realized what I was doing. It wasn't easy to live with myself, believe me."

"If Marilee found out . . ."

"Hell," he said, "I knew, and that was bad enough. I ended it. It was a huge relief. I think maybe I'm a better man for it. Showed me my weakness. I'm ashamed to this day." He shrugged. "And that's the whole story. The thing is, Brady, there aren't any juicy details or anything. One of those things that happens."

"One of those things that gets nominations rejected," I said.

He bowed his head and held up his hands in a gesture of surrender. "Aside from your prurient interest, there's nothing for you to know here. Nothing for anybody to know. It happened a long time ago. A moment of weakness. So I'm human. Should that disqualify me?"

"Not as far as I'm concerned. But I'm not responsible for making a federal judge out of you."

"Brady, it's an old story, that's all. It's embarrassing. My main concern is Marilee and the girls, here, not the appointment. There's nothing that should disqualify me from being a federal judge. Maybe from being president or something, but not judge. It could, but it shouldn't. But if this business ever got back to Marilee—well, I don't need to tell you that the qualifications for being a husband are sometimes more stringent than those for being a judge. Can we leave it at that?"

I shrugged. "Who is she? Where is she? Is there a chance that she'll come forward, make things embarrassing?"

"She—she was just this girl. I have no idea where she is now, or what's become of her. Last I heard she got married. I assume she's got as many reasons as me to keep this quiet. I am very certain that she will confirm nothing about this. It's over. Ancient history."

"But somebody seems to think differently."

"Brady," said Pops, "listen to me. I want you to tell this guy to stuff it, okay? He's got nothing to blackmail me for, and I won't be bluffed. I don't give a shit what kinds of threats he makes. He thinks he's got something for the press or for Marilee, tell him to go ahead. He gets nothing out of me. Nothing. Okay? Does that satisfy you?"

I nodded. "Okay. Yes, it does."

"Well, good."

"You're not holding back on me, Pops?"

He held up his right hand, palm out. "Honest to God, Brady. I know better than to hold anything back from my lawyer. It's just, when your lawyer is your friend, and you value his good opinion of you . . ."

I nodded. "Okay. I still think you're a helluva man. So how'll I recognize this guy?"

He hesitated. His eyes swung away from me for a moment. Then he leaned forward toward me. "You won't." He grinned at me. "He'll recognize you."

I stared at him. He shrugged. Then I laughed. "You're unbelievable."

"I had a hunch you'd offer to go."

"You knew goddam well I'd offer to go. You set me up."

"If you hadn't offered, I would never have asked."

I shook my head. "Okay, okay. So how will he recognize me, then?"

"I told him you'd be drinking bourbon and smoking Winstons. Told him you'd be the handsome guy alone at the bar."

"So I better not let any ladies sit with me."

"At least not until after you finish with our friend."

"That's gonna be hard, keeping the ladies at bay."

"It's tough work like that I pay you a fat retainer for," said Pops.

· TWO ·

THERE WERE TWO WOMEN at Skeeter's when I got there a little before nine. They were seated on stools at the end of the bar near the door, as far from the giant-size television down the other end as they could get. One was dark-haired and one was blond. Both wore blazers over silky blouses, with dangling earrings and gold chains at the throat and dark narrow skirts that showed a great deal of sleek thigh. The female yuppie uniform. Both appeared to be in their early thirties. They could have been secretaries or stockbrokers or lawyers or hookers. There was an empty stool between them, and they didn't appear to be talking with each other. Both were drinking white wine and smoking long, skinny filtered cigarettes and studying the rows of bottles lined up in front of the mirror over the bar.

I took one of the several empty seats in the middle, halfway between the women and the cluster of men around the TV.

The women ignored me completely.

Skeeter's Infield was a long, narrow tavern at the end of a short alley off State Street within walking distance of my waterfront apartment. The entire length of the left side was taken up by the bar. Along the right wall were ten or a dozen high-backed booths. The walls were hung with posters of old major leaguers—superstars like Yaz and Willie and Mickey, Skeeter's heroes, and others, too, who had been his friends—José Tartabull, Dalton Jones, and Joe Foy.

Along the back of the bar artifacts of Skeeter's game were displayed. Bats and gloves, shinguards, baseballs, even the protective cup once worn by a pitcher named Gary Bell, who had the unhappy penchant of stopping hard-hit grounders with it. The cup had a dent in it. Skeeter told me that Bell had been nicknamed "Ding Dong" by his teammates. Skeeter said when you got hit by a ball off the cup it clanged.

Skeeter's was famous for its half-pound ground sirloin hamburgers and five-alarm chili. Mostly, though, people went there to drink. To drink and talk with Skeeter and maybe rub elbows with a sports celebrity.

Skeeter O'Reilly was a kid from Southie who had actually made it to the big leagues. In the course of his twelve-year major-league career, he played with seven different teams. He was pegged early as a backup infielder—steady glove but limited range, a Punch-and-Judy hitter, a feisty kid who could move a runner over, steal a base, and wasn't afraid to turn a double play with someone like Don Baylor bearing down on him. He spent one season on the Red Sox bench—1968, the year after they were in the World Series. That was the closest Skeeter O'Reilly ever got to real glory.

When bone chips in his ankle ended his career he came back to Boston and bought the run-down joint in the alley off State Street. He installed indirect lights, lots of glass and brass and leather and dark wood and that five-foot television screen, and himself behind the bar. Skeeter wore the same droopy red mustache he grew when he played ball in the sixties, and a long shag of red hair spilled from under the shapeless old Red Sox cap he always wore when he was tending bar. Only a select few of us knew that under his cap Skeeter's dome was as hairless as a baseball.

Skeeter smiled a lot, and when he did he revealed the empty place in his mouth where one of his eye teeth used to grow. It was a battle scar of sorts, the product of a headfirst slide into Elston Howard's shinguard, and Skeeter wore it proudly.

He ran a modest book on professional sports, too, which the Boston cops blinked at out of respect for Skeeter's status as a local sports hero.

I unzipped my ski parka and fished out a cigarette. Skeeter was down with the guys at the television, moderating an argument. I glanced at the two ladies to my left. Neither of them glanced at me.

"But the *Broons* are playin' the *Whalahs,* fah crissake," said one voice from near the TV.

"Screw the Broons," said another. "Buncha loosahs. Get the Celts on fifty-six. They're playin' the Knicks. I wanna see Pat Ewing."

"Ahh, basketball's fer wimps."

"You wanna see blood, fah crissake, go lookit yourself shavin'. Them basketball players're *ath-a-letes.*"

Skeeter glanced at me, arched his eyebrows, said something to the sports fans, and came my way. He held his hand across the bar to me. "Hey, Mr. Coyne. Great to see ya again."

"How's business, Skeets?"

He turned down the corners of his mouth and wiggled his hand, palm down, over the bar. "Metsa-mets," he said. "You know, Mr. Coyne, in the old days it was simple. You'd play baseball in the day and talk about girls. Then at night you'd go to a bar with a girl and talk about baseball. Now? Boy, I don't know. You tell me. What'd you do? Show 'em the hockey or the basketball? I never have this problem in the summer. Baseball's all there is. But there are times in October, for God sake, you got the Celtics and the Bruins and the Patties and the World Series all at once. Makes me want to shoot holes in the damn tube. Boys don't get to watch what they want, they don't stay around to drink my booze."

"I understand the Boston Symphony's playing Beethoven on Channel Two," I said. "I got my money on Beethoven."

Skeeter cocked his head at me and grinned. "Somehow I don't think that's the answer." He produced a rag and swiped at the bar in front of me. "Special drink this week's the Whitey Ford. Wanta try it?"

Skeeter had earned modest fame in Boston with his inventive concoctions, which he named after old ballplayers. I had once tried a Don Drysdale, which Skeeter said was guaranteed to "knock you on your ass and keep you there." He didn't lie. He boasted that his Wee Willie Keeler would "hit 'em where they ain't."

"What's a Whitey Ford?" I asked cautiously.

"Dark rum, Guinness stout, papaya juice," he said. "It's sneaky fast. Before you know it, you're back in the old dugout. Just like when you tried to hit Whitey's curve."

"Think I'll pass this time. Give me a shot of Rebel Yell on the rocks."

"Always the bourbon, huh, Mr. Coyne?"

I didn't tell Skeeter that Pops' mystery man would recognize me by my bourbon. "I don't want to be snuck up on," I said.

He grinned, showing my the gap in his teeth. "Oh, and happy Groundhog Day," he said.

"Thanks." I decided not to share my newfound lore about Candlemas Day with Skeeter.

Skeeter brought me my drink with a side of water, gave the bar a final swipe with his rag, and wandered back to the controversy at the television. It appeared that the Bruins had won the day. Boston has always been a hockey town.

The ladies to my left continued to gaze into the mirror. I glanced at my watch. Nine-fifteen. I lit another cigarette and sipped the southern sour mash and watched the hockey players zip around the big screen.

He was wearing a Ben Hogan tweed cap, dark shades, snug-fitting blue jeans, and a fleece-lined sheepskin parka. Wisps of longish blond hair showed under the cap. He had a bushy blond mustache a shade darker than the hair on his head. "Mr. Coyne, is it?" he said.

"Yes. Who're you?"

He grinned, showing perfect teeth that might have been capped. "It's not important, who I am," he said. His voice was deep and well modulated, with no trace of any sort of regional accent. It seemed faintly familiar, and I had the feeling that had he taken off his sunglasses I would have recognized his face.

Skeeter came over. My companion ordered a St. Pauli Girl. We sat in silence until his beer and frosted glass arrived. After Skeeter moved over to refill the ladies' wineglasses, the man said, "You know why I'm here?"

"I don't even know why I'm here," I said.

He gave me what looked like a well-practiced smile. "It's really quite simple, Mr. Coyne." He touched his mustache with his forefinger. "I have a commodity that is very valuable to your client."

"And what is this commodity?"

"My silence."

"It's my belief that your commodity has no value whatsoever," I said. "To my client or to anyone else."

"He told you that, huh?"

I shrugged.

"Did he tell you about Karen Lavoie?"

"Yes," I said.

He grinned and spread his hands. "Well, then."

"Look, friend," I said. "You're running quite a risk here. Blackmail is against the law, in case you didn't know it. Neither my client nor I is interested in violating the law. Technically, you have already broken the law. So my sincere advice to you is to finish your beer, shake my hand, acknowledge that I have misunderstood your intention, and be on your merry little way."

"Blackmail," he said, arching his eyebrows in mock surprise. "Oh, dear."

I nodded. "Fine. Excellent. So I have misunderstood your intention."

"Your client, I assure you, has not misunderstood my intention, Mr. Coyne. And I know that you know that there's not a damn thing you can do about it. Except do business with me." He played with his mustache again.

"What is it you want?"

"Convey the figure of ten thousand dollars to your client."

"If I were wearing a wire, you could be arrested right now, do you realize that?"

He smiled lazily. "Perhaps. Perhaps not. In any case, if I were arrested tonight, tomorrow's papers would be full of the story of Chester Popowski and Karen Lavoie. That's why you're here. That's why His Honor didn't hang up on me. He wasn't always quite the proper judge everybody thinks, you know. And that's why I know you're not wearing a wire."

"We appear to be at a stalemate, then," I said.

He leaned close to me. "Look. My source is impeccable, believe me. I've got the proof. The ball's in my court. If I weren't sure of what I had, do you think I'd've risked meeting you this way, in person? Do you think the judge would've had you come here to meet me?"

"I think the judge could survive all of this much easier than you could."

He sat back and took a long draft from his beer. "Ten grand," he said. "Tell that to the judge. And tell him I'll be in touch."

"Don't bother."

He whirled quickly on the barstool and grabbed a handful of my jacket. He put his face close to mine. "I'm gonna call day after tomorrow," he hissed at me. "Make sure Chester Y. Popowski knows that."

I tried to twist out of his grasp. "Let go," I said softly.

He leaned back and held his palms in front of him in a gesture of surrender. He smiled. "Take it easy, friend. No offense, huh?"

Skeeter appeared. "Everything okay, Mr. Coyne?"

I nodded. "No problem, Skeets."

He looked from me to the man beside me and shrugged. "Okay. Another?"

"No, thanks," I said.

"No," said the man.

Skeeter wandered away. I hunched my shoulders back into my jacket. The guy beside me swiveled off his barstool. "Tell him I'll be in touch," he said. "Ten grand. Just tell him I said ten grand."

He headed for the door. "Hey," I yelled at him.

He turned. "Yeah?"

"You didn't pay for your beer."

"It's on you," he said as he went out the door. "The judge's paying your expenses."

I sat there simmering. Skeeter came back. "Who was that?" he said.

"I don't know. You ever see him before?"

Skeeter cocked his head. "Seemed familiar. Not a regular. Dunno. Can't place him."

"I'd like to know who he is," I said.

He shook his head. "Nope. Can't place him. He giving you a hard time?"

"Nothing I couldn't handle."

"I get all kinds in here. Guy has a fight with his old lady, doesn't dare take a swipe at her, he comes in here looking for someone he can slug. Fella has a few down the street, they shut him off, he comes in here looking for another. Sorry he picked on you."

"Not your fault," I said.

"Look, Mr. Coyne," said Skeeter. "I'm gonna give you a refill on the house for your trouble."

"You don't have to do that, Skeets."

"I want to. I like to take care of my customers."

"You talked me into it. Thanks."

I sipped my second shot of Rebel Yell. I caught the dark-haired woman watching me in the mirror. I smiled at her. She looked away and said something to the blonde beside her. A minute later she slid a couple of bills onto the bar and both women left.

As I had said to Pops, keeping the ladies at bay was a problem.

· THREE ·

I T TOOK ME TWENTY MINUTES or half an hour to stroll back to my apartment from Skeeter's. All the rain that had fallen and the slush and crud that had melted into puddles during the day had frozen and glazed the sidewalks. It made the walking tricky. Sullen heaps of gray snow remained mounded against the buildings. The February air smelled moist and organic and complex, a combination of low tide and industrial waste and automobile exhaust and a winter's accumulation of garbage that had frozen and thawed too many times. City smells. Not objectionable at all.

Up in my apartment on the sixth floor of the stark concrete building on the harbor, I dropped my parka on the floor and kicked off my boots. I checked my machine for messages and, as usual, found none. I put on the heat under the teakettle and flicked on the television. I clicked it over to Channel 56 and pushed last week's newspapers onto the floor to make room for myself on the sofa so I could watch the end of the Celtics–Knicks game.

When the old black-and-white tube warmed up, I realized that the game had ended. I watched a few minutes of an old Richard Burton movie. Judging by the costumes, we were back in sixteenth-century England. Burton was riding a horse. I figured I'd missed the premise, so I changed the channel to 38. The Bruins were in overtime, so I watched the toothless young men glide over the ice, colliding with each other as they pursued the little rubber disk around the rink.

The teakettle began to sing at about the same time the game ended, still tied. I turned off the television and went to the stove. I dropped a bag of Sleepytime into a mug and poured the boiling water over it. I stared through the floor-to-ceiling glass sliders at the harbor while my tea steeped. In the moonless night, I couldn't distinguish the line between sky and ocean. A few lights blinked dully through the haze.

I retrieved my tea and took it to the phone. I dialed Pops' home number. He lived in West Roxbury, which is not to be confused with Roxbury, although both are sections of Boston. Roxbury is a black ghetto situated between Huntington and Columbus avenues in the heart of the city next to the Northeastern campus. You go to Roxbury to buy drugs. You live in Roxbury only if you have to.

West Roxbury is a swanky white enclave. It's located in the southwest corner of the city, hard by Brookline and Newton and Dedham. It's separated from Roxbury by the Jamaica Plain and Roslindale sections of the city. West Roxbury is bounded, roughly, by the Charles River and several golf courses, including The Country Club, one of the oldest and most exclusive in the nation.

Judges tend to live in West Roxbury. The people who appear before them often come from Roxbury.

I got Pops' answering machine. Marilee Popowski's voice repeated the number I had dialed and invited me to leave a message at the beep. "It's Brady," I told the machine. "Just got back from my meeting. I'm home now. Give me a call."

Pops hardly ever answered his phone, whether he was sitting beside it or not. He used the answering machine to screen his calls. I hung up after delivering my message to his tape and sat beside my telephone, sipping my tea, smoking a Winston. I assumed he'd call me back instantly.

I finished my tea and rinsed out the mug, glanced through the latest issue of *Newsweek*, and smoked a couple of cigarettes. When Pops still hadn't returned my call, I shucked off my clothes and took a shower. I luxuriated in the hot needles that blasted relaxation into my muscles. I went through my entire repertoire of old Johnny Mathis make-out ballads. I was in good voice.

I got out, dried myself, and slipped into a pair of jeans and a sweatshirt.

When I went into the living room, I saw the red light on my answering machine blinking. Blip-blip. Pause. Blip-blip. Two messages. I played the tape. "It's Gloria," she said. "Hope I didn't interrupt something. Please give me a call when you get a chance."

The voice of my ex-wife never fails to constrict my throat a little. We've been divorced about as long as we were married, but she still gets to me.

The second blip was Pops. "Returning your call," he said. "I'm here."

I called Pops first.

"So what happened?" he said.

"Let me ask you something, first."

"Shoot."

"Your home phone's unlisted, right?"

"You betcha," he said. "Be pretty stupid, a judge having a listed phone number. I change it every couple months, too."

"So who knows your number?"

"Marilee and the girls. Some of their friends, I suppose. You. Some of the folks at the courthouse. Hard to keep a phone number a secret, even if it's unlisted. Tends to keep away the creeps, though."

"You said our friend called you this morning, am I right?"

"Hell, yeah. I never thought of that. Yes, he called me here, at this number. What do you make of that?"

"I don't know. Either it's someone who you know well, or it's someone who knows how to find out things."

"Well," said Pops, "I guess we know he knows how to find out things. He came up with Karen Lavoie's name."

"And he seems to know more about her than I do," I said.

"He knows nothing you don't know, Brady, believe me. There's nothing else to know, I told you."

"Well, he seems to think it's worth ten thousand dollars."

"Sure. He would. Nice try, fella."

"You were right. He wants to blackmail you."

Pops hesitated. "Ten thousand bucks, huh? That's the figure he mentioned?"

"Yes. Ten grand."

"I hope you told him to fuck off."

"Indeed I did. I don't believe I used that expression. He said he'd be in touch with you."

"You have any idea who or what he is?"

"Nope."

"Well, I guess we'll just have to see what happens."

"You don't sound worried."

"I'm not," he said. "Nothing to be worried about."

"Pops," I said, "I think it's time to come clean with me."

"I did. I always have."

"Reluctantly."

"Granted."

"Is there something else? Does this guy know something I don't know?"

"Nothing else to know, Brady. It was what it was."

"I got the feeling he was way ahead of me."

"Look, Brady. I didn't give you the locker-room version. I think you understand."

"If you mean I don't judge you, pass judgment on the things you do, things you've done, you're right. I understand. If you mean I understand what this guy thinks he's got, I'm not so sure."

"A long time ago, something happened, and then it was over. Okay? Can we please just leave it there?"

"And that's it?"

I heard a loud explosion of breath. "Christ," he said. "That's it, Brady. Leave it lay, will you?"

"This guy seems to think it's worth ten grand."

"It's not. You told him that. End of story."

"Okay," I said. "If you say so. You going to need me for anything else?"

"You told the guy I'm not going to give him money, you did your job. I appreciate it. Would've told him myself, but the position I'm in, I can't very well sit around barrooms meeting with strangers who want to blackmail me. Folks see me, they might get the wrong idea."

"Ah, the price of fame."

"It's a bitch, ain't it?"

"I wouldn't know," I said.

"Ten grand, huh?"

"That's what he said."

"Ain't worth a penny."

"He seemed to think it was."

"Trust me," said Pops. "It ain't."

"Sure," I said. "I trust you."

After I finished talking with Pops, I dialed the familiar number in Wellesley.

My number two son, Joey, answered. "Hi, pal," I said.

"Hey, Dad. How you doing?"

"Fine. You?"

"Terrific."

"What're you up to?"

"Not much. I watched the Bruins, worked out a little. Thinking of hitting the sack."

"What about your homework?"

"Under control."

"The Bruins, huh. The Boston Symphony played Beethoven tonight, you know."

He chuckled. "Who won?"

"Dead even, same as the Bruins. Ozawa and his orchestra ended at the exact same time. Always amazes me, how they do that. Your mother still awake?"

"I'll check. Hang on."

I heard him yell, "Hey, Mom. The old man's on the phone."

A moment later I heard a click, and Gloria said, "I've got it, dear."

" 'Night, Dad," said Joey.

"Good night, pal."

I heard him disconnect.

"Hi," I said.

"Hi, there."

"The old man, he calls me. God."

Her laugh tinkled in my ear. "You want maybe he should call you the young man?"

Gloria has a husky voice on the telephone. Gloria's voice exudes intimacy. It promises ecstasy. But I suppose that's me. The ear of the beholder. Gloria's voice conjures up a whole kaleidoscope of memories whenever I hear it. It makes my bachelor apartment seem sterile and alien to me. Fortunately, the feeling passes quickly. It would be worse if I talked with Gloria more frequently, which is one of the reasons I don't.

"So what's up, hon?" I said. "Everything okay?"

"Oh, sure. Everything's fine."

"Whenever you call, I always worry that something's wrong."

"Nothing's wrong. I don't do that, do I?"

"Do what?"

"Call you to lay my problems on you."

"No. It's me. I think about you and the boys, that's all. Wondering if everything *is* okay. Imagining that it's not, and then wondering why you didn't call me. And then when you do call, I think . . . I mean, if something *was* wrong, you would call me, wouldn't you?"

"Sure."

"So. That's how I think."

"Jesus, Brady."

"I can't help it."

"I mean, if you're worried all the time, you can always call me, right?"

"Not really," I said. "It's not that simple."

I heard her sigh. "It was almost easier being married to you, know that?"

"I don't think you mean that."

"No," she said. "No, I don't. Anyway, nothing's wrong. This is something good. I've got a line on a magazine job, and I'm going to be in town on Friday, and I just wondered if you might want to meet me for a drink."

"Friday," I said. "Let me check my calendar."

She laughed. "You're such a bullshitter, Brady."

"No, really. I've gotta check my busy schedule."

"Hey, forget it, then."

"Nope. You're in luck. It's clear Friday."

"Oh, lucky me," she said.

"I can squeeze you in."

"The hell with it," she said.

"Aw, it's just a joke, Gloria."

"I don't always think your jokes are that funny."

"Don't I know it."

"And what the hell is that supposed to mean?"

"Look," I said. "I'd like very much to meet you Friday for a drink, okay? I was just fooling around, about my busy schedule."

She paused. I heard her sigh. "Well, okay. So I'm lucky."

"Where do you want to meet?"

"You name it."

"Skeeter's," I said. "He's got a new drink. A Whitey Ford."

"What's a Whitey Ford?"

"Oh, boy. No wonder we didn't make it. Whitey Ford was a very great left-hander for the Yankees. Always gave the Sox fits. Skeeter has concocted a drink in his honor."

"I'll probably have a glass of wine. If the interview goes well, maybe a Scotch. Say eight o'clock?"

"Eight's good. Will you have eaten?"

"No. Skeeter still have those great hamburgers?"

"Yes."

"Maybe I'll let you buy me one."

"What's the job, Gloria? Something exciting?"

"Very. I'll tell you about it when I see you."

I hung up with Gloria, had one last cigarette, and went to bed. I had a date with my former wife. February no longer seemed like such a shitty month. Perhaps that little groundhog in Pennsylvania hadn't been frightened by his own shadow after all.

· FOUR ·

I WAS IN MY OFFICE on the telephone at three o'clock the next afternoon when Julie scratched at my door and poked her head in. She flashed a complicated set of hand and facial signals at me that I interpreted to mean either the building was burning down or my fly was open. I sniffed the air and glanced downward and knew that I had failed to translate her meaning. I beckoned her to come in.

She sat in the chair opposite my desk and drummed her long nails on the glass desktop while I finished my conversation. She crossed and recrossed her fine legs impatiently.

When I hung up, I said, "What's wrong?"

"There's two men out there to see you. They're cops."

"Christ. I thought there was a problem."

"They're policemen, Brady."

"We lawyers deal with the police now and then, you know."

She shrugged. "I don't like them."

"Cops?"

"Not cops in general. These two. They don't smile."

"They're trained not to smile. It probably gets easy for them. They hardly ever do happy business. Am I free now?"

She nodded.

"Well, you might as well show them in, then."

She cocked her head and arched her brows.

"Please, I mean."

She nodded and smiled. Then she went to the door and looked out into the waiting room. "Mr. Coyne can see you now," she said.

She stood aside and the two cops came in. Both stood around six feet tall, give or take a couple inches. One wore a brown topcoat. He was a bearish, rumpled guy, mid-fifties, I guessed, with thinning silver hair, big jowls, and small rheumy eyes. He reminded me of Walter Matthau. The other wore a black leather flight jacket with a fur collar. He was younger and trimmer, with short dark hair and a flattened nose. Robert De Niro.

I came around from behind my desk. Julie hesitated, then closed the door behind her. I extended my hand to the two men and shook hands with each of them. "Brady Coyne," I said.

The cop in the shapeless topcoat flipped open a leather folder showing me his shield. "Sylvestro," he said. "Boston cops. Homicide."

"Homicide," I repeated.

Sylvestro shrugged. "This is Finnigan. State police."

Finnigan showed me his detective's shield, too.

I gestured to the sofa. They sat beside each other, not bothering to take off their coats. I took the chair across the coffee table from them.

Sylvestro leaned toward me. "Sorry to barge in on you like this, Mr. Coyne. Hope maybe you can give us a hand."

"That's okay," I said. "What can I do for you?"

Sylvestro was carrying a large manila envelope. He reached into it and extracted an eight-by-ten glossy black-and-white photograph. He put it onto the coffee table and turned it around to face me. "I wonder if you recognize this man, Mr. Coyne?"

It was a studio portrait of a very handsome man who was smiling comfortably into the camera lens. He was perhaps thirty, with a high smooth forehead and a thick mane of light hair, worn modishly long. His features were regular and ordinary. A movie star, I guessed. His looked like hundreds of faces I had seen on television. One of the romantic leads in *The Young and the Restless,* maybe.

I looked up at the cops. Sylvestro had his eyebrows arched. He was smiling apologetically. Finnigan was frowning.

I shrugged. "He certainly looks familiar. But I can't place him."

They exchanged glances. "You sure, Mr. Coyne?" said Sylvestro. "Take another look."

I looked at the picture again. "It's a face I've seen somewhere. But I can't place it." I lit a cigarette, then looked at Sylvestro. "This man kill somebody or something?"

"Wayne Churchill. That name mean anything to you?" said Sylvestro.

I nodded. "Yes, it does. But I can't place it. Showbiz? Movies? A singer or something?"

Finnigan sat back in the sofa and folded his arms. Sylvestro scratched his neck.

I looked at Finnigan, then Sylvestro. "I think you should tell me what this is all about. You're obviously showing me a picture of this Wayne Churchill. It's a face I've seen, a name I've heard. That's the best I can do for you."

"You ever watch Channel Eight?" said Sylvestro to me.

"I hardly ever watch television," I said. "Sports now and then. Sometimes the eleven o'clock news. I generally watch Channel Four for the news, don't ask me why. Habit, I guess. I like the sports guy. I suppose I'll watch something on Channel Eight once in a while."

"Wayne Churchill's on Eight," said Finnigan.

I snapped my fingers. "Right. Newsman. You usually see him interviewing a fire chief at an arson scene in Lynn or a cop at a shooting in Dorchester." I glanced down at the photo that still rested on the coffee table. "That's why he looked familiar, and why his name rang a bell." I looked up at the cops. "Why are you asking me this?"

"Do you mind telling us where you were last night, Mr. Coyne?" said Sylvestro.

I frowned. "Yeah," I said. "I think I do mind. I think you better tell me what's going on."

"Of course," said Sylvestro. "I apologize." He glanced at Finnigan, who looked up at the ceiling. "This man—this Wayne Churchill—he was, ah, killed last night."

"Murdered?" I said.

Sylvestro nodded.

I whistled. "Jesus!"

"It would help if you would tell us where you were last night, please, Mr. Coyne," said Sylvestro.

"I don't get it. What's this got to do with me? I mean, you show me this picture of some guy I've seen on television, you tell me he got murdered, you want to know what I was doing last night. I don't get it."

Sylvestro smiled. He looked like a basset hound when he smiled. He reached across the coffee table and touched my knee. "Relax, Mr. Coyne. Take it easy. Come on. Trust me. We're just a couple cops trying pull some facts together. It'd really help us if you could tell us where you were, what you might've seen last night, okay?"

I shrugged. "Okay. I guess so. I got home—that's my apartment in the Harborside down near Commercial Wharf off Atlantic Avenue, apartment 6E, hell, you probably already checked that out—I got home from work around six, six-fifteen. Could've been six-thirty. Changed my clothes. Opened a can of Friend's pork and beans. Listened to Mozart and read *Field & Stream* while I ate. Left a little after eight-thirty. Walked to Skeeter's. You know Skeeter's Infield, down off State Street? Had a couple drinks there.

Probably stayed no more than half, three-quarters of an hour. Got home, I don't know, ten, around there. Showered. Went to bed."

"What were you doing at Skeeter's?" said Finnigan.

I hesitated. They noticed it. I couldn't help it. I couldn't violate the privileged status of Chester Y. Popowski by telling these cops my business at Skeeter's. "I'm sorry," I said. "I can't tell you that."

They nodded, as if they knew I was going to say that.

"Why can't you tell us?" said Sylvestro.

"Look—"

"You protecting a client?" said Finnigan.

I nodded. "I suppose you could say that. If *protect* is the word. I was at Skeeter's for a client. You know I can't tell you about that."

Finnigan turned to Sylvestro. "Come on, Jack. I mean—"

Sylvestro held up a hand and Finnigan stopped. Then Sylvestro turned to me. "Mr. Coyne, would you mind going over those times for us again."

"Last night, you mean?"

He nodded.

"I really wasn't paying much attention. Like I said, I got home maybe six-thirty. Left at eight-thirty, I'm quite sure of that, because . . . ."

I stopped. Sylvestro was watching me. Finnigan had a notepad on his knee and was making notes.

I lit another cigarette. "Because I wanted to get to Skeeter's at nine," I finished.

"Why?" said Finnigan.

"Come on," I said. "I already explained that."

Finnigan frowned. Sylvestro nodded and smiled. "Sure. That's okay. Go on, Mr. Coyne," he said.

"Well, I had two drinks. When I left, the Bruins were still playing. The game was on the TV in the bar. By the time I got home, it was just ending. Whatever time that was."

"What time was it?" said Finnigan.

"I don't know. I didn't notice."

"So you got home as the game was ending," said Sylvestro.

I nodded. "Yes. I had a cup of tea, took a shower, and went to bed."

"Were you with anybody last night?"

"Skeeter and I chatted at the bar."

"Nobody else?"

I flapped my hands. "Can't tell you."

"What about when you got home?" said Finnigan.

"Nobody."

"Any phone calls?"

"I talked with my wife."

"Your wife?"

"My ex-wife, I mean."

"What time was that?"

"Eleven, maybe?"

"Can she confirm this?" said Finnigan.

"Of course."

"Gloria Coyne, right? Lives in Wellesley?"

"I give you credit," I said. "You've done your homework. I wish you'd fill me in a little."

"You didn't talk with anybody else on the phone?"

"I talked with a client."

"And you can't tell us who, naturally," said Finnigan.

"Right."

"For crissake, Jack," said Finnigan to Sylvestro.

Sylvestro ignored his partner. "Why don't you take another look at this picture," he said to me.

I looked at the photo of Wayne Churchill again. That's when I saw it. The smile, the hair. In my imagination I sketched in a bushy mustache over his lip and a pair of dark glasses over his eyes and a Ben Hogan cap covering those lanky blond locks on his head. "Okay," I said. "Now I see it. He was at Skeeter's last night." I glanced up at Sylvestro. He was watching me intently. "That's why you're asking me where I was last night. Trying to figure out where Churchill was. He was at Skeeter's. Yes."

Sylvestro and Finnigan both stared at me. They were not smiling.

"This man was murdered?" I said.

"Yes," said Sylvestro.

I let out a breath. "Oh, boy."

Sylvestro nodded. "You're sure you saw him there, now, Mr. Coyne? This is pretty important."

"I'm sure. He—he looked different."

"Different how?"

"He had a mustache, dark glasses, one of those caps like golfers wear. A disguise, I suppose, though I didn't know it at the time."

"And you didn't know who he was."

"No."

"Did you talk to him?"

I nodded.

"What about?"

"Sorry. I can't tell you that."

"It's pretty important, Mr. Coyne," said Sylvestro.

"I can't help you there. Sorry."

"You his lawyer?" said Finnigan. "You doing business with Churchill?"

"Please," I said. "I can't tell you my business. You know that."

Sylvestro nodded. "Sure. You're right. That's okay. Was Churchill there when you got there?"

I shook my head. "He got there a few minutes after me."

"Did he leave before or after you?"

"Before me. I left maybe ten minutes after he did."

"About what time was that?"

"Nine-thirty, quarter of ten. I didn't really notice."

"Did you notice if he talked to anybody else when he was there?"

"No, he didn't. Ordered a drink from Skeeter. Otherwise, just me."

"He came in alone?"

I nodded.

"And left alone too?"

"Yes."

"So," said Finnigan, "you were there before him and stayed after he left. All the time he was there, he was talking with you."

"That's right," I said.

"You know it could help a lot if we knew what you talked about," said Finnigan.

I nodded. "I understand. You know I can't discuss it with you."

"Sure," said Sylvestro.

The two cops glanced at each other and exchanged nods. Sylvestro picked up Wayne Churchill's photo and slid it back into the envelope. They stood up.

"Thanks for your time," said Sylvestro. "You've been a big help."

"Anytime," I said. "Wish I could help you more."

"You helped."

I shook hands with both of them and we moved toward the door. I opened it and we stepped into the reception area. Sylvestro turned to me. "I'm sorry if we made you uncomfortable, Mr. Coyne."

"I must admit, you put me on the defensive."

"Didn't mean to. It's just, we need to backtrack the man. Placing him at Skeeter's at that time, that really helps us."

"No problem. Glad to help."

They turned to walk away. Finnigan hesitated, then turned back. "You smoke an awful lot, Mr. Coyne. You know that?"

I shrugged and glanced at Julie. She was grinning. "You nervous?" he said.

"Life makes me nervous," I said.

He smiled at me.

"Come on," said Sylvestro. "Let's leave the man alone." Finnigan nodded and joined his partner. They marched past Julie, nodding to her as they left.

After the door closed behind them, I said to Julie, "Any calls?"

"Somebody named Rodney Dennis?" It was a question.

I shrugged. "Nobody I know. What'd he want?"

"He wouldn't say. Left a number. Asked for you to call back."

I grinned. Julie knew that I didn't return calls to strangers. Some of them were people looking for counsel. I had all the clients I wanted. Most of them turned out to be officers of nonprofit organizations looking for donations or after-dinner speeches. They knew if they left that message with Julie, they'd never hear from me. My approach to them was strictly democratic—I ignored them all, without regard to race, color, creed, gender, or national origin. "Anything else?" I said.

"Nothing I couldn't handle," she said. "What was that all about?"

"You ever see Wayne Churchill on television?"

"Sure. He's a hunk."

"He was murdered last night."

Her eyes widened. "Wow! No kidding."

I nodded.

Suddenly she frowned. "So why were those cops talking to you, huh?"

"I talked to Churchill last night. I was helping them pin down his movements before he got killed."

"What were you talking to Wayne Churchill for? He interview you or something?"

"Something like that."

"So who killed him?"

I shrugged. "I didn't ask. I don't know if they know."

"How'd those cops know you'd been talking with Wayne Churchill?"

"I never asked that, either. They did most of the asking."

"Well," said Julie, nodding her head in that emphatic way of hers, "I didn't like them. They made me nervous."

I grinned. "Nothing to be nervous about. A couple of cops, doing their job. I was just helping them retrace a murdered man's movements before he was killed, that's all. I don't mind helping out the police. In the name of good citizenship and all, you know."

She rolled her eyes. "My hero."

· FIVE ·

I WENT BACK TO MY DESK. I tried Pops' number at the East Cambridge courthouse. His secretary said he was still in court. She expected he'd adjourn within the next fifteen minutes. I asked her to have him call me as soon as he came out.

I swiveled my chair around so I could look out my office window. It faced westerly, out over the old churches and new office buildings of Copley Square toward Cambridge and beyond, if I could see that far, as I liked to imagine I could, to the Swift River in Belchertown and the Deerfield beyond it, a hundred miles and a different world away, where I could count on escaping city problems like the murder of a handsome young newscaster who wanted to blackmail a Superior Court judge whose name had been submitted to the United States Senate for a seat on the Federal District Court bench. The same newscaster with whom I had had a drink the same night he was killed.

What kind of a world was this, anyway?

Dreaming of catching rainbow trout on the Swift and the Deerfield didn't work. I was still sitting there in my office, and it was a dreary dimming afternoon in February, and the fishing season was months away.

My phone buzzed. I rotated back to face my desk and picked it up. "Yes, Julie?"

"It's Judge Popowski."

"Thanks. I'll take it."

"I'm leaving now, okay?"

"Sure. See you tomorrow."

I depressed a button on the phone and said, "Pops."

I heard him sigh. "What's up, Brady?"

"You ever hear of a guy named Wayne Churchill?"

"Sure. Newsman on Channel Eight."

"Did you know he was murdered last night?"

"Of course. The courthouse is all abuzz."

"What have you heard?"

"Gossip, mostly. Girlfriend found him in the proverbial pool of blood. Two small-caliber bullet holes in him. One in the chest, one in the forehead. No sign of forced entry. They have not recovered the weapon. Understand the girl's being quizzed closely."

"Same old story, huh?"

"Usually works that way." I heard him clear his throat. "This is interesting, Brady, and I like gossip as much as the next guy. But may I ask, so what?"

"You hear anything about someone he had a drink with shortly before the estimated time of death?"

"No, nothing like that."

"Guy he argued with in a bar?"

"No."

"Skeeter's?"

There was a long silence. "Oh, Jesus, Brady."

" 'Oh, Jesus' is right, Pops."

"This Churchill . . . ?"

"Yes. Our friendly neighborhood blackmailer. One and the same."

"You didn't—?"

"What, kill him?"

"Don't be ridiculous. That's not what I was going to say. How'd you hear about this?"

"The police visited me. Asked me some questions. Trying to figure out where Churchill had been, I guess."

"How'd they track you down?"

"I don't know. I was there and so was he. Only he was wearing a mustache and shades, so I didn't recognize him. They showed me Churchill's photograph, and I drew a blank. They told me his name and I couldn't place it. Asked me where I was last night and what I was doing there. Queried me closely on my comings and goings. The thing is, I'm not sure I gave them good answers. I mean, they came in just trying to backtrack Churchill's whereabouts. But I gave them lousy answers, looking back on it. I mean, for all I know they left with a new suspect. That's how I'm beginning to feel."

"My God, Brady. I don't blame you for being upset."

"I'm not exactly upset, Pops. I mean, mainly, it's weird, thinking there I was, talking with the man, and he walked out of there and went home and somebody shot him."

"Murder is always weird," said Pops.

"I feel so—so guilty, Pops. They asked me these questions, and I couldn't answer them very well, and somehow they made me feel as if I had done something wrong."

"Good cops can do that."

"These guys are good cops, then."

"So, what'd you tell them?"

"I told them what I did last night. I mean, I just told them the truth, as best I could. You don't pay attention to things when they're happening. What time you do this or that, exactly who said what to whom. After a while they started to question me more closely, trying to pin down the times. Looking back, I think I was pretty vague. I felt as if I was being interrogated."

"I've got to ask," he said.

"You should know better, Pops. You don't even need to ask. You're my client, and you're privileged. I didn't utter your name to them. I did admit I was there with him on behalf of a client. But now I can see how damn suspicious I must've appeared to them. I mean, they got me to admit I'd had a drink with this Churchill just last night, yet when they showed me his picture I didn't even recognize it, and I couldn't place his name, which I guess makes me suspicious right there. I gather everybody in Boston's heard of Wayne Churchill except me."

"Anybody who watches the news on Channel Eight," said Pops.

"I don't. I like the sports guy on Channel Four. But how do you explain that? So anyway, then they asked me why I was there at Skeeter's with him, what we talked about. Naturally, I refused to say. I must've sounded pretty evasive."

"You sound upset, Brady."

"It's been slowly dawning on me how it seemed."

"Christ, what a mess. I'm really sorry I got you into this."

"Hey," I said. "This is why lawyers make a lot of money."

"What can I do?" he said.

"Nothing. Pat my head. Tell me I'm overreacting."

"Well, of course. You are. You know you are." He hesitated. Then he said, "Brady, I know you realize how important our privileged status on this is to me. My God, if my name were connected with a murder just now, there's no way that nomination would happen. I mean, a peccadillo a long time ago, that's one thing. But a murder? After all the crap that's been happening with judicial appointments . . ."

I arched my neck against the stiffness that stress always brings. "Don't worry about it, Pops. This is not an issue."

"I do appreciate it, Brady, and I know it makes things more awkward for you. But, hell, you didn't kill the man, did you?"

"Is that a question?"

"No. Of course not."

"I'm not gonna tell them anything about you, Pops."

"Hell, I know that."

"I didn't tell them that you and I talked on the phone last night, either."

"It never occurred to me that you would."

"Well," I sighed, "anyway, that's the story. That's who sent you the note. Wayne Churchill."

"Unbelieveable," he muttered.

"Look on the bright side," I said.

"There's a bright side?"

"Sure. This Churchill's the guy who wanted to blackmail you. He's dead. So you don't have that to worry about anymore."

"Christ, Brady. What kind of a thing is that to say?"

"I'm always on the lookout for bright sides."

"Boy, I'm sorry about this, friend."

"Me too."

"Let me know if there's anything I can do."

"I will, Pops."

After supper that evening I walked to Skeeter's. I had to get out of my apartment. I felt a compulsion to do something, and I didn't know what. I was beginning to feel like a character in a Kafka novel. In retrospect, it seemed to me that Detectives Sylvestro and Finnigan had not questioned me as if I were simply a witness. The deeper we had gotten into the interrogation, the more I had begun to feel as if I were a suspect. I had to admit that I must have sounded suspicious. They probably thought I was hiding something, copping out behind the client privilege plea. Why did I meet Churchill at Skeeter's? Sorry. Can't say. Client privilege, don't you know. So what'd you talk about with this guy who was about to get snuffed? Terribly sorry, gentlemen. Client privilege, of course. What about phone calls when you got home, help us know you were there when somebody was shooting Churchill? Sure. Talking with a client. Can't tell you who, you understand.

Christ, it sounded bad.

It was ridiculous, of course. The product of my own overwrought imagination. It's what I do when I spend too much time by myself. I invent troubles for myself that don't exist. I visualize my boys speeding around the back roads at high speeds, colliding with telephone poles. That's one of my standbys.

I tried to console myself with the thought that cops were trained to deal with everyone as if he were a suspect. Wayne Churchill probably had plenty of enemies. Everybody does. I had happened to cross his path at an unfortunate time.

But I didn't kill him. Someone else did.

None of this succeeded in consoling me very much.

Skeeter's was crowded, and it was several minutes before he noticed me. He came at me with a grin, brandishing his rag. "Hey, Mr. Coyne. Two nights in a row, huh?"

"How are you, Skeets?"

"Good. Busy. More of that Rebel Yell?"

I nodded.

"Can't talk you into trying an Early Wynn?"

"I hesitate to ask," I said.

"Old Early was one tough son of a bitch," said Skeeter. "I faced him plenty of times. Felt lucky if I fouled off a couple. Actually, I had it easy, being as how I wasn't much of a hitter. The good hitters he always knocked on their ass. He'd give 'em this high-riding fastball. It'd explode inside on you. Whoosh! Old Early's fastball, you could hear the seams hissing when it went under your chin. Loosen you up quick. Set you back on your heels, believe me. Then he'd tuck that curve over the outside corner. Most hitters, though they wouldn't admit it, were scared to face Early Wynn in a close game with somebody on base. Early used to say, 'I got the right to knock down anybody holding a bat.'"

"So what's in an Early Wynn?"

"Blackberry brandy, champagne, and vodka," he said. "Knock down anybody holding a glass."

I smiled. "I'll stick with a shot of Rebel Yell, I think."

He was back in a minute with my drink. He watched me while I sipped it. Then he said, "I hope I didn't get you in trouble, Mr. Coyne."

"How's that?"

"There were a couple cops in here this morning. I wasn't even opened up. They pounded on the door while I was out back working on my accounts. They showed me a picture of that guy you were with last night."

"You recognized him?"

"Sure. That fake mustache fooled me last night when he was here. Like I told you then, I couldn't place him. But when they showed me that picture, I remembered the guy that was with you. Knew it was him right off. I seen

Wayne Churchill on the tube plenty of times. They had a picture of you, too."

"They did?"

"Yup." Skeeter shrugged apologetically. "I had to tell them the truth."

"Of course you did."

"I told them it looked like you and Churchill had planned to meet here. I mean, I didn't know that, but that's how it looked."

"That's all right."

"I told them you had some kind of argument."

I nodded. "I guess that's accurate too."

"They wanted to know when he left, and when you left. I was able to pin down the times pretty close, because of the hockey game. I told them that Churchill left at nine twenty-five. You had another drink and left about fifteen minutes later." Skeeter arched his eyebrows at me. "You got a problem, Mr. Coyne?"

"Nothing I can't work out."

"That guy got murdered, you know."

"Yes, I know."

"Channel Eight did a big thing on it on the six o'clock news. They're saying the police have a suspect."

"Suspect? Did they say suspect, singular? Or did they say suspects?"

"They said suspect, Mr. Coyne. Singular. Actually, I think they said possible suspect. Or maybe alleged possible suspect." He smiled. "You know how they think they gotta talk."

I nodded. "That's how they have to do it."

"From what I hear, the suspect is the girl who phoned it in."

"I heard that too."

"Hope I didn't get you in trouble, Mr. Coyne."

"Nah. You did what you're supposed to do. No problem."

"Well, hell," said Skeeter. "Man like you. Lawyer and all. Christ, they can't suspect you, can they?"

"No, I don't think they suspect me. I'm not worried about that."

"I mean," persisted Skeeter, leaning toward me on his forearms, "They talked to me, too."

I sipped my bourbon. "They were just backtracking his movements, that's all. That's why they talked to both of us."

Skeeter leaned across the bar to me. "Looked like the guy was giving you a hard time."

I shrugged. "We had a little disagreement."

"I had to mention that to the cops. Felt bad, but I had to."

I nodded.

"They already knew," he said.

"Knew what?"

"They knew that you were here with him. I mean, even before I told them anything, they already had his picture and your picture. They didn't even ask if you were here together. Just, did I know who the two of you were, whether you came in and left together, what you had to drink, did I know what you talked about. They knew you were here, and they knew you were here with each other."

"Don't feel bad," I told him.

"I didn't tell them that I heard anything you said to each other, though."

"Did you?"

"What, hear anything?"

"Yes."

He grinned. "Not me. Bartenders only hear what they're supposed to hear."

When I got back from Skeeter's, the red light on my answering machine was winking. I played the tape. "This is Gloria," she said. "Please call me."

She answered on the second ring. "It's me," I said.

"Brady, what the hell is going on?"

"What do you mean?"

"Two cops showed up on my doorstep just about suppertime."

"Sylvestro and Finnigan."

"Yes. And aside from that Finnigan practically raping me with his eyes—"

"He did?"

"He sure as hell did."

"He hardly glanced at Julie."

"Oh, I'll bet."

"What'd they want, hon?" I said.

"They started asking me all about our phone conversation last night. I mean, wasn't that about the most innocuous conversation you can imagine?"

"I don't think they cared about the content of it."

"No. You're right. They wanted to know the times."

"So what did you tell them?"

"Well, in spite of the way that Finnigan kept running his eyes over my body, Mr. Sylvestro was really quite nice and polite. Of course I told them the truth. I know enough to do that. Besides, I had no idea what they were getting at." I heard her take a deep breath and let it out with a nervous whoosh. "Brady, are you in some kind of trouble?"

"Nah," I said, with more conviction than I was beginning to feel. "Not to worry. I didn't do anything. It probably just looks different to the police from the way it is right now. It'll get straightened out. Tell me what they asked you."

"They asked if I talked to you on the phone last night. I told them that I did. They asked if you called me or if I called you. I told them that I called first, but you weren't in, so—"

"I was in," I said. "I was in the shower."

"Whatever," said Gloria. "I didn't know that. I just said that I called and left a message on your machine, and that you called me back about half an hour later."

"What times did you tell them?"

"I called you at eleven. It was right before the news came on, and I was hassling Joey to go to bed but he said he had to watch the news for something he was doing in his history class. You called me back at eleven thirty-five. The news had ended and Joey thought he was going to watch Johnny Carson and I told him like hell he was. So he said okay and turned off the set. I went upstairs. He was having a piece of cake and a glass of milk. Promised he'd be right up. That's when you called. He answered it in the kitchen, then I took it upstairs in the bedroom."

"You're sure of those times?"

"Sure I'm sure."

"I had them wrong," I said, more to myself than her. "It probably looks like I didn't get home until eleven-thirty or so, and I was lying about it."

"What did you tell them?"

"I think I said we talked at around eleven. I didn't say you called and left a message and I called you back. Just that we talked at eleven."

"Brady," said Gloria, "what is this all about?"

"You heard about Wayne Churchill?"

"Well, sure. He was murdered."

"I was with him last night. Right before he got killed."

"You mean, if you weren't home when you said you were . . . ?"

"Right, hon."

There was a long pause. "My God, Brady," said Gloria finally.

"Nothing to worry about."

"But when you told them you talked to me at eleven . . . ?"

"Sure. Contradiction there. I'll clear that up."

"Well, there's one thing," she said.

"What's that?"

"I did tell them I left a message on your machine. And I did tell them that when you called me you mentioned the message. So at least they know you were home when you called me."

"There you go," I said. "No problem."

"Is there anything I can do?"

"Just tell the truth, Gloria. Don't worry about this."

"Oh, sure."

"Well, it's nice to know you're worried, I guess."

"Nothing ever really changes, does it?"

"Not really. Anyway, we've got a date Friday. If I'm not behind bars by then."

"Don't make jokes, Brady."

"I should know better," I said. "Our senses of humor never meshed very well."

I was brushing my teeth when the phone rang. I caught it on the third ring. My answering machine kicks in after the fourth.

"Mr. Brady L. Coyne, please," came a man's voice.

"This is he," I said, trying to match his formality.

"My name is Rodney Dennis, sir. I tried to reach you in your office today."

"I don't make speeches."

"Excuse me?"

"I give lots of money to Trout Unlimited, the Nature Conservancy. That's it for charity. I am taking on no new clients."

I heard him chuckle. "I'm sorry. Let me explain. I'm the station manager at Channel Eight." He paused. He wanted me to say something. I didn't.

After an awkward moment he said, "You know about Wayne Churchill, of course."

"I heard, yes."

"Well, Mr. Coyne, you, I understand, were the last person to see Wayne alive."

Damn those cops! Less than twenty-four hours, and already the media had gotten hold of my name. "Look," I said, "Maybe you'd better tell me what you want, Mr. Dennis."

"An exclusive interview, Mr. Coyne," he said promptly. "Give you a chance to tell your story in your own way. What do you say?"

"I say: Fuck you. And you can quote me."

He laughed. "I'm afraid the FCC might not approve." He cleared his throat. "You should give this some serious thought, Mr. Coyne. It could do both of us a lot of good, you know."

"I don't see how."

"Please think about it, Mr. Coyne. The Wayne Churchill murder is a very big story for us, naturally. Big story for you, too."

"Let me correct you on one thing."

"Please."

"I wasn't the last person to see Churchill alive. Somebody killed him, you know."

He chuckled again. "The one doesn't exclude the other, Mr. Coyne."

"Good evening, Mr. Dennis," I said. Then I hung up.

· SIX ·

THE SKY OVER THE HARBOR was changing from soot to pewter. I dropped an English muffin into the toaster and retrieved my *Globe* from outside the door. Then I retrieved my muffin, spread it with peanut butter, and took it and the paper to the table. The story was on the front page, beside the same picture of Wayne Churchill that Sylvestro had showed me. NEWSMAN FOUND MURDERED, read the headline.

I skimmed the story. My name was not mentioned, nor, for that matter, was the fact that Churchill had visited Skeeter's Infield shortly before his death. Rodney Dennis, the Channel 8 station manager, evidently had better sources than the *Globe*. Still, it seemed to me a matter of time before the rest of the media would catch on. And then, inevitably, someone would connect me to Pops. And then . . . I went back and read the article more closely.

Drugs had not been discounted as a possible motive. There was no evidence of theft, although that wasn't discounted either, nor did the police find evidence of a forced entry into Churchill's condominium. He had been shot twice with a .32-caliber handgun, according to preliminary reports from the state police ballistics laboratory. The first shot, according to a spokesman from the Medical Examiner's office, was to the chest, and had probably killed him instantly. The second shot had come from the muzzle of the same gun placed directly against the dead man's forehead.

Gretchen Warde, the young lady who found Churchill's body, was quoted as saying, "Everybody liked Wayne. He was a down-to-earth guy. He didn't fool around with drugs. And he was a very good newsman."

She didn't mention that this down-to-earth guy dabbled in blackmail.

My friend Rodney Dennis said in a prepared statement, "Wayne Churchill was one of the best investigative reporters in the country. He was working on a big story when he was killed. We are all shocked and saddened by his sudden and violent death."

Boston homicide detective Jack Sylvestro was quoted as saying, "We have some good leads in this case."

I wondered if that meant me.

The story was continued on page six. Beside it was a sidebar outlining Wayne Churchill's career. BA from Stanford in 1980, where he was graduated cum laude in English Literature and was honorable mention on the Associated Press All-American soccer team. Master's from Northwestern in communications two years later. Brief stint with a radio station in Omaha. Then he took a job with the Miami *Herald* as a political reporter. A year later he was in Cleveland, reporting political news for a television station. Shortly thereafter he became news anchor. And a little over a year ago, he came to Boston's Channel 8 as a reporter.

He had won an award from the Florida Press Club for a story on illegal Cuban immigration in Miami. He had been nominated Newscaster of the Year in Cleveland.

A handsome, talented young man with a bright past and a brilliant future. Except now he was dead.

Why the hell would this guy try to blackmail a Superior Court judge for a paltry ten thousand dollars? The *Globe* offered me no answer to that one.

I got to the office early, around eight-thirty, as I often do. Julie doesn't get in until nine. She is never early. Never late, either.

Boston homicide detective Sylvestro and state police detective Finnigan were leaning against the wall in the corridor, waiting for me. Sylvestro was wearing the same brown wool topcoat he had worn on our previous get-together. Finnigan had dressed up for the occasion. He had on a beige trench coat affair, with epaulets and a belt and the collar turned up around his neck, looking like someone out of a Ludlum novel.

"Good morning, gentlemen," I said, shaking hands with each of them.

Sylvestro shrugged apologetically. "Sorry about this, Mr. Coyne. We've got to go over some things again with you."

"It's all right," I said. "I'm glad to see you. I've been expecting you." I unlocked the door to the office suite and stood aside. "Enter, please."

They went in and I followed them. I hung up my coat and got the coffee started. Then I showed them into my inner office. They unbuttoned their coats but didn't take them off.

"Sorry, but the coffee won't be ready for a few minutes," I said.

"Thanks, Mr. Coyne," said Sylvestro. "Don't worry about coffee. I hope this isn't a bad time. We figured we'd try to catch you before you got started."

"This is fine."

"Hate to bother you. Few odds and ends . . ."

I gestured to the sofa where they had sat before. They sat down. I took the same chair across from them that I had sat in during their first visit. "You want to talk about the other night again."

Sylvestro nodded. "Appreciate your cooperation. We got a few questions."

"Me first," I said. "I've got a couple questions."

Sylvestro frowned. "Yeah, okay."

"Number one, why the hell did you give my name to Channel Eight? You've got no right—"

"Whoa," said Sylvestro, holding up his hand like a traffic cop. "What are you talking about?"

"This guy, this Rodney Dennis, called me. Twice. Once, for God's sake, while you two were here with me yesterday. Then again at home last night. Why'd you tell him I was at Skeeter's with Churchill?"

Sylvestro looked at Finnigan, who shook his head. Then he frowned at me. "We didn't. We didn't mention your name to anybody."

"One of your colleagues did, then. Because he sure as hell got it from somebody."

"Not the cops," said Sylvestro. "Guaranteed. No way. Look, Mr. Coyne. I won't say our operation doesn't get leaky sometimes. Sometime down the line, sure, maybe your name might dribble out. But not yet. We've got a good lid on this so far. I promise you. Dennis got nothing out of us."

I stared at him. "He got it from somebody."

"Well, seems to me," said Sylvestro, "Churchill worked for Dennis. Probably told him what he was doing. Whatever it was, which we wish you'd tell us, but if you won't we still got a chance of getting it out of Dennis. Though he'd probably rather keep it for himself, get a big exclusive story, which Channel Eight could certainly use."

"I don't like being pursued by the media any more than I like being interrogated by the police," I said.

"Nobody does."

I sighed. "Another question."

"Go ahead."

"Am I a suspect here?"

Sylvestro shrugged. "Everybody's a suspect."

"That's not what I mean."

"We're just trying to get some things clear. So we can understand."

"But am I a suspect?"

"Right now, Mr. Coyne, you're a witness. Actually, an important witness. Okay? If you were a suspect, we'd Mirandize you, bring in a tape recorder. Right now, we just want to ask you a few questions."

"Well, okay then," I said. "Shoot." I grinned. "Bad choice of words."

Sylvestro smiled appreciatively and glanced at Finnigan, who nodded but did not smile. Finnigan, I noticed, rarely smiled, and when he did it was not a pleasant smile. I tried not to take it personally that he didn't smile at me.

Sylvestro extracted a notepad from the depths of his topcoat and consulted it for a moment. "Okay, Mr. Coyne," he said, looking up at me. "Now let's talk about the night you met with Wayne Churchill at Skeeter's Infield. You did meet with him there, am I right?"

"Yes."

"And why was it you met with him?"

"I told you before. I can't say."

"For a client, I believe you told us."

I smiled. "I believe I did."

"And you don't want to tell us who this client is."

"Right. I don't. I can't. You know this."

"Was the client Wayne Churchill?" said Finnigan.

I turned my head and looked at him. He shrugged. "I tried," he said.

"Are you protecting this client?" said Sylvestro.

"Well, sure. That's what the client–lawyer relationship is all about. That doesn't mean he's involved."

"Then why . . . ?" began Finnigan.

Sylvestro turned to him. "Come on," he said. Finnigan shrugged.

"Mr. Coyne," said the older cop, "you can see how this looks, you refusing to answer our questions."

"This has nothing to do with self-incrimination."

He nodded. "Sure. Incriminating somebody else, then?"

"If that's supposed to be a question, you know I can't answer it."

Sylvestro sighed and nodded, as if he expected these answers. "Okay, then. Let's go over the times again, Mr. Coyne. Now, what time did you arrive at Skeeter's?"

"Nine o'clock, give or take a couple minutes."

"And Churchill arrived—?"

"A few minutes after that."

"And you had a discussion with him."

"Yes."

"What did you discuss?"

"I can't answer that."

"Why?"

"Come on. I already explained that."

"Privileged information," said Finnigan. He made the words sound vulgar.

"That's right," I said.

Sylvestro nodded. "Okay. Sure. Did you argue with Churchill?"

"I'm not going to tell you what we talked about."

"A witness said it appeared that you argued."

I shrugged.

"You don't want to comment on that?"

"No."

"And what time did you leave?"

"Around nine-thirty."

"When did Churchill leave?"

"Ten or fifteen minutes before me."

"Did you observe anybody leave with him?"

"No. Wait. There were two women at the bar. They left after him, and before me."

"Why didn't you tell us about them before?"

"I didn't think of it. It didn't seem relevant, anyway."

"Can you describe these women?"

"One was blond, one brunette. Both maybe thirty. Good-looking. Well dressed. That's all I really noticed."

"Did you know either of these women?"

"No. Never saw them before."

"Did Churchill appear to know either of them?"

"He didn't seem to even notice them."

"Okay. Now, what time did you get home?"

"It must have been around ten. I walked home. I didn't notice the time. But I did turn on my TV. The Celtics game had ended. I watched the very end of the Bruins. They were in overtime. Whatever time that was."

"You told us that you talked to your wife—"

"My former wife. We're divorced."

"Right. You talked to your wife at eleven. That right?"

"No. It was about eleven-thirty."

"You told us before that it was eleven, Mr. Coyne."

"I told you I wasn't really aware of the time. After the Bruins game I had a shower. Gloria called me while I was in the shower, left a message on my machine. I called her back around eleven-thirty."

Sylvestro frowned. "Now, hang on. I'm a little confused here. You got home at ten. Watched a couple minutes of the Bruins. Had a shower. While you were in the shower, your wife called you, and you didn't call her back until eleven-thirty?"

"I didn't get into the shower the minute the Bruins were over."

"Well, what did you do before you got in the shower?"

I called Pops, for one thing, I thought. He could easily verify I had left a message on his machine somewhere around ten. But I couldn't tell Sylvestro that. "I made some tea. Relaxed. Called a client. It was probably closer to eleven when I got into the shower."

"This client. Wanna say who it was?"

I shook my head. "Come on. You know better."

Sylvestro waved his hand, as if it were not important. "Mr. Coyne, the last time we talked, you told us that you phoned your wife at eleven. Now you're saying it was eleven-thirty. Why have you changed your mind?"

"I'm not changing my mind. I'm just remembering it differently."

"Had a chance to talk it over with her, huh?"

"Yes. She and I talked after you visited her."

"She called you, then, right?"

"Yes. She left a message on my machine."

"But you weren't home when she called."

"I was home. I was in the shower."

"The previous time we talked, you didn't tell us that she had called you and left a message."

"I didn't think it was important."

"Do you own any weapons?" said Finnigan.

"Yes, as a matter of fact. I do. I bet you already knew that."

Finnigan gave me his unpleasant smile. He had small, pointed teeth, like a northern pike.

"I own a Smith & Wesson thirty-eight," I said. "It's in my safe. Want to see it?"

"What about a thirty-two handgun?" said Finnigan.

"No. Just the thirty-eight."

"We don't have a warrant, Mr. Coyne," said Sylvestro. "Are you offering to show us your thirty-eight?"

"Sure."

I got up and went to the wall safe that the architects of my building evidently felt every office suite should have. I have found no use for it except as a place to store my Smith & Wesson. I rarely remove the gun from its hiding place. I don't like carrying it around with me. Once I shot a man with it, and the state police kept it for three months. When they returned it to me, I wasn't that happy to see it.

I lifted up the calendar I had hung over the safe, twisted the dials, and opened it up. I reached inside and found the chamois cloth that I kept the gun wrapped in. I took it out and brought it over to the cops. I handed it to Sylvestro.

He unfolded the chamois. "You got a license for this weapon, Mr. Coyne?"

"Of course."

"Thirty-eight," he said to Finnigan. He sniffed the muzzle, popped the cylinder, and held it up to the light to peer into the barrel. Then he handed it to Finnigan, who also sniffed it. Finnigan wrapped the chamois around it and gave it back to me. I sat in the chair with the gun in my lap.

"Own any other weapons?" said Finnigan.

"No. Just this one."

"Did you kill Wayne Churchill?"

"No."

"Did you follow him to his house after he left Skeeter's?"

"No."

"Did you have an appointment to meet him there after your discussion at Skeeter's?"

"No."

"Did you threaten him when you argued with him at Skeeter's?"

"I told you. I can't discuss what he and I talked about."

"He threatened you, then."

I didn't say anything.

"How well did you know Churchill?" Finnigan was leaning toward me. Every time he asked me a question he pounded his right fist on his thigh.

"I never met him before that night."

"Why did you meet him that night?"

"I can't tell you."

"Oh, sure. Protecting a client."

Sylvestro put his hand on Finnigan's shoulder. Finnigan was shaking his head back and forth. He leaned back and folded his arms. "You're in big trouble, friend."

"Come on," said Sylvestro to him. "Lay off."

"Are you intending to arrest me?" I said.

Finnigan glowered.

"No, Mr. Coyne," said Sylvestro. "We didn't come here to arrest you. We came here hoping you could help us understand what happened the night before last."

"Then you gentlemen are out of line."

Sylvestro nodded. "You're right." He shot a sideways frown at Finnigan. "I apologize, Mr. Coyne."

"Apology accepted," I said. "I'm sorry I couldn't help you more. I don't know who killed Wayne Churchill or why. But it wasn't me."

Finnigan shook his head slowly back and forth and glanced at Sylvestro, who nodded. He stood up and Finnigan followed suit.

Sylvestro held out his hand. I shook it. "Appreciate your time, Mr. Coyne," he said.

I shrugged. "I want to help."

"Sure," said Finnigan.

· SEVEN ·

I STOOD IN THE DOORWAY and watched them leave. Julie was at her desk with the telephone tucked against her neck. She watched them too.

After the door closed behind them, I went back into my office. I sat at my desk and swiveled my chair around to stare out the window. I hadn't seen the sun in four days. The cityscape was painted in tones of gray. It was sullen and grouchy, just like me.

Julie scratched at the door. Without turning, I said, "Come in. And I hope you brought coffee."

"I did," she said.

I turned around. She came and sat in the chair beside my desk. She had had her black hair cut short, which did good things for her fine cheekbones. She wore gold hoops in her ears. Her green eyes tried to smile but fell short. She put the old mug that Joey had made for me three years earlier in eighth-grade ceramics class in front of me. It was steaming. I picked it up and sipped from it. Julie had brought her own mug with her.

"So what the hell is going on?" she said.

I sighed. "I really can't even talk to you about it."

"Oh, come on, Brady."

"That's what's so frustrating. I can't discuss it with anybody."

"But this is me," she said.

"This is I."

She widened her eyes. "Hoo, boy. Look who's correcting whose grammar."

"Reflex," I said. "Sorry."

"Those guys look mean."

"They're not that tough."

"They look tough to me."

"They're no tougher than me," I said.

"Than I," she said.

I lit a cigarette and touched her wrist with my hand. "What's on this morning?"

"A bunch of desk work. We've got a pile of correspondence to answer. You've got some calls to make. Several clients who need to hear your reassuring voice. Then there's Mrs. Covington."

"Huh?"

"Mrs. Covington. Suing her dentist, remember?"

"Oh, right."

"Christ, Brady. Where's your mind?"

"I'm sorry."

"Those guys're getting to you, huh?"

"I guess they are."

"Nothing you can tell me?"

I shook my head. "No. Look. I've got to make a couple calls first. Then we'll get to work."

After Julie left my office, I called my friend Charlie McDevitt. He's a prosecuter for Uncle Sam, in the Boston division of the Justice Department. He's got an office at Government Center. I had to be careful what I said to Charlie, because he knew Pops at Yale when I did. But Charlie's my best friend. He's the guy I talk to when I need to talk. He's also a fine lawyer who understands a prosecutor's mind better than I do. He's been on that side of the fence a long time.

I exchanged flirtations with his secretary, Shirley, who's a dead ringer for the round-cheeked white-haired lady pictured on the frozen-fish packages. I made her giggle and admit she was blushing, as I always did, and then she put me through to Charlie.

"Belize," said Charlie, instead of hello.

"Christmas Island," I answered.

"Either one. When?"

"Would that I could," I said. "Bonefish. Permit. Barracuda. One of these days."

"The other side of the world, Christmas Island," he said dreamily. "Heaven."

"Which makes this side of the world . . ." I said, leaving the obvious thought unfinished.

"That bad, huh?"

"That bad."

"You've looked out your window, then," said Charlie.

"I have. Grim out there."

"We gotta get away."

"Agreed. That's not why I called."

"Business, huh?"

"Sort of. Charlie, I've got a delicate problem."

"Your hemorrhoids kicking up again?"

"Yeah, but that's not it. Charlie, you're sort of a cop."

"Coyne, I find the comparison both spurious and odious."

"Pardon me. Let me put it this way. You think like a prosecutor."

"Hell, I *am* a prosecutor. What's this all about?"

"I think a couple cops are convinced I killed somebody."

I heard him chuckle. Good old Charlie. Just that chuckle gave me perspective. Brady Coyne, kill somebody? What a laugh.

"Did you?" he said. He snickered again.

"I'm not kidding. The thing is, my alibi, if that's what you call it, is mixed up with a client."

"Aha," he said. "Client privilege."

"Yeah. It makes me sound kind of guilty."

"It's the price we pay sometimes. Generally we are well reimbursed."

"Yeah, well, in this case it's damned awkward."

"Your client can release you, you know."

"I can't ask him to. Not under these particular circumstances."

"Because he—?"

"No, nothing like that." If I told Charlie it was Pops, he'd understand. But I couldn't tell him that, and I knew he wouldn't ask.

"So these cops are on your case," he said.

"Yes. And already there's a television guy who's got wind of it."

"These cops actually tell you they think you did it?"

"Not in so many words, exactly."

"That's cops for you," said Charlie. "They accuse enough people enough times, somebody's gonna cave in. Reminds me of something Burleigh Whitt was telling me recently. You remember Burl?"

"The game warden?"

"Right. Tiny Wheeler knows him. Burl's way up there in the screaming Maine wilderness risking his life trying to track down jacklighters and those dirt-poor folks who shoot themselves a couple cow moose and three or four deer a year to feed the kids. Anyhow, Burl was telling me about this one particular old coot who he knew was poaching deer. Burl pretty well had it figured out that this guy'd get up before dawn and get himself a deer and have it all dragged in and skinned out and butchered before the sun came up, and it was pissing Burl off that he could never seem to nail the guy in the act.

Everybody knew he was poaching, and it was bad for Burl's credibility that he couldn't catch him."

"Charlie—"

"No, listen. This is relevant. Burl decided he was gonna nab the old geezer red-handed. So he got up at two A.M. one morning and hid himself in the bushes by the old-timer's cabin. Sure enough, about maybe four the light went on inside the cabin, and a few minutes later wisps of smoke began to come out of the chimney. Then the old guy came out onto the porch. 'Mr. Warden,' he called. 'No sense of you layin' out there gettin' all cold and damp in them bushes. Whyn't you come on in here and get yourself a nice cup of coffee.' So Burl cussed himself and got up and went in there, had a cup of coffee with the old guy.

"Burl remembered he'd told a couple guys in his office what he was gonna do. Figured one of them must've let it slip. So he waited a few weeks, and this time he didn't tell anybody what he was up to. Again, got up early and hid outside the cabin while the moon was still high. The cabin was dark. He huddled there, freezing his ass off, and finally a light went on in the cabin. Then smoke appeared from the chimney. Then the old poacher came out onto his porch. 'Hey, Mr. Warden,' he yelled. 'Don't go catching cold out there in them bushes. You come on in here, have some coffee and get warm.' So Burl, very embarrassed, went in and had coffee with the old codger, and after that he gave up trying to catch him. He just admitted to himself that the old guy was too smart for him. You still with me, Brady?"

I sighed. "I'm with you, Charlie. Is this going someplace?"

"Course it is. Well, about a year later, Burl hears the old poacher's had himself a coronary. He's laid up in the county hospital. The scuttlebutt is that he's not gonna make it. So Burl goes to visit him. 'Nice you could come visit me,' wheezes the old guy from his bed. 'Sorry to hear about your sickness,' says Burl. 'Ain't gonna make it, they tell me,' says the poacher. 'Sure gonna miss the woods.' Burl hitches his chair closer to the bed. 'You've got to tell me something,' he says. 'Those times when I was hiding out there in the bushes waiting for you. How in hell did you know I was there?' The old geezer turns his head and grins. 'I didn't know you was there, son. Every mornin' for thirty years I went out on my porch and yelled the same damn thing.' "

I lit a cigarette and didn't say anything.

"You still there, Brady?"

"I'm here, Charlie."

"You get my point?"

"You're saying these cops're like that old poacher. They go out on their porch every morning, so to speak, and yell accusations, and sooner or later someone's going to be hiding in the bushes, thinking they've been found out. You're saying I should ignore what they say to me. Just stay hunkered in the bushes."

"You got it, pal."

"Difference is, I'm not guilty of anything."

"That doesn't make it different at all," said Charlie.

"Okay. Thanks for the advice."

"That's why you called, wasn't it? For advice?"

"Yes."

"Well, remember about that old poacher, then."

"Thanks, Charlie. Anything else I should be thinking about?"

"Sure. Though I hesitate to mention it to you."

"What is it?"

"Well," he said. "If I know cops, they think they've got themselves a hot one."

"Me."

"Right. And while they're chasing you around, the real bad guy's feeling better and better about things. Because nobody's chasing him around."

"And somebody ought to be chasing him around," I said. "Like, for example, me."

"Jesus, Brady. I didn't say that."

"Who else?"

Charlie had no answer for me.

After I hung up with Charlie I tried Detective Horowitz's number at State Police headquarters at 1010 Commonwealth Avenue, not really expecting him to be in. But he was. I gave my name to his secretary, and a minute later he came on the line.

"Horowitz," he mumbled.

"You got a mouthful of Bazooka?" I said.

I heard a bubble pop. "Nasty habit," he said.

"You should try cigarettes."

"Coyne," he said, "I ain't got time for a bunch of shit. What do you want?"

"What do you know about the Churchill killing?"

He popped a bubble. "I know what there is to know. Just for one thing, that you seem to have stepped into some moderately deep shit."

"I hope you told your friends about me."

He snorted through his nose. "Would you really want me to do that?"

"Come on, Horowitz."

"You've been in plenty of weird scrapes, Coyne. Christ, you killed a guy with your gun a few years back."

"You know about that. You investigated that one."

"Sure. You were defending the virtue of a woman. Still, you can see how it looks."

"What've they got on me?"

"Look, Coyne. You are pushing what is already a tenuous friendship to its limits. You follow me?"

"Spell it out."

"Hell, you're a witness in a homicide."

"That's it?"

"Okay," he said. "You're a possible suspect. How's that?"

"That's not very good."

"They haven't got anything more than circumstance right now. They come up with much more . . ." He paused. "Will they?"

"Will they what?"

"Come up with something else?"

"Of course not."

"Well, I didn't really think so. Still . . ."

"Look," I said. "What the hell is going on?"

He sighed. "I guess I won't be screwing anything up if I tell you what I've heard. The papers got most of it anyway. You got the right to know."

"Thanks."

"This'll cost you something fancy at the Ritz when it's all over."

"Fine. Gladly. It'll be worth a celebration."

He cleared his throat. "This girl found Churchill's body on the living room floor in his condo on Beacon Street. He was—"

"What girl?"

"His girlfriend, I gather. She had a key to the place. Name of Gretchen Warde. Warde with an *e*. Works over at Channel Eight. Assistant producer or something, which means glorified gofer. Anyhow, she went in and found the body. Called the cops."

"What time?"

"Little after midnight. Gather she and Churchill spent the night together now and then."

"She's not a suspect?"

"Of course she is. She's the main suspect. She's a better suspect than you. They grilled her. She didn't seem to have her times straight. Holes in her story. Nothing like hard evidence, from what I hear. Like they didn't find a weapon. The M.E. looked at the body, estimated how long it had been dead, and I guess they figure she could've done it after she left the station. They're shy motive, but they've got opportunity."

"Same as me," I said.

"That's what I hear."

"So how'd they glom on to me so quick?" I said.

"This is why I don't think you did it," said Horowitz.

"Why?"

"Churchill had a piece of paper in his pocket. It had your name, the name of the bar you met him at—"

"Skeeter's."

"Right. And the time. Nine o'clock."

"How's that get me off the hook?"

"It gets you off the hook with me. Not with Sylvestro and Finnigan. See, I know you, and for all your shortcomings, I know you ain't dumb. If you shot Churchill to death, you would've gone through his pockets. You sure as hell wouldn't have left that piece of paper there. In fact, it occurred to me that whoever did shoot him might've stuck the paper into his pocket afterwards."

"Who'd do a thing like that?"

Horowitz laughed. "Make a list of your enemies, Coyne."

"He had that paper there because we had a meeting set up at Skeeter's for nine o'clock. That's how the cops knew to go and question Skeeter."

"Whatever you say," said Horowitz.

"So they went to Skeeter's, and they found out that I had been there with Churchill, that we'd had a discussion that wasn't exactly amicable, and that we both left around nine-thirty. And since I was basically unable to account for my time between then and eleven-thirty, by which time Churchill was already dead, I could easily have followed him home, or gone with him, and plugged him, and had plenty of time to get back to my place by the time I called Gloria."

"Well, all of that sounds about the way I'm hearing it around here. They haven't got a weapon and they haven't figured out your connection to Churchill. They do have this Warde woman. But they've also got you. I know Finnigan. I've worked with Sylvestro a couple times, too. They're good. Dogged. They think they've got a hot one, they don't give up. They'll work their asses off till they dig something up. I hear you weren't especially cooperative when they braced you yesterday."

"They were back this morning." I said. "I tried to be cooperative."

"Well, good. You should be."

"I told them what I could," I said.

"I gotta tell you, Coyne," he said. "They came away from that little interrogation more suspicious than when they went into it."

"I imagine they did."

"The way I hear it, you fudged awhile before you admitted you'd been with the guy."

"They showed me his picture and told me his name. When I met Churchill he was wearing sunglasses and a fake mustache. I didn't know his name. Once I figured out he was the guy I met at Skeeter's, I readily admitted it."

"They thought it was odd, you didn't recognize his picture or latch onto his name."

"Suspicious, you mean."

"Whatever. I hear Skeeter recognized the guy right off by his picture. They figure you should have, too."

"I guess Skeeter's better at faces than me."

"And then you refused to tell them what you and Churchill were doing together."

"Yes, I did."

"Well, shit. How do you think that looks?"

"That looks to me the way it was. I was there for a client. To them I guess it looks bad. I can't help it."

"You talk to this client of yours?"

"Of course." I hesitated. "Why?"

"You ask him where he or she was?"

"What're you trying to say?"

He popped his gum. "Maybe I was wrong."

"About what?"

"Back there I said you ain't dumb. Now I'm not so sure."

"I'm not dumb," I said after a moment. "I know what you're thinking. What you're thinking is dumb."

"If you say so."

"I do."

Horowitz hesitated. "You wanna know something, Coyne?"

"What?"

"I don't think I better talk to you anymore."

"Why?"

"In fact, I don't think I should've told you this much already."

"Come on, Horowitz."

"I mean, look, as a friend, if that's what I am, I gotta tell you it does look bad."

"I didn't kill him, for God's sake."

"Well, why the hell don't you tell them the truth, then?"

"I can't."

· EIGHT ·

WHEN I HUNG UP with Horowitz, I lit a cigarette, sighed deeply, and prepared to make a pass at the stack of paperwork in my desk. The console buzzed unpleasantly. I picked up the phone. "Yes, Julie?"

"Boy, do you sound grouchy."

"I'm sorry. What is it?"

"Mickey Gillis called. She'd like you to call her."

"She say why?"

"No."

"Okay. I'll call her."

Mickey Gillis is a columnist for the *Globe*. The city and its people are her beat. She has more snitches than the cops on *Hill Street Blues*. She has the tenacity of an angry pit bull, the eclectic knowledge of a *Jeopardy* champion, the commonsense smarts of a down-east lobsterman, and the mistrust of human nature of a maximum-security prison guard. What comes to her as a strand of idle gossip leaves her typewriter as hard, well-fortified fact. She has been sued a dozen times. She has never lost. I have defended her several of those times. It has always been a simple matter of reminding a jury of Mickey's peers of the intent of the First Amendment.

Mickey and I went to high school together. We had been lovers, if that's what you call two adolescents engaged in violent chemical reactions with each other. She married a guy named Gillis, left the state for several years, and then came back, divorced, to write society for the *Globe*. Within two years she had her own column and carte blanche from the editor to write about what and whom she chose. Mickey Gillis pisses people off. She tells the truth. And she sells a helluva lot of newspapers.

She has two phones in her office. One is listed with the *Globe*. The other is a private number known only to her snitches. Sometimes she talks on both phones at once and hammers at her word processor at the same time. I've seen her do it.

The number I dialed was the snitches' number. She answered, "Gillis."

"Mickey," I said. "It's Brady."

She chuckled in that raspy, throaty way of hers. Mickey smoked little cigars and drank a lot of whiskey. "Glad you called back, Counselor."

"What's up, Mickey? You in trouble again?"

"Nope. You are."

"Oh, boy. Word gets around, huh?"

"To some of us it does. I bet you want to know about Wayne Churchill, huh?"

"Whatever made you think that?"

"Sylvestro and Finnigan've been giving you a hard time, I hear."

"Do you hear everything, Mickey?"

"You bet your ass I do."

"You planning to write about me in your column?"

"Hey. A story's a story."

"Come on, Mickey."

"Just joshing, Brady. There's nothing to write, yet. You didn't kill Wayne Churchill, did you?"

"Of course not."

"You been arrested or anything?"

"No."

"I knew that. Hey, I'm just being friendly here. I hear things, I've got sources most people don't have. I figure, hey, I hear my friend Brady's name bandied about, I oughta see what I can do for the guy. Right?"

"Right, Mickey."

"So I figure I'll give him a call, remind him old Mickey's here."

"I appreciate it."

"So," she said, exhaling loudly. I pictured her puffing on one of her little cigars. "What would you like old Mickey to find out for you?"

"I'm not sure, to tell you the truth. Somebody killed the man. It wasn't me. But the cops seem to be focused on me, which means that whoever did it is getting no attention. If I could just come up with a motive, or an enemy, or some niche in his armor . . ."

"He was a golden boy, for sure. But you're right. There was something about the man." She paused. "You know something about him, don't you?"

"No, not really," I lied. Of all people, Mickey Gillis was the last one I could mention Judge Popowski and Wayne Churchill to in the same breath.

"But you wouldn't mind if Mickey did a little checking, just for old times' sake."

"Mickey, listen. I don't want to find my name in your column tomorrow morning."

"Aw, Brady . . ."

"I don't want to be quoted. You want to write about the Churchill murder, I can't stop you. Go ahead. But leave me out of it."

"You're in it, pal."

"Then let's forget the whole thing."

"You misunderstand, Brady. Christ, I know you didn't kill anybody. I figure it'd be good for both of us if we figured out who did, that's all. I intend to pursue this story. I just figured I might share with you. Out of friendship. If you want to share with me, hey, great." She paused. "If not, well, okay. Either way, I'm gonna pick a few scabs. Would you mind if I did that?"

"I guess I wouldn't mind, Mickey."

She paused. I heard the click of a lighter. Then she exhaled loudly. "Remember Granny Hill, Brady?"

"You were a sexy one, all right."

"Were," she repeated. "Fuck you, Coyne."

"You've still got great legs, Mickey."

"I wear the same size dress I did then."

"Terrific body. You always had a great body."

"It's the face, ain't it?"

"You look wonderful, Mickey. Come on. Granny Hill was a very long time ago."

"Yeah," she sighed. "You ain't the same lean stud you once were, either, you know."

"Don't I know it."

"Well, hell. This Churchill thing's interesting. Maybe I'll just roll over a few rocks, see what crawls out. I'll keep you posted."

"Appreciate it."

"You take care of yourself, Brady," she said softly. "You're not used to being on the other side."

"Ain't it the truth," I said.

Mickey called back the next morning. "I got some dirt," she said.

"On Churchill?"

"Yup."

"Let's have it."

"Rather not on the phone."

"Lunch, then."

"Can you deduct it?"

"No. It won't be business."

"We could do some business."

"Couldn't justify it," I said.

"You are so goddam ethical sometimes, Counselor. Okay, then. I'll pay. I can deduct it."

"No you can't. Not unless you're working on a story. And if you're working on this story, then I better not be one of your sources. In which case, you can't deduct my meal."

"Okay, okay," she said. "I know a little place around the corner from the courthouse, right next to the bakery that makes dirty cakes. It's cheap and quiet and they have great hot turkey sandwiches. We'll go dutch."

"Dirty cakes?"

"Oh, yes. They're a riot. X-rated cakes. They have their regular assortment, or you can have them custom designed. Breasts, asses, phalluses, or any combination thereof."

"What's this restaurant like?"

"Not much if you're looking for ambience. Hole in the wall, actually."

"Why don't we meet at the Oyster House, instead," I said.

"You wanna go for ambience, then."

"I can't get excited about a turkey sandwich, that's all."

"Ambience it is. Twelve-thirty?"

"Twelve-thirty is fine."

I thought of calling Pops, then I thought better of it. He couldn't help me. I thought of calling Xerxes Garrett, the good young defense attorney who had clerked for me for a year while studying for the bar. But at this point, I didn't figure I needed an attorney. Not yet. If they decided they wanted to arrest me . . .

I did want to get a line on Wayne Churchill. I wanted to find out something I could give to Sylvestro and Finnigan so they'd leave me alone, something that would provide somebody with a motive to murder him, an enemy, a weakness, a secret. I knew there was something. After all, somebody *had* murdered him.

Mickey was waiting for me at the bar at the Union Oyster House when I got there. Her slim, muscular legs were crossed, and she had hiked her skirt up over her knees to display them to their best advantage. She was hunched over a glass of Scotch. A thin black cigar was burning in the ashtray by her elbow. I eased onto the stool beside her. The young woman behind the bar said, "Sir?"

"Jack Daniel's on the rocks, please."

Mickey turned to look at me. Her monkey face broke into a grin, spreading tiny crinkles at the corners of her eyes and mouth. I bent to kiss her cheek, and she managed to get her mouth in the way of my aim. Before I could pull back, she had flicked her tongue out, licking my lips.

"Come on, Mickey. Behave."

"Ah, you old fart, Coyne. Always were a prude."

"I never particularly thought so."

"Trust me," she said. "You always were a prude."

My drink arrived. I lit a cigarette. She puffed on her cigar. I noticed that she inhaled it. The blush on her cheeks and the glitter in her eyes told me that the Scotch she was sipping wasn't her first.

The Union Oyster House is down near Haymarket Square. It's more than a hundred years old, and it has managed to retain its somewhat down-at-the heels mystique, which tourists and natives alike continue to find charming. The narrow warren of burnished wood-paneled rooms, the uneven plank floors, and the general aura of earthy good nature are features that, I'm certain, the management nurtures.

I like the food. The seafood is always fresh, well prepared, and priced right. And I confess, I like the ambience, too.

Mickey and I inquired after each other's health and sex lives. She was a good deal more forthcoming than I on both subjects. When I finished my drink, I said, "Want to eat?"

She nodded, so we found the hostess, who led us upstairs into one of the dining rooms. We ordered more drinks from the waitress. After she left, I said, "What'd you find?"

"Get right down to business, eh, Counselor?"

"It's important to me, Mickey."

She nodded. "I suppose it is. Okay. You want to know about Wayne Churchill. Sorry to report, I didn't learn who killed him. Man in his business, of course, was bound to have enemies. I oughta know. Unfortunately, so far none of them has stepped forward to take credit for it. He had a girl-friend—"

"Gretchen Warde."

"Right." She nodded. "The one who found his body. She appears to be the cops' number one suspect."

"Where's that put me?"

"Number two."

"What's supposed to be the girl's motive?"

Mickey shrugged. "The usual, I suppose. Jealousy, whatnot. Rumors I hear are that there were probably other women."

"Rumors?"

"You know. Things people say. Nothing you can print. I also hear the cops found some coke in his apartment. The man evidently was your average yuppie cokehead. They're keeping that out of the papers."

"But you heard it."

She grinned.

"Isn't that significant?"

Mickey rolled her eyes. "This day and age, Brady, it'd be more significant if they didn't find that little Baggie with white stuff in it."

I sighed. "I guess I'm naive."

"You said it, pal."

I shook my head. "And you found out all this overnight?"

She shrugged. "Sure."

"How?"

"It's my business to know how to find out stuff like that."

Our waitress arrived with our drinks. "May I take your order?" she said.

Mickey ordered the scrod. I settled for a big bowl of lobster stew and a tossed salad.

When the waitress left, I said, "So far you haven't really helped me."

"Eliminating possibilities helps, doesn't it?"

"I guess it does. Why do you think they're keeping the drug angle out of the papers?"

"Usually it means they've got their eye on somebody and don't want to alert them. It could also be stupidity. With cops you never know."

I nodded. I hadn't figured out Sylvestro and Finnigan yet. I was reluctant to consider them stupid. "Was there anything else?" I said.

She smiled. "Of course there's something else. There always is, isn't there?"

I shrugged.

"Before he came to Boston, Wayne Churchill was anchorman for the evening news on Channel Eleven in Cleveland. Very popular there. Young, photogenic, sincere, with a history of being a solid reporter. He won a couple awards, even."

"I read that in the paper, Mickey."

"Sure. Then he came to Channel Eight here in Boston as a news reporter."

"Right."

"Well, that struck me a little funny."

"Why?"

"Think about it. Why would a guy with the best job on television give it up to go back to wearing out shoe leather?"

"Obviously you're going to tell me," I said.

"Eventually," she said. "Anyhow, that's what struck me. Okay, so Boston is a better market than Cleveland."

"By a long shot."

"Not only that, but Channel Eight doubled his Cleveland salary. Not bad, moving from anchorman to reporter. See, Brady, Channel Eight's in very dire straits. Competition's tough in Beantown. So they decided to take this flier on Churchill. Gave him this huge salary, plenty of incentives, expecting him to do for them what he'd done in his previous jobs."

"Which is what?"

"Get dirt. Channel Eight's committed itself to becoming the tabloid of television. Sex, violence, scandal. Tell the stories the more responsible stations wouldn't touch. Baby born with a wooden leg, Elvis spotted in drag in a Vegas nightclub, Florida woman impregnated by green two-headed alien."

"And this is what Churchill did?"

"The political stuff. What I hear, Cleveland was happy to let him go. Oh, he was zealous as hell. Had a blockbuster for them. Corruption in the mayor's office. Churchill had it figured the mayor himself was in on it. He broke the story before he got corroboration. Turned out he was wrong. Tried like hell to back and fill, only got in deeper. The mayor threatened him and the station with a lawsuit. He retracted on the air. As I hear it, they were delighted to let him out of his contract to come to Boston."

"Well, I didn't even recognize him when I saw him."

"He's been a grave disappointment. This guy Rodney Dennis—he's the station manager over there—"

"I've talked to him," I said. "He came up with my name."

"Oh-oh," she said.

"I didn't tell him anything."

"They're not all that responsible at Channel Eight, Brady. Little lawsuit, they might be willing to buy the publicity. You be careful."

"I'm trying," I said glumly.

"Anyhow," said Mickey, "Rodney Dennis went way out to the end of a thin limb, hiring Churchill. I understand Dennis's job's in jeopardy. Largely because they were stuck with this huge contract and Churchill hadn't come up with anything for them and the station's slowly going down the ratings tubes."

"No babies with wooden legs."

"No scandals, Brady. Your political equivalent." She smiled at me.

"Funny thing here is, Wayne Churchill's murder is the best story they've had in a long time. You can expect them to milk it dry. And they've managed to divest themselves of a dead-weight reporter and a monster salary at the same time."

"Food for thought," I mused.

She looked up. Our waitress had arrived. "Better yet," said Mickey, "food for our bodies."

The waitress placed our salads in front of us. We munched them in silence. When I was done, I lit a cigarette and said, "This is interesting, Mickey. But I'm not sure how it helps."

She reached across the table and patted my cheek. "Think about it."

The waitress came and took away our salad bowls. In a minute she was back with Mickey's scrod and my stew. Mickey didn't like to talk while she ate. She ate fast and enthusiastically. She finished her vegetables, even. So I slurped the rich stew and waited for her. And thought about it.

When we finished eating, I said, "I've been thinking about it."

She wiped her mouth on her napkin, sipped her water, and said, "And?"

"Why don't you tell me what I should've been thinking."

"Okay," she said. She lit one of her skinny cigars, dragged heavily, and exhaled. "Churchill's getting pressure from Dennis. Go earn your salary. So he digs. Doesn't have to be a legitimate story. Or if it is, he doesn't have to get it all. Something to keep Dennis off his ass. So he does what he's so good at. He gets something on somebody, and that somebody finds out about it, and whatever it is is so bad that this somebody wastes our intrepid reporter to keep it off the air. How's that sound?"

I nodded. It's what I had been thinking. It was possible that Pops had killed Churchill. Except for the absolute fact that Pops could not possibly murder a man, it fit together neatly.

Motive. Churchill had learned about Karen Lavoie. Probably, somehow, from the woman herself, what he had called when we met at Skeeters an "impeccable source." Pops killed him to keep him quiet.

Opportunity? Hell, it was elegant. He set me up. He arranged the meeting with me and Churchill. I was seen publicly with him. I'd even inadvertently cooperated by exchanging angry words with the man. Then Pops could've simply followed Churchill home and shot him. I'd be the logical suspect. And, as Pops well knew, I couldn't implicate him. Client privilege, or at least my own stubbornly rigid interpretation of it, forbade it. Pops knew me well enough to know that I would never violate our confidence.

Mickey was frowning at me. "Brady, you okay?"

I nodded. "Yeah. I know what you're thinking. It sounds good. But it's wrong."

She shrugged. "You're in a better position to know that than me, I guess. Anyhow, keep the other thing in mind."

"What's that?"

"Haven't you been listening to me?"

I smiled. "I always listen to you, Mickey."

"Wayne Churchill dying? Channel Eight's gained a story and lost an albatross. Only better thing, they break the case before the cops."

· NINE ·

O NE SUMMER MORNING IN 1973 Pops and I were having a Coke in the clubhouse at Stow Acres, waiting to tee off. The television in the corner showed a man striding across the lawn toward a waiting helicopter. The man mounted the steps, turned, and lifted his arms into the air. He was making vees with his fingers on both hands. His smile, which was intended to convey courage and confidence, looked like a death rictus.

"That rotten sonofabitch," muttered Pops. "I refused to believe it. All this time, I couldn't allow myself to consider that he had done those things. Christ! I voted for that prick."

"Well, I *always* knew he was a crook," I said.

Pops turned to me. He wasn't smiling. "Laugh if you will. But that man had a sacred trust. I can't tell you how betrayed I feel."

"Aw, hell. He's just a man."

"Bullshit!" Pops shouted the word. The other golfers turned their attention from the television to look at us.

"That's bullshit," he repeated to me, his voice lower. "That's no man. That's a president. We cannot tolerate anything less than perfection."

"Come on, Pops. Lighten up. The system works. That's enough."

He shook his head. "The system failed. People will never trust lawyers again. Things'll never be the same. That bastard has taught the cruel lesson of cynicism to every American boy and girl, and I pity us all."

That was Pops. And as far as I knew, he conducted his life according to the same standards he imposed on presidents. I had never doubted that as an assistant district attorney, and then as a judge, he was carrying out a one-man crusade to restore the faith of the public in lawyers and public officials.

He had a firm, even rigid, concept of justice. He could sometimes be self-righteous. I remembered the fury in his bleeding face that time in New Haven, when I had to pull him off the bully who had been beating up the black teenager. Could Pops kill a man? Perhaps. Could he kill a man to protect his own reputation? I doubted it.

But, I had to admit to myself, it was possible.

I pondered this as I walked back to my office from the Oyster House. It was a long walk, and I paid little attention to the grimy slush that lined the sidewalks, or the dingy gray clouds that hung low over the city, or the grimy, dingy, gray people who hunched along the sidewalks.

I was thinking of Pops.

Once, when we were in New Haven, he and I and Charlie McDevitt were sitting on the rickety wraparound back porch of the run-down Victorian by the water that Charlie and I rented. Our feet were propped up on the railing and we were sipping beer while in the kitchen Gloria and Marilee and Charlie's date were laughing and drinking wine and steaming a bushel of clams. It was in the fall, I recall. We were wearing sweaters. A breeze was stripping the yellow leaves from the big maple beside the house and spinning them around the yard like miniature tornadoes.

We were discussing the war, which was then still raging in Vietnam. Pops had been there. Charlie and I hadn't.

"Before I went in, I marched," Pops said, gazing thoughtfully out over the water. "I sat in and I taught in and I loved in. I hated that war. I thought it was evil. I cast my first ballot for L.B.J. because I thought Goldwater would take us to war."

"But you enlisted," said Charlie.

"Damn right I enlisted. I thought it was wrong for ghetto kids and poor people to go over there to die while I went to law school because my old man had enough money to send me there. I couldn't have lived with that."

Charlie and I said nothing. We had escaped the lottery. We had not enlisted. And yet it was clear that Pops was not judging us. He only judged himself. And he judged himself rigorously.

"I expected to die over there," he continued, running his fingers through his thick thatch of prematurely white hair. "I absolutely knew that I was going to be killed. And I feared it, believe me. I was no kind of hero. My abiding thought all the time I was in Nam was that I didn't want to miss it. My own death, I mean. All around me the boys were injecting heroin into their blood and sucking grass into their lungs and gulping alcohol into their stomachs, and all I could think was they're going to die, the most important event of their lives, and they're going to miss it. I wanted to be wearing clean underwear when the truck hit me."

That was the Pops I knew. If ever a man deserved the word *Honorable* before his name, it was Chester Y. Popowski.

Until my lunch with Mickey Gillis, I had never doubted it.

I got back to the office a few minutes before three. Julie was at her desk, pecking at her word processor. A man I did not recognize was sitting on the sofa, a magazine spread over his knees. I pegged him for a salesman. He was not a client. Both of them looked up when I shut the door behind me. I hung up my coat. Julie said, "Oh, Brady—"

"Not now," I said. I went into my office.

I called the courthouse, and the switchboard put me through to Pops' office. A young man's voice answered the phone. "The Honorable Chester Popowski's office," he said.

"This Robert?"

"Yes, sir."

"This is Brady Coyne. I'm the judge's lawyer."

"Oh, yes, sir."

"I must speak to His Honor."

"I'm sorry, but—"

"When he gets out of court, tell him he must call me immediately. It's extremely important."

"I'm sorry, Mr. Coyne. The judge isn't in today."

"Is he sick?"

"Actually, sir, he's on vacation."

"Vacation?"

"Yes, sir."

"He never mentioned any vacation to me."

"He flew down this morning. He's joining his wife for a few days in Florida."

"Oh," I said. "Do you have a phone where he can be reached?"

"I'm afraid I don't. They chartered a boat. I expect him back at the beginning of the week. I'll have him call you then. Will that be all right?"

"I guess it'll have to be. Leave him a message to call me instantly when he gets back."

"Certainly, Mr. Coyne. I'll do that."

I hung up and muttered, "Damn!"

Doubt was gnawing at my mind. I wanted Pops to reassure me. I needed answers. Pops had them. And now he was gone, incommunicado. Damn convenient.

With the police and Channel Eight both at my heels, I couldn't sit around waiting for Pops to decide to come home.

I lit a cigarette and tried to think it out. Churchill had told me he had what he called an "impeccable source." Since it wasn't Pops, it had to be Karen Lavoie herself. She was the key.

I guessed that she, like I, had read of Pops' nomination to the federal seat. Still bitter from having been jilted, even after all these years, she saw a chance to get even with her former lover. She knew Wayne Churchill's reputation. She approached him, told him about herself and Pops. Maybe she lied a little. Exaggerated. Made it sound even jucier than it already was.

Churchill liked her story. Maybe he paid her for it.

Maybe Karen Lavoie changed her mind. Tried to back out of it. And Churchill laughed at her.

Or maybe they were in it all the way together.

Maybe Wayne Churchill and Karen Lavoie were lovers.

Maybe she had even killed him.

Too many maybe's. I needed some answers.

I found the big Greater Boston telephone directory in the bottom drawer of my desk. I looked up Lavoie. There was nearly a full column of them. No Lavoie, Karen. No Lavoie, K.

I closed the directory. There was no reason to assume Karen Lavoie lived in or around Boston.

I thought about it. Pops had known her. He had known her in several ways. Perhaps Karen had been a defendant who had come before him. Or a witness. It was a long shot. But no longer than finding her by telephoning every Lavoie in the phone book. It was something Zerk could help me with.

My console buzzed. I picked up the phone. "Yes, Julie?"

"I saw your light go off."

"Okay. What's up?"

"You came storming in here like a bear."

"I'm sorry."

"There's a man here to see you."

"What's he selling?"

"He's not selling anything. His name is Rodney Dennis. He's the station manager at Channel Eight?" Julie made it a question.

"Right," I said.

"He'd like to talk to you."

I sighed. "Okay. Send him in."

He had a high forehead, plastic-rimmed glasses, and a bushy sand-colored mustache. He was short and solidly built. When Julie let him in, he strode to my desk. I stood up and held my hand to him.

"Mr. Dennis," I said. "You are persistent."

"Thanks for seeing me, Mr. Coyne."

I gestured to one of the chairs beside my desk, and he sat down.

"No interview," I said.

He spread his arms. "No camera. No tape recorder. I want to talk to you."

"Off the record," I said.

"Absolutely." He cocked his head and examined me. I judged that he wasn't much over thirty. Bright, ambitious, single-minded, to have become station manager so young. "We'll be frank, okay?"

"Go ahead, Mr. Dennis."

"Wayne Churchill worked for me. He was murdered. Maybe it had something to do with a story, maybe not. Either way, his murder is a story." Dennis touched the end of his mustache with his thumb. "Your name, ah, is connected, Mr. Coyne."

"Where'd you hear that?"

He smiled. "I've done some investigative reporting myself."

"Be specific."

"Look," he said. "I was his boss. He had to account to me."

"You knew he was meeting me that night?"

He shrugged. "Your name was scribbled on his calendar."

"You didn't get it from the police?"

"I've gotten nothing from the police. That's one reason I'm here."

"Do you know why we met?"

"That's what I'm asking you."

"Forget it," I said. "What else can I do for you?"

"Actually, of course, I want to know if you killed Wayne."

"That's easy. I didn't."

"But you were with him the night he died."

I stared at him and said nothing.

"What did he tell you?"

"You're out of line, Dennis."

"You're a suspect, Mr. Coyne. A helluva suspect. Police're gonna let it out, sooner or later. I want to get there first with the story. I've got a personal interest in it. I'll repeat my offer. Exclusive interview. You'll get all the time you need, tell your story in your own way. Guarantee you don't get edited, misquoted, taken out of context. Put your case in front of the public. Best defense, believe me."

"Can I ask you a question, Mr. Dennis?"

"Sure." He opened his arms and showed me his palms. "Ask away."

"Did you kill him?"

He grinned. "Me?"

"Are you a suspect? Have the police questioned you?"

"Sure the police questioned me. I don't believe I'm a suspect, however. Anyway—"

"End of interview, Mr. Dennis."

"I don't think you understand—"

"You want a story. I'm not it." I stood up. "Now, if you don't want . . ."

Rodney Dennis stood. "I'm an impatient man," he said. He narrowed his eyes. "It would be to your advantage to be candid with me, Mr. Coyne."

"Is that a threat?"

He smiled. "Goodness, no. Call it an offer."

"Offer declined. Thanks anyway."

He looked at me for a moment, then shrugged. "If you change your mind, give me a call."

I held out my hand and he took it. "Good day, Mr. Dennis."

He nodded. "We'll be in touch."

Xerxes Garrett was the young black attorney who had clerked for me during the year that Julie was on maternity leave, in exchange for my tutelege. When he passed the law boards he turned down my offer to join up with me, which was a relief to both of us. I liked my independence too much to work with a partner. He retained the idealism that I had lost along the way. He wanted to work with the poor and downtrodden. He did not want a career like mine, helping, as he saw it, "rich white folks get richer."

So he opened his own office in Cambridge near the Somerville line, not far from Tufts University where he had earned modest fame as a Little All-American linebacker and running back. Poor folks, white as well as black, flocked to him, folks whose landlords allowed apartment building pipes to freeze in the wintertime, folks whose sons got nabbed stealing cars or selling coke, folks who didn't know how to negotiate bureaucracies to complain about insufficient welfare payments or runaway husbands.

Zerk was a big, handsome guy. He was also smart and articulate and principled. He had become an excellent lawyer. He was one of those impressive men who grew even more impressive when you got to know him. He had even helped me through a few scrapes.

Zerk did a lot of business at the big ugly concrete courthouse in East Cambridge. He knew all the ADAs and secretaries and judges there. From what I could gather, they all shared my impression of him.

"Yo," he said, when his secretary connected us. "Bossman."

"I need a favor, Zerk."

"I didn't figure you were calling to offer one to me. You in trouble again?"

"Not really," I said. "At least, not yet. I just have a question for you."

"If you're in trouble, you oughta tell your lawyer."

"I know that."

I heard him yawn. "Let's have it."

"Okay," I said. "Supposing, just hypothetically, a person wanted to look up an old case, and all he had was the name of the defendant. How would he go about it?"

"It's in the computers. It could be dug out."

"How?"

"If you're prosecuting a case, you just go to the nearest terminal in one of the D.A.'s offices and punch it up."

"If you're not?"

"If you're defending a case, it's a little more complicated."

"And if you're neither prosecuting nor defending a case?"

He hesitated. "This isn't really hypothetical, is it?"

"No. Not really."

"You need to check on a name?"

"Yes, I do."

"A defendant in a criminal case?"

"Possibly."

"Or possibly something else?"

"Possibly a defendant or plaintiff in a civil case. Possibly a witness. Possibly a prosecutor or a defense attorney. I don't know."

"Jesus, man."

"I know." I thought for a minute. "I could probably associate this name with a particular judge."

"That wouldn't help."

I sighed. "You can't help me, then?"

"I didn't say that. You think this name might have been a defendant in a criminal case?"

"Might've been. It's one possibility. It's a place to start."

"Let me call you back."

I hung up.

I got some coffee and apologized to Julie for my earlier rudeness and my extended lunch with Mickey. She said she expected as much of me. She had left a neat stack of manila folders on my desk. My afternoon assignment. Without Julie, I would tend to spend my days swiveled around with my back to my desk—both literally and figuratively—staring westward out of my window and dreaming of fishing. Periodically I would telephone Charlie McDevitt or Doc Adams to swap stories and lay plans for trips to places like Alaska and Idaho where large trout swam in clear rivers and great snow-peaked mountains rose in the distance and the air was clean and murder was someone else's concern. Without Julie, the GONE FISHIN' sign would hang from my doorknob most of the time.

Without Julie, I would soon be broke. Then I couldn't afford to go to those places.

Julie keeps me as busy as she dares. She forces me to do all the little things that keep my wealthy clients happy, like phoning them weekly and paying them house calls and occasionally doing real legal work for them, all of which persuades them that the shamefully large retainers they pay me are a good bargain.

So I shuffled through the manila folders she had left for me. But I couldn't concentrate. The knot in my stomach was too persistent. It reminded me that I had smacked my nose against a brick wall.

How in hell could I find Karen Lavoie?

Julie came into my office half an hour later. She queried me on the contents of the folders. I answered her. She patted my shoulder, told me I was a good boy, and gave me some more stuff to look at. The phone rang a couple of times. Julie made a few calls and then turned them over to me. Around four-thirty she came in with some letters for me to sign. She had composed them herself.

A little after five my phone buzzed. I picked it up and Julie said, "It's Zerk."

Julie admired Zerk. Zerk had two secretaries, and kept them both overworked.

I pressed the button that connected me to Zerk. "Hi," I said.

"I figured this was important," he said.

"Yeah, it is."

"You seemed to be in a rush."

"I guess I am."

"Listen carefully, bossman. Tomorrow you should take the elevator to the fifteenth floor of the courthouse. Go to the Clerk Magistrate's office. Be

there at one-thirty. Some of the folks will be at lunch. Look for Sarah. She'll
be expecting you."

"I don't want to get anybody in trouble."

"Tell her you need the case number. Give her the year and the name.
She's a friend of mine. She said she could do it as a favor to me. I told her
you were a lawyer."

"I *am* a lawyer."

"More or less," he said.

I left the office at one the next day, rescued my car from the parking
garage in the bowels of my office building, and wended my way onto Storrow
Drive. I negotiated the rotary by Charles Street and crossed the Charles
River Dam on the Monsignor O'Brien Highway. The river was iced over.
Every winter a heedless child or a drunken Harvard or MIT undergraduate
tries to walk across the river, crashes through the ice, and drowns. I passed
the Museum of Science, took a left onto First Street, and parked in the
Lechmere Sales lot. Then I walked the two diagonal blocks to the court-
house.

I emptied my pockets of loose change, cigarette lighters, and car keys and
passed through the metal detector. Good thing I left my .38 in the office.
Then I retrieved my things and rode the elevator to the fifteenth floor.

The Clerk Magistrate's office was a large open room. There were forty or
fifty desks and several banks of file cabinets that all sat behind a chest-high
countertop that extended the full width of the room and served to barricade
the public from the Clerk's operations. Some of the desks had computer
terminals on them. Some didn't.

Perhaps half of the desks were occupied by secretaries, talking on the
phone or shuffling papers or typing at their keyboards. One of them was
reading a paperback novel. Very little was happening in the Clerk's office. I
guessed the Clerk himself was probably out to lunch.

A series of signs hung over the countertop for the convenience of citizens
with business there. TRAFFIC/DOG VIOLATIONS. JUVENILE. INFORMATION &
HEARINGS. CRIMINAL. CIVIL & RESTRAINING ORDERS. SMALL CLAIMS. CASHIER
WITNESS FEES.

I stood under the CRIMINAL sign and looked from one secretary to another. None of them noticed me. I cleared my throat and coughed. One of
the secretaries glanced up at me and I caught her eye. Her skin was the color
of dark maple syrup. She had a short Afro that looked like a helmet on her

head. She wore rimless eyeglasses. She was very beautiful. She looked like a young Lena Horne. It was the cheekbones and the finely chiseled nose.

"Sarah?" I said to her.

She looked at her wristwatch. Then she cast what looked to me like a furtive glance at the other secretaries in the big room. They were ignoring us.

She got up and came to the counter. "May I help you, sir?" she said. I detected the trace of a Jamaican accent.

"I'm a friend of Xerxes Garrett. My name is Brady Coyne."

She nodded. "Yes. Zerk said you might be in. What can I do for you?"

"I need a case number," I said. "Defendant's name is Karen Lavoie."

She peered at me for a moment, then said, "Okay. Spell the name, please."

I did.

"What year was the case?"

Not too recent, I guessed. Probably from Pops' days as a District Court Judge. "I can't remember exactly," I said. "Around 1979, 1980, maybe."

She shrugged. "I'll see what I can do for you."

She went to a desk and began to peck at the keyboard. Then she sat back, watching the monitor. After a minute or two she looked up at me. "Sorry," she said.

"Try '77 or '78," I said. "Please."

She made another entry on the keyboard.

I noticed one of the other secretaries watching us. This one was older, perhaps forty. She had straight black hair, shoulder length, liberally flecked with gray. Deep creases were etched into the corners of her mouth. She was resting her chin on her fists, propped up on her elbows, and she was frowning.

When she saw me glance her way, she got up and walked over to the desk where Sarah was sitting.

"Whatcha looking for?" she said to Sarah.

Sarah didn't look up. "Case number. This gentleman's old case."

The older woman glanced at me. "How old?"

"We're not sure. That's the problem."

"What's the name?"

Sarah peered over at me. I nodded.

"Lavoie, Karen."

"That's funny," said the woman. "Used to be a Karen Lavoie who worked right in this office. Couldn't be the same one, could it?"

Sarah glanced at me. I shrugged.

"Probably not," she said, returning her attention to the computer screen.

"Karen was here for only about a year," went on the older secretary. "Gee, that must've been sixteen, eighteen years ago. When you were still a baby. Right, Sarah?"

Sarah looked up and smiled. "Maybe not a baby, Helen."

"You know," said Helen, "there *was* something with Karen." She frowned for a minute, then shrugged. "Probably not. She left to get married. I guess that's all."

"Where did this Karen live?" I said.

Helen looked at me as if she were noticing me for the first time. "Medford, I think. Yes, I'm sure it was Medford. She used to talk about Medford High School. She came to work here right out of high school. She had a boyfriend who had graduated a year ahead of her. He was some kind of athlete at Medford High. Karen used to talk about him."

"Well, that's not my client," I said. "Funny coincidence, though."

Helen cocked her head at me, then nodded. "Yeah, funny."

She wandered back to her desk. Sarah looked at me and shook her head. "Not here, either. Want me to keep looking?"

"Boy, I should've checked the year before I came over here," I said.

"That certainly would've made it easier."

"I didn't realize," I said. "Let me go back to my office and look it up."

"Good idea," she said. "Zerk should've told you."

She switched off the computer and stood up.

"Well," I said. "Thanks for your trouble. I'll get the date and be back, if that's okay."

"Sure," she said.

I turned and walked out of the office.

· TEN ·

As soon as I left the Clerk Magistrate's office, I punched my palm with my fist and whispered "Yippee!" to myself.

Karen Lavoie was not someone who had appeared in Pops' courtroom. She had worked in the same building with him. And if it had been, as Helen remembered, sixteen or eighteen years earlier, it was when Pops was still an assistant district attorney.

She had been there for a year. Then she left to get married. She lived in Medford. It was a start.

When I got back to my office, I told Julie to hold my calls for a few minutes. Then I went to my desk. I spread open the telephone directory to the page with all the Lavoies on it. With a felt-tipped pen I made a check beside every one of them with a Medford address.

Then I started calling. I asked if I could speak to Karen. The first two told me there was no Karen living there and, no, they knew no Karen Lavoie. Then I got a no-answer. Then an answering machine, on which I left no message. I made a note to try that one again.

The fifth number was listed for John W. Lavoie on Centralia Street. A woman answered. "Hello?" she said. Her voice was soft and cheerful. I could hear the muffled sounds of television voices in the background.

"May I speak to Karen, please," I said.

There was a long pause. "She's not here," said the woman, finally. I thought a note of caution had crept into her voice.

"When do you expect her?"

"Who is this, anyway?"

"My name is Brady Coyne. I'm a lawyer."

"What do you want?"

"It's a business matter. It concerns a mutual friend. A client of mine."

I had contemplated an evasion. The Massachusetts Lottery Commission, congratulating Karen on a Megabucks windfall. An insurance salesman. A doctor with a laboratory report to deliver. But I don't do that sort of thing very well. The vague "business matter" was as close as I could come.

"Karen doesn't live here," said the woman.

"Mrs. Lavoie," I said. "Are you her mother?"

"Yes, that's right. Is this some kind of bad news?"

"No, no. Nothing like that. Would you mind telling me how I can reach Karen? It is rather important."

There was another pause. Judging by the television voices and the music that accompanied them, Karen's mother was watching an afternoon soap. I pictured her in a humble but neatly kept flat with her ironing board set up in the living room in front of a giant color tube.

"I'm sorry," she said finally. "I don't believe you."

I began to protest. But she hung up.

I thought of redialing her number, pleading with her, explaining that it was, quite literally, a matter of life and death that I contact Karen. My life. Wayne Churchill's death.

But I didn't. I copied the phone number and Centralia Street address into my little breast-pocket notebook, then swiveled around to gaze out my office window.

If Karen had left the Clerk Magistrate's office sixteen or eighteen years earlier to get married, as the secretary, Helen, had said, then I'd never find her by looking through the phone book. Because she'd have a different name. Mr. and Mrs. John W. Lavoie of Centralia Street in Medford would know where she was. Somehow, I'd have to persuade them to tell me.

My phone console buzzed. I rotated back to my desk and picked up the telephone. "Yes, Julie?"

"You got a call."

"Who is it?"

"It's a young woman, of course."

Julie disapproved of just about all the women in my life, or at least all the young ones, and most of the middle-aged ones, too, excepting a few carefully screened clients. It was Julie's belief that the only significant woman in my life was Gloria, and the fact that Gloria and I had been divorced for about a decade did not diminish her conviction that any woman I knew was a predator, and that my various liaisons with them constituted adultery. For Julie, it was an article of faith that one day Gloria and I would, as she put it, "get back together."

So any woman under the age of seventy who called me on the phone was regarded by my secretary as a potential threat to my ultimate destiny of a joyous reconciliation with Gloria. Julie tended to be frigidly polite with such women. I kept reminding her that Gloria and I were permanently and completely divorced. I even told her that Gloria, from time to time, saw men other than myself socially. I suggested to Julie that it was conceivable that Gloria actually slept with some of them.

It made no difference. To Julie, all my interactions with women constituted marital infidelity.

The funny thing was that I kind of saw it that way too.

Not that it stopped me.

"What's this young woman's name?" I said.

"Suzie," she said, scornful disapproval dripping from her voice, as if no woman who called herself "Suzie" deserved respect. "No last name. Shall I tell her you're busy?"

"No. Put her on."

I heard her sigh. "Well, you're the boss," she said, somehow implying that I wasn't.

I pressed the blinking button on the console and said, "This is Brady Coyne."

"Are you the gentleman who was at the Clerk's office a while ago?" Her voice was soft and guarded, as if she was trying not to be overheard.

"Yes."

"Listen. I think I better talk to you."

"About what?"

"Wayne Churchill."

"What about him?"

"Look. I can't talk now. Can you meet me?"

"Yes, of course. Where and when?"

She mentioned a little restaurant near the courthouse that I had never heard of. She gave me directions. I agreed to be there at five-thirty.

"Does this have something to do with Karen Lavoie?" I said.

"I can't talk," she said.

"How will I recognize you?"

"I'm very beautiful," she said. "Look for a beautiful blonde."

I did Julie's bidding for the rest of the afternoon, carefully ignoring the hints she left here and there that she wanted to know about Suzie, and at five o'clock I set forth on my second trip of the day across the river to East Cambridge.

The restaurant was several blocks from the courthouse. It was dimly lit and virtually deserted at five-thirty. I stood inside the door and blinked at the darkness. A hostess appeared and asked if she could seat me. I gazed past her and saw a hand wave from a booth along the wall.

"I'm with someone," I told the hostess.

I walked past her and slid into the booth. Suzie had not lied. She was beautiful. She wore her blond hair long and straight, with bangs cut straight across at eyebrow level. Her eyes were widely spaced and icy blue. Her nose was straight and narrow and just a bit long for her face. Her mouth was wide, her lips full. She wore no makeup except for a touch of liner on her eyes. She didn't need any.

I held my hand across the booth to her. She grasped it quickly and dropped it. "Brady Coyne," I said.

"I'm Suzie."

She was sipping on a draft beer. I lit a cigarette and waited. Her eyes kept darting from me to the foyer of the restaurant. She sipped, then her tongue flicked out to lick her upper lip. I reached across the table to touch her hand. "You're nervous," I said.

She smiled quickly. Perfect teeth. "Yes, I guess I am. I'm not sure I should be doing this."

"Are you in trouble?"

"I could be."

A waitress appeared with menus. I ordered a bourbon old-fashioned. Suzie said she was fine. When the waitress left, Suzie opened her menu and began to study it. Evidently, I was expected to buy her dinner. I looked at my menu. I would wait for her.

My drink appeared. Suzie ordered scallops. I chose the haddock. Seafood was usually safe in a Boston restaurant.

When the waitress wandered away, Suzie said, "Before I talk to you, I've got to know that you won't tell anybody what I'm going to tell you."

I nodded. "Okay. You got it."

"I know lawyers are supposed to be able to keep secrets," she said. "But they don't always do it."

"I always do it."

"I can retain you, right?"

"Yes. Do you want to?"

She nodded. I tore a page from my notebook and began to write. I stopped. "I need to know your last name."

"Billings," she said after hesitating.

I finished writing. I slid the paper across the table to her. She read it and glanced up at me. "It's Suzanne. Not Susan."

I shrugged and wrote it again. I gave it to her. She nodded and I passed her my pen. "I, Suzanne Billings, do retain Brady L. Coyne as my attorney" was what it said. She signed her name.

"Put the date beside your name," I said. She did, and gave the paper back to me. I signed underneath her name and handed it back to her. "You keep it."

She tucked it into her purse, which was on the seat beside her. Then she sighed deeply.

"Okay, Mr. Coyne. Here it is. Ever since—since it happened—I've been worried sick. Scared. Feeling guilty. See, Wayne and I—"

"Churchill," I said.

She waved her hand. "Yes. I was sort of his girlfriend."

"Sort of?"

She smiled quickly. "He had lots of girlfriends. I always knew that. I never thought I was his one-and-only, or anything like that. Oh, Wayne would tell me that. But that was him. He was a very exciting man. Very charming, very handsome. Sexy. And he liked to take me to nice places. He was proud to show me off, I think. Banquets, openings of shows, political happenings."

"You weren't the one—"

"Who found his body? No. That was another one. Oh, I had a key to his place. A lot of us did, I guess. But no, that wasn't me." She hesitated, then frowned at me. "You don't think . . . ?"

I spread my hands. "A man is murdered. A girlfriend calls a lawyer, wants his confidentiality. She has a key to the condominium where his body was found. If you killed him, you can tell me. I may not agree to defend you, but I will be happy to advise you. And I will not violate your confidence."

She was shaking her head. "It's nothing like that, Mr. Coyne. I mean, if it was, I know a lot of lawyers I could call. That's not why I called you."

I shrugged. "Okay. I had to ask."

She stared at me for a minute, then smiled. "Good. You're not a bullshitter, are you? I like that. I'm not either. I'm just scared."

"That someone will accuse you of his murder?"

"Well, maybe that, too. But that's not why I'm scared. I mean, it's scary to think the police might come and start questioning me and all. But I didn't do it. I didn't kill Wayne. Sometimes I felt like it, believe me. But I didn't." She leaned toward me. Her hand touched my wrist. "If it ever came out what I did do, though, I'd lose my job. That's what I'm scared of. Maybe I even did something illegal, I'm not really sure. It wasn't murder, but it was wrong, and I feel terrible." She paused. "Maybe what I did got Wayne killed, even. I don't know."

I patted her hand. She withdrew it. "Tell me," I said.

"This afternoon Helen was talking to me. She's the world's biggest gossip. I mean, I wouldn't tell her a thing. Anyway, she started telling me about this guy who came in trying to track down Karen Lavoie, and how she used to know somebody by that name, and how she was wondering if old Karen had done something wrong, because Karen used to be this wimpy little girl, or maybe it was somebody else named Karen Lavoie, which it probably was, because the Karen she used to know wouldn't do anything wrong, she was a nice little Catholic girl who quit her job to marry her high school beau. . . . Anyhow, that's how Helen talks, on and on, around and around, just these words coming out, as if anyone really cared. I mean, ninety-nine percent of the time, nobody does. Helen's just a busybody. But when she mentioned Karen Lavoie, my ears perked up."

"You know Karen?"

"Oh, no. I've only been in the Clerk's office for four and a half years. Anyhow, after Helen wandered away—"

Our waitress suddenly materialized at our table with our salads. Suzie kept her head bowed until she left, as if she didn't want the waitress to get a good look at her face.

When we were alone, she looked up at me. "Where was I?"

"After you finished talking with Helen."

She took a bite of her salad. "Right. Helen said this guy—you—were talking with Sarah. So I found a chance to talk to Sarah. I just asked her who was the good-looking guy that came in while we were at lunch. She didn't want to tell me at first, but then she gave me your name, said you were an attorney trying to get some information about a former client. Anyway, I looked you up and called you."

"Suzie, you still haven't told me about Wayne Churchill and Karen La-voie."

"I know. It's hard." She cut a piece of cucumber and put it into her mouth. Then she put down her fork and dabbed at her mouth with her napkin. "Okay. About a week ago Wayne asked me what happened to criminal complaints when they're dropped before they go anywhere, when there's no process to issue. That's the official term. No process to issue. I told him they're filed away, alphabetically."

"Alphabetically by what?" I said.

"By the name of the respondent. So Wayne asked me if these files were open to the public. Well, of course they're not, Mr. Coyne. These particular files are not part of the public record. They're just complaints. Not like cases. Anyway, what happens is that the application-for-complaint forms are filed, and a hearing is scheduled in the book, and after a couple years the files are emptied and the books are removed. Presumably they're destroyed. But actually, the file cabinets are emptied into cardboard boxes and stored away."

"Churchill wanted to look at these old files?"

She nodded. "That's right."

"And you let him?"

She bowed her head. "Yeah, I did." She looked up at me. "It was wrong. It's not that I'm this wide-eyed innocent kid. But it was important to Wayne. He said he was working on a big story, it was real important. Not just to him, but it was something the public had a right to know about. Wayne is—was— a very persuasive guy. And I guess I had fallen for him. I wanted to help him. It didn't occur to me that he was using me, which I guess he was. I mean, pretty convenient, me working in the Clerk's office, having access to those old files, huh?"

I shrugged. "So what happened?"

The waitress came back, took away our salad bowls, and delivered our plates. Suzie waited for her to leave. She ignored her scallops. "Wayne came in late one Friday afternoon. Everyone else had left for the weekend. I took him to the storeroom where all the cartons are stored, then I kind of stood guard outside. Maybe ten minutes later he came out with an old complaint application in his hand. Asked me to photocopy it. Which I did."

"How old was the application?"

"Seventeen years ago."

"Did you look at the application?"

She nodded.

I took a deep breath. "Who filed it?"

"The complainant's name was Karen Lavoie."

"And the respondent?"

Suzie frowned at me. "It was Chester Y. Popowski."

"Oh, boy," I breathed. "What was the complaint?"

"It said, 'Assault with intent.'"

"What does that mean?"

Suzie picked up her fork and poked at her scallops. "Usually, that means with intent to rape."

"What was the disposition?"

"No process to issue," she said. "Nothing happened."

"Did the form indicate why?"

"The box that was checked said, 'At request of complainant.'"

"Karen Lavoie changed her mind."

Suzie nodded. "Yes."

I took a bite of my haddock while I tried to digest all of this. The fish was a bit overcooked. The information didn't settle that well, either. I squeezed some lemon onto the haddock. "So you photocopied this form and gave it to Churchill?"

She nodded. "Yes. Then I put the original back where it belonged. And the next thing I knew, Wayne had been murdered. Maybe it had something to do with that form and maybe not. But ever since then I've been petrified that someone would find that photocopy and wonder where it came from. I mean, sooner or later someone's gonna tell the police that Wayne and I were seeing each other. So when I heard you were in talking about this Karen Lavoie, whose name was on that complaint application, and Sarah said you were an attorney, I knew I had to talk to you. I mean, I was about ready to burst. I had to talk to somebody."

"You know who Chester Y. Popowski is, don't you?"

"Sure. He's the Superior Court judge. Look, Mr. Coyne. There was no process to issue on that complaint. And it was seventeen years ago. I can't see what good it was to Wayne."

I did. But I wasn't going to tell her. "Nothing, I'm sure. One more thing. Did you, by any chance, give your friend the judge's home phone number?"

She looked down at her hands and nodded. "All the judges have unlisted home phones," she mumbled. "The secretaries know 'em."

"Jesus, Suzie."

She looked up at me. "I know. That's another thing. I feel like such a fool. I just didn't think—"

"No. You didn't think." She appeared to be on the verge of tears. I'm a sucker for a teary woman. I reached across the table and took her hand. "What's done is done," I said. "You're not a criminal."

"I feel like a criminal, believe me."

"Suzie," I said, "I want to ask you a question."

She looked up at me. "Yeah, okay."

"I heard that Wayne did coke."

She lowered her head. "What difference does it make?"

"It could make a great deal of difference."

She nodded, still staring at the table in front of her. "Yes, I see that." She sighed. "Sure. Wayne did coke. Nothing, you know, out of control. I mean, lots of people . . ."

"Where did he get it?"

Her head jerked up. "Why?"

"Do you know where he bought it?"

She shrugged. "How should I know?"

"He might've mentioned it to you."

"He didn't. I don't know. Look, Mr. Coyne. I'm kinda upset about that other thing. Really, just because Wayne and I might've done a line now and then doesn't make us big criminals or something."

"Actually," I said, "it does."

"You're not gonna . . . ?"

I smiled at her. "Don't worry. You've retained me. I can't say anything."

"Okay. Good." She ran her fingers through her hair. It seemed to compose her. "Well, you've made me feel a little better, Mr. Coyne. I just hope those police . . ."

"Look," I said. "If anybody should try to question you about that photocopy, don't tell them anything. Just call me, okay? I will serve as your lawyer if you need one."

She smiled. Dazzlingly. "Thank you. That's what I needed to hear. How much trouble am I in, do you think?"

I shook my head. "At worst, you used poor judgment. There've been a lot worse things done than what you did."

"Boy," she said, "I'll say. Somebody killed Wayne, just for one thing."

They sure did, I thought.

"Mr. Coyne?"

"What, Suzie?"

"Helen?"

"The gossip. Yes."

"Well, she was talking, you know, and she mentioned something. About Karen Lavoie?"

"What was it?"

"She said that a couple times just before she quit, Karen came to work with like bruises on her face? And wearing long sleeves and high necks, as if she was trying to cover up her skin?"

"Now look, Suzie—"

"I was thinking, you know, that complaint? I mean, assault?"

"Forget it, Suzie."

She shrugged. "I mean, if Wayne knew about that . . ."

I wasn't sure what she was thinking. But I had my own thoughts. Because now I knew that Pops had lied to me. And now the conclusion I had rejected became more convincing. He had more to hide than an innocent affair a long time ago. He had a motive for murder.

And there was nobody I could tell.

· ELEVEN ·

JULIE HAS LEARNED over the years not to schedule me for anything important on Fridays. Hanging the GONE FISHIN' sign on the door on Friday is one of the most important perks of being a lone-wolf attorney. During the season I usually do go fishing on Fridays. Except when I play golf. Four days a week at the office is plenty.

Occasionally I am obliged to do unpleasant things on Friday. Like appear in court. I have learned, however, that judges, like lawyers, like to go fishing on Friday too. It's rare that I can't at least get the afternoon off.

Julie doesn't like it. Julie worries that I don't take my practice seriously enough, that I won't, as she puts it, "generate sufficient income" to support the life-style I have chosen. As a result, she works a full day on Friday to compensate for my sloth.

Julie generates lots of income for both of us.

So when she walked into the office at nine the next morning, she looked me up and down and said, "Going fishing, huh?"

I was wearing a pair of corduroys, a green flannel shirt out of the L.L. Bean catalog, and my comfortable old pair of cowboy boots.

"In a manner of speaking, yes, I'm going fishing," I said.

"Mrs. Covington is anxious to see you, you know."

"You can, I'm certain, soothe her savage and ample breast."

Julie sighed. "You're the boss."

"Who are you kidding?"

She grinned. "I'll schedule her for next week."

"Need me for anything else?"

She rolled her eyes. "You have a nice day, Brady. You planning to go sit on the ice somewhere with Mr. McDevitt or Dr. Adams, drinking bourbon and waiting for those little flags to pop up?"

I shook my head. "No, nothing so exotic. I'm going to Medford."

"How exciting."

"You can do one thing for me. If I bring you a cup of coffee, one sugar, no cream, will you see if you can get directions to Centralia Street for me?"

"Centralia Street in Medford?"

"Please."

"I suppose this isn't a client or something."

"Well," I said, "it's not exactly a vacation trip, but no, it's not, strictly speaking, business either."

She shrugged. "Go get my java."

I went to the coffee urn. She went to her desk. In a moment she was deep in conversation on the telephone. I placed her mug in front of her and she looked up, smiled, and blew me a kiss. I placed both hands flat on my chest and feigned a swoon. Then I poured some coffee for myself and went into my inner office. Before I had finished my first cigarette, Julie came in. She put a piece of paper in front of me. It told me how to get to Centralia Street.

"It's not actually very central to anything," she said.

I looked it over. Pretty straightforward. I stubbed out my cigarette, took a final slurp of my coffee, and got up. "How do you do things like this?" I said.

"Like what? Getting directions?"

"Yes."

"The good old NYNEX Yellow Pages. I called a real estate agency in Medford and asked. They told me."

"I could've done that."

She patted my arm. "Sure you could," she said.

I retrieved my parka from the coatrack and descended through the building to my car.

Julie's directions confused me a little at an intersection outside of Medford Square. When I realized I had taken a wrong turn, I pulled over and reread what she had written. She had it right. I had misread it.

Mounds of dirty old snow covered the sidewalks along Centralia Street. Empty trash barrels stood in clusters at the ends of short driveways. Cars were lined solidly on the right side of the street. Winter parking regulations were in effect. The houses were large, square, and old. They were crammed close to each other, separated only by the driveways. Multifamily, most of them, with a pair of front doors side by side. Porches jutted off the fronts of all of them, some screened, some open. Most of the porches were cluttered with bicycles and toys and brown Christmas trees.

I found the street number that the telephone directory had given for John W. Lavoie. I parked on the wrong side of the street, locked the car, and mounted the porch. There were two doors, and two bells by each door. A four-family. John W. Lavoie and his wife, the parents of the elusive Karen Lavoie, lived on the bottom floor of the left side. I rang the bell.

After a minute or so the door opened. "Yes?" said the man who stood there.

He was small, compact, perhaps sixty. He was wearing a red plaid shirt buttoned right up to his throat and tucked into a sharply creased pair of brown wool pants. His sparse white hair was slicked back on his skull. His face was pink from a recent shave, and he wore plastic-framed glasses.

"Mr. Lavoie?" I said.

He nodded. "Yes. That's right." His voice was soft, almost apologetic.

"I wonder if I might talk with you for a minute."

He peered at me through his glasses. His pale blue eyes were magnified through them. "Are you selling something? My wife handles all that."

"My name is Coyne, sir. I'm a lawyer."

He frowned. "A lawyer?"

I gave him my best, most reassuring smile. "I need to talk to your daughter."

"Karen doesn't live here. She was married some time ago."

I nodded. "I know. But—"

A woman appeared behind the man. Her long black hair was just beginning to go gray, and she had fine cheekbones and clear, pale eyes. Only the complex cross-hatching of lines on her face betrayed her age. "Who is it, John?" she said, frowning past his shoulder at me. She was a few inches taller than her husband.

He turned to her. "It's, um—" He looked back at me. "I'm sorry . . ."

"Brady Coyne," I said to her. "We spoke on the phone."

She frowned for an instant, then smiled. She touched her husband on the shoulder. "Well, for heaven's sake, John, invite the gentleman in. You're letting out all the heat." She smiled at me. "Come in out of the cold, sir."

John W. Lavoie opened the door wide for me, and I stepped into a small foyer. To the right a flight of stairs led up to the second floor. I blew into my hands. "Chilly out there. Thank you."

"Let me take your coat," said Mrs. Lavoie.

I slipped out of my parka and handed it to her. She carried it with her into the living room and laid it carefully on a chair. I followed her. Her husband came in behind me.

"Please, have a seat," she said. "May I get you some coffee?"

I nodded. "Please."

"How do you like it?"

"Just black."

She disappeared through a doorway that opened into a dining room. Beyond that, I assumed, lay the kitchen.

The living room was large. Several oversize windows looked out onto the street and to the side of the house next door. Venetian blinds had been folded up to let in the daylight. The furniture was old and threadbare and decorated with crocheted yellowing antimacassars. A twenty-four-inch television squatted in one corner. All of the furniture was aimed at it. Several framed color pictures sat on top of it. The largest and fanciest frame displayed a bride and groom. The bride had dark hair and the same cheekbones I had seen on Mrs. Lavoie. She looked very young and, aside from those cheekbones, quite plain. The groom was a big blond guy. He looked bulky in his tuxedo. He had a large, meandering nose and a wide expressive mouth.

Karen Lavoie, in her wedding picture, looked grim. Her husband looked frightened.

There were a half-dozen or so other photos atop the TV. All were of a child in varying states of growing up. All seemed to be of the sort one gets at bargain prices by standing in line in a K mart on a Saturday morning. The child was of the male persuasion. Fair like his father as an infant, but in what appeared to be his most recent photo he had grown into a dark and brooding adolescent. I could almost hear him complaining about being dragged to K mart to stand in line with a bunch of squalling infants to be photographed. The photo failed to hide the acne pits on his cheeks.

The only other decoration in the room was a framed painting of Jesus Christ hanging from the cross. Beams of light played from behind His emaciated body. Crimson streaks of blood dribbled down His arms. A dried palm frond had been stuck behind the picture.

The room was tidy and clean. I was struck by the complete absence of reading matter. Just a copy of *TV Guide* along with the photos on top of the television console.

I sat on one of the soft chairs. John Lavoie settled on the sofa diagonally across from me. "I'm sorry to barge in on you like this," I said to him.

He smiled softly and waved his hand. "It's no problem. It makes her happy." He jerked his head in the direction of the kitchen. "She'd invite Jack the Ripper in for coffee," he added with an impish grin.

"I hope you can help me," I said, wondering if he had equated me with a mass murderer.

"I'm sorry. I didn't quite catch your name?"

"Coyne. Brady Coyne." I took a business card from my wallet and handed it to him. He glanced at it and dropped it onto the coffee table in front of the sofa. I reached toward him with my hand extended. He took it and we shook.

"John Lavoie," he said, nodding as if to reassure himself.

"If you could just tell me how I could reach your daughter . . ."

"What's your business with Karen?"

"It's a legal matter."

"Has she done something wrong?" He frowned. "Is Karen in trouble?"

"Oh, no. I have a client who she knew several years ago. There's a possibility that she can help him."

"How?"

"I'm really not at liberty to say," I said, working on being agreeable and low-key. "I'm sure you understand."

He nodded. "Confidentiality and all."

"Yes. That's it. The problem is, I don't know Karen's married name. She knew my client before she was married."

"Mr. Coyne, Karen's my daughter. If there's some sort of problem—"

He stopped when his wife entered the room. Mrs. Lavoie carried a tray bearing three cups on saucers, a silver pot, and matching cut-glass containers of sugar and cream. She placed the tray on the coffee table and sat down beside her husband on the sofa. She handed me a paper napkin. Then she poured coffee into the cups and passed one to me.

I balanced it on my knee. She looked from me to her husband.

"He's looking for Karen," he said to her.

She returned her gaze to me. She cocked her head. "I know. He called yesterday."

I shrugged. "It's really very important that I contact your daughter."

"Yes, you said that before." She glanced sideways at her husband. He was staring past me, evidently happy to defer the situation to his wife. "Well, Mr. Coyne," she said, swiveling her head to look directly at me, "I haven't changed my mind. We are simple people. We mind our own business. It seems to me that much of the trouble in this world comes from people not minding their own business. We mind our business, we like it when other people mind their business. Now, I understand you've probably got some kind of job to do, and that's why you're here. Doing your job. But we don't like to get involved in other people's problems. And neither does Karen. And when a lawyer comes around, it's pretty obvious there's some kind of problem. We've had nothing but trouble from lawyers. When John got laid off, we talked to a lawyer. It didn't seem right, what they did to him, a hardworking man all his life, loyal to the company, never out sick. And that lawyer was happy to take a lot of our money. And you see what he did for us. John didn't get his job back. A hardworking man, a good provider, proud of his family, and now he has to do part-time things, using none of his talents. It's just not right. That lawyer took our money and nothing changed. Only difference is, now we're out two thousand dollars, too."

I nodded my head. I had nothing to say. I had heard it too many times. Ambulance chasers. Crooked politicians. Sleazy guys in shiny suits on television, advising grinning men with crooked noses and big diamond rings on their pinkies not to answer questions. I remembered what Pops had said many years earlier. Since Nixon, nobody trusted lawyers.

"Look, Mr. Coyne," she said. "I'm not blaming you for our problems. And I'm not saying that Karen shouldn't cooperate with you. But I am saying that we're not going to be responsible for any problems you might cause her."

"I have no intention of causing her a problem, Mrs. Lavoie," I said, although even as I said it, I recognized that it could be untrue.

She sipped her coffee. "My husband and I will not help you. I hope you will understand."

"Perhaps you'd be willing to answer a few questions?"

"No," she said. "No, we would not. I invited you in, offered you coffee. I don't want to be impolite. But we do not want to help you."

"My wife is right," said John Lavoie.

"Perhaps you should leave," she said.

John Lavoie looked at me, gave me a shrug and a small smile, and nodded.

"Okay," I said. I downed the coffee and stood up. I went to the television and picked up Karen's framed wedding picture. "A pretty girl."

Mrs. Lavoie got up and came to me. She gently took the picture from my hand and placed it back on top of the television. "She's a pretty woman, now. She lives quietly. She likes it that way."

"I understand," I said. I picked up my parka from the chair and slipped into it. I turned and held my hand to the man, who was still seated. He stood up hastily and grasped it. "Thank you for your time, sir," I said.

He nodded. "You're welcome."

I went to the door. Mrs. Lavoie followed me. I turned to her. "If you folks should change your mind, I left my business card. Please call me."

"Sure," she said.

"Please think about it."

"Mr. Coyne," she said, "I hope you won't be holding your breath."

· TWELVE ·

WHEN I WALKED INTO SKEETER'S at six-thirty that evening, he was leaning his forearms on the bar deep in conversation with a very attractive woman. Brown, wavy hair cut short. Big expressive dark eyes. Wide mouth, heart-shaped face. She perched elegantly upon the barstool, tall, slender, poised, firm of rump and sleek of thigh, politely attentive to Skeeter's charm but with a bemused smile gleaming in her eyes.

I took the stool beside her. "Excuse me, ma'am," I said to the woman, "I wonder if we've met."

She turned and frowned at me. "I'm afraid not," she said. She swiveled back to face Skeeter.

I touched her arm. "I'm sure we know each other from somewhere."

"I don't think so," she said without looking at me.

"You're extremely attractive."

"Oh, boy," she said. But she smiled.

"Really. Gorgeous."

"Mr. Coyne," said Skeeter, frowning at me. "I don't think—"

"It's okay," said the woman. "I can handle it." She turned to me. "So you find me attractive, then?"

"Yes," I said. "Extremely."

"Would you like to kiss me?"

"I sure would."

I bent to her and pecked her cheek. She turned her head so that I could nuzzle her neck just below her ear. I heard her murmur in her throat. Her hand moved up to touch my face.

I pulled away from her. "Thank you," I said.

She drew her head back and frowned at me. Then she said, "Oh, wow!" and threw both arms around my neck and kissed me on the mouth. We held it for a long moment. The woman's fingers played at the back of my neck. She made little moaning sounds.

Skeeter snatched the Red Sox cap off his head and scratched the top of his gleaming skull.

Finally we broke off the kiss. The woman wiped her mouth on the back of her hand and said, "Oh, boy."

I looked at Skeeter. "Evening, Skeets," I said.

He shook his head slowly back and forth. He frowned at me. He twisted his Red Sox cap in his hands. Then he shrugged. "Evening, Mr. Coyne. Drink?"

"What's the special tonight?" I said.

He looked at the woman, then back to me. "Ah, a Willie Mays. It's my Willie Mays. Look—"

"What's a Willie Mays?"

"You take a big scoop of coffee ice cream, Mr. Coyne. One shot of Old Grand-dad, one shot of Tia Maria. Mix it in a blender. Real smooth. Graceful drink. Reminds you of Willie chasing one down in center field or going from first to third on a base hit." He glanced again at the woman beside me. "It's really a lady's drink."

"May I buy you one, ma'am?" I said to the woman.

She touched my cheek with her fingertips. "Anything at all," she said in a soft, husky voice. "Whatever you want."

Skeeter was still absentmindedly holding his Red Sox cap in his hand. "The usual, Mr. Coyne?"

"I like that Rebel Yell, Skeets."

He twisted his cap onto his head and turned to get our drinks. "Oh, Skeets," I said to him.

He stopped and faced us. "Yeah?"

"Did Gloria introduce herself?"

He cocked his head at us. "This your wife, Mr. Coyne?"

"This ain't no wife, Skeets. This is a lady."

Skeeter wandered away, shaking his head. Gloria put her hand on my shoulder and grinned. "That poor man."

I kissed her nose. "You are looking terrific, Gloria."

She frowned and smiled softly. "I'm okay."

"What's the matter?"

"Really nothing. I'm just a little disappointed. I had an appointment with *Life* magazine today. They're doing this feature. 'The Face of the City,' they're calling it. New York, Chicago, L.A., Houston, New Orleans, and, da-dum, Boston. They're assigning a local free-lance photographer in each city to capture the essence of the place. People, buildings, skylines, everything and anything. It's a photographer's dream." She lifted her chin and gazed at the ceiling for a moment. Then her eyes shifted to my face. "I thought I had a real good shot at it."

"You didn't get it?"

She shook her head. "I spent about four hours with these guys, going over my portfolio, talking about art, style, sociology, lenses and filters, truth and justice and the American way. They had it narrowed down to, I think, about six of us."

"You were a finalist. That's damn good."

"Right. I know. It's what I keep telling myself. I'm getting there."

"It's true."

"The way we were talking, all the time I thought they loved my stuff. Loved me. When they told me—ah, shit, Brady."

"You've come a long way. I'm proud of you."

"Yeah, I'm proud of me, too. Hell, ten years ago . . . ."

Ten years ago, I thought. Ten years ago Gloria was a tense and unhappy housewife with two prepubescent sons and a barely postpubescent husband, living the suburban nightmare in Wellesley. What had been, before her marriage, a promising career as a photojournalist, had devolved into documenting family birthday parties and vacations.

Divorce had been difficult for both of us. Difficult for me because I had never stopped loving the woman she had once been, even though marriage to me had transformed her into someone I stopped loving. Difficult for her because it took her a long time to visualize a life any different from the one she had allowed herself to get stuck in. For Gloria, marriage had been more than surrendering her career. She had surrendered a piece of her soul—had surrendered it to me. I had mindlessly accepted it, mistaking it for a gift, and too late realized it could never belong to me. Splitting with Gloria was the only way I knew of forcing it back on her. For a long time she hadn't wanted it. For a long time I was reluctant to part with it.

Now she had almost nailed down a breakthrough assignment with *Life*. She had lost out. But she seemed undaunted. Now, in spite of her disappointment, I saw her reemerging as the vibrant girl with the ironic grin who had maneuvered a meeting with me outside a courthouse in New Haven a long time ago. "The man with the three-piece-suit face," she had called me. There was some hippie in her then. Now there was some yuppie. But there was no mistaking it. It was the old Gloria, soul restored. I was proud of her, happy for her.

And at the same time, profoundly saddened, too. It felt like a loss to me. I didn't like that feeling.

Skeeter brought our drinks. Gloria's was served in a tall glass with a straw.

Mine was in a squat glass with a side of branch water. "Better have another one ready for me," I said.

Skeeter arched his brows at me, then nodded. "Sure thing," he said.

I downed my bourbon in one long, burning swallow. Then I took a sip of the water.

Gloria touched my arm. "What's the matter, Brady?"

I shook my head. "I don't know. Nothing."

She put her face close to mine. "Hey," she said. "I'm okay. This is a little setback. Nothing to get all morose about."

"I know. I'm sorry. It's not you."

Skeeter brought me another drink and took away my empty. I drained it, too. Gloria sipped her Willie Mays through a straw.

"This is delicious," she said.

"Go slow. Skeeter's concoctions have a way of creeping up on you."

"So does that stuff."

"Barkeep," I called to Skeeter. "One more, *s'il vous plaît.*"

Skeeter turned and frowned at me, then shrugged. In a minute he brought me my third drink. I decided to sip this one.

Gloria leaned away from me and seemed to study me. Then she began to nod her head. "I get it," she said slowly. "This is really a big relief for you, isn't it?"

"What is?"

"Your—what do you call it, your mood."

"What the hell are you trying to say?"

"You couldn't stand to see me make it. You want me to suffer in your absence. Your goddam ego. You don't believe I can function without you. If I'd gotten that assignment, it would shatter your illusion of yourself. It'd force you to see that I don't need you."

I smiled. My face felt stiff. "Shit, Gloria. It's nothing like that. I want the best for you."

She looked down at the bar. "Part of you does. But there's that other part of you . . ."

I reached to touch her hair. She drew away from me. I shrugged and pulled my hand back. "I can't speak for the different parts of me. Maybe you know them better than me." I paused, trying to pin down the thoughts that tumbled around up there. "The only part I can speak for is the one that is so damn proud of you . . ."

I put my forearms on her shoulders and crossed my wrists behind her neck. I leaned toward her until our foreheads rested against each other. I had the odd feeling that I might cry. After a moment Gloria moved her head so that our noses touched and our eyes were staring into each other's. She crossed hers and giggled. We rubbed noses. "I can't stand you," she whispered, grinning.

"Me either," I said.

She bent to her drink. I sipped my bourbon.

"Brady," she said. "What is it? Really?"

"I'm kind of in trouble, Gloria."

"Tell me."

"Hey," I said. "Shall we have a burger?"

She frowned, then nodded. "Sure. I'm starved."

"I think I'm drunk," I said. "Hey, Skeets."

He came over. "No more, Mr. Coyne."

"Hey—"

He folded his arms. "I never seen you drink like this before. You've had enough. Want some coffee?"

"We want burgers, Skeets."

He held up both hands, a gesture of surrender. "Sorry, Mr. Coyne. You want yours pink, right?"

"Right. Pink and hot in the middle. Like Gloria, here."

Skeeter looked at Gloria. "If you want me to call a cop, ma'am . . ."

"I think I can handle this bum," she said. "Make mine pink and hot too."

Gloria chatted about Billy and Joey, our two sons, while we sipped our drinks and waited for our burgers to arrive. Joey had made the high school honor roll again. His only discontent was his inability to conquer a certain member of the volleyball team named Debbie. Billy, a sophomore at UMass, was still talking about dropping out. He had a new career goal, Gloria told me, about the fifth since he had started college. Now he wanted to be a fishing guide in Idaho.

"I'd like to do that," I said. "That's a very realistic goal."

"Well," she said, "don't think I don't know where he gets his sense of reality."

"He should do what will make him happy," I said.

"You are so supportive, Brady."

"You say that with just a faint trace of sarcasm."

"I do?" she said.

"Life is too damn short," I said. "Before you know it, it's something you can only look back on. The best thing is to be able to look back and nod your head and smile and say, 'No regrets.' "

"So what about you?"

I nodded. "So far, plenty of regrets. I shoulda been a fishing guide, for one thing."

"And us?"

"What, regrets?"

"Yes."

"Honestly, no. We've done the right things. Getting married was the right thing. Just look at the boys. They exist because of us. Getting divorced was the right thing, too. Otherwise I bet you wouldn't have even taken a shot at that assignment from *Life*. Being here together is right, too. Don't you think?"

She leaned toward me and kissed my mouth softly. "Yeah," she said, "I guess."

Our burgers arrived. We ate without talking. When we were done, Skeeter came over. "Coffee, Mr. Coyne?"

"Another bourbon," I said.

"Aw," he said, "if I serve you and you go smash up your car, I lose my license. Don't put me on the spot, huh?"

"I'm not driving, Skeets. Gloria will drive me home."

"I will?" she said.

"Won't you?"

"What, so you can get sloshed?"

"Yes."

She shrugged. "Sure. Why not."

"Tell you what," I said to Skeeter. "Give me half a cup of coffee. Fill the rest of it up with bourbon."

He shook his head. "It don't work."

"It doesn't matter, does it?"

Skeeter studied me for a minute. "Okay. I guess so. Ma'am?"

"Just coffee," said Gloria. "I'm driving."

When Skeeter brought our coffees, mine liberally laced with Rebel Yell, Gloria said, "Now sip it slowly and tell me what's on your mind, what this thing is that's making you so weird."

"I guess I can tell you. I can't say names. You understand."

"Something involving a client?"

I nodded. "I think one of my clients might've murdered a man. He set it up so it would look like I did it. That's why those cops visited you the other day."

"Checking on your alibi."

"Yes. So I'm stuck here, maybe knowing who did it and the cops thinking it was me, and I can't really even talk to them. Makes me seem suspicious as hell. Anyhow, I've been trying to get a handle on it. I mean, if I can make the link between the dead guy and my client—"

"You need evidence to give the police."

"Right. But it has to be evidence that is separate from anything my client has told me. I can't violate his privileged status with me."

"So you're playing sleuth again."

"Mmm," I said. "It's getting a little drunk around here, did you notice?"

She smiled. "I noticed."

"So I have a name. A woman. I gotta talk to her. Trouble is, the name I got is the name she had before she got married. I can't find her unless I know her name. I found her parents. They won't tell me."

"So you're stuck. And that's why you're acting stupid."

"Yup." I grinned at her. "That's why I'm acting stupid. Because I am stupid. And because they might want to arrest me. And if they arrest me and put me in Walpole, I would be unhappy. The fishing is shitty at Walpole."

"But you didn't do it, Brady."

"Ah, I love the delusions of laypeople. The delusion that only guilty people are convicted of crimes."

"The same reason doctors overreact to their own symptoms, right?"

"Yeah. Doctors know that people really die."

Gloria tipped up her coffee cup and drained it. "Come on, big guy. I'm gonna tuck you in."

I finished my drink. I fumbled for my wallet. "I got it," said Gloria.

"No, no . . ."

"Yessir. This is party. I invited you. I got you drunk."

"Talked me into it," I mumbled. I had begun to feel sleepy.

Gloria paid Skeeter. We climbed off our barstools. Gloria put her arm around my waist and we made our way to the door.

"Hey," called Skeeter.

We turned.

"You gonna be okay, Mr. Coyne?"

"I am in excellent hands, barkeep. Excellent hands. Excellent."

He was shaking his head when we left.

I tipped my head back during the short ride to my apartment. I struggled to stay awake.

Gloria parked in the garage in the basement of my building. She helped me onto the elevator. When we got off at the sixth floor, she said, "Which one is your key?"

"The gold one."

"There are four gold ones."

"It's round on the end."

"Forget it. I'll try them all."

She got the door open and helped me in. "Oh, Jesus, Brady Coyne. What a mess."

"It's how I like it."

"Do you ever do laundry?"

"Nah. I just buy new stuff."

"That's how it looks."

I dropped my parka on the floor by the door. Gloria picked it up and draped it over a kitchen chair. I went into the living room and sat on an old newspaper on the sofa. I began to tug at my boots. I couldn't seem to keep a grip on them. My hands kept slipping away, and when they did I fell backward against the sofa.

"Let me help you," said Gloria.

She had removed her coat. "Nice blouse," I said. I reached out and touched the sleeve with my forefinger. "Silky. Like skin."

"You hardly ever used to get drunk," she said, kneeling in front of me and pulling off a boot.

"Uptight," I said. "I was always too uptight."

She grunted at the other boot. It slipped off. "You're not uptight anymore, huh?"

"Nope. Not me."

"Come on," she said, holding her hands to me. "Let's tuck you in."

She helped me up. We went into the bedroom. She took the old clothes off the bed, shook them, and piled them on the chair. I sat on the edge. She worked at the buttons of my shirt. I leaned forward and put my face in her hair. She looked up at me and smiled. "You used to get drunk in New Haven," she said.

"You remember that."

"Of course I remember."

"That was before we got married."

"Before you got uptight."

She peeled my shirt off. She undid my belt. She unzipped me. I tried to prop myself up so she could shuck off my pants. I kept collapsing.

"Stand up," she said.

I did. She got my pants down around my knees, and I fell onto the bed. I closed my eyes.

It was a black sleep, like death. I awoke sometime in the middle of the night. My head hurt. I tried to hitch myself into a sitting position. My hand brushed bare skin. It wasn't mine. I reached beside the bed and flicked on the light.

Gloria blinked at me.

"What are you doing here?" I said.

"Trying to sleep."

"I didn't know you were going to stay."

"You expect me to walk home?"

"My head hurts."

"Serves you right."

I closed my eyes. It helped my head. "Did we——?" I said.

"You passed out, lover."

I touched her hip experimentally. She was wearing panties. Nothing else. "What are you doing?" she said.

"Sometimes . . ." I shook my head. "I don't know. Sometimes I . . ."

She touched my chest. "I'm here," she whispered.

I turned and she moved against me. I held her close to me. She tucked her face into the hollow against the side of my neck. Her hands moved on my back. After a moment she tilted her head back and looked at me. "Do you want . . . ?" she said.

"Yes, I do."

All the moves were from memory, and yet somehow it was new. There was little passion to it. We explored, we made discoveries. Making love with Gloria seemed inevitable and logical, something we had been pointing to for ten years. Afterward we lay beside each other on our backs, staring up at the ceiling.

"How's the head?"

"It still hurts. The rest of me feels much better."

"I was thinking," she said.

"What, Gloria?"

"Your problem."

"Do I have a problem?"

She turned to look at me. She smiled and touched my leg with her hand. "Not that kind of problem, dummy. You don't have that problem. The one that was bothering you, I mean. The one that made you feel like you had to get drunk."

"Funny thing," I said. "For a while there, I had forgotten about it."

"That woman who got married, whose name you don't know?"

"What about her?"

"There are records, aren't there? When someone takes out a marriage license?"

I turned and held her face in both of my hands. "The smartest thing I ever did was marry you."

"And," she said, "divorce me."

I held her for a while. We were a familiar, comfortable fit. I began to drift. Then I sensed her moving away from me.

"Hey," I said softly. "Where are you?"

"I'll be back," she said.

I blinked into the darkness. I saw her pale naked body move out of the room. I waited to hear bathroom sounds, but none came. After a few minutes I climbed out of bed. I staggered for an instant against a sudden pain in my head. Then I went into my living room.

Gloria was standing silhouetted against the big glass windows overlooking the harbor. She was hugging herself and her head was bowed. I moved beside her. "Hon?" I said.

"Hi."

"You all right?"

"Sure. Fine."

"Coming back to bed?"

"You go ahead. I'll be along."

I touched her bare shoulder. She seemed to pull away. I let my hand trail down her arm. "Come on. It's chilly out here."

"I'll be there."

I detoured to the bathroom. Then I returned to my bed. Gloria had not come back to it. I lay on my back and stared blankly at the ceiling, waiting for her. But sleep returned to me before she did.

· THIRTEEN ·

I DIDN'T DARE OPEN MY EYES. I didn't dare move. Someone had driven an ice pick into my left temple, all the way through so that it came out at my right temple. By squeezing my eyes shut I found I could minimize the pain.

I lay there, immobilized by my monster hangover, and remembered that I had dreamed of Gloria. We had made love. It was like the old days. No, it was better than the old days. An ancient feeling had been recaptured. I had forgotten that old feeling. It was something I hadn't felt since before we were married.

Experimentally, I allowed my eyes to open to slits. Gray light suffused my bedroom. I creaked my head around to check the time. My digital clock-radio said 8:48 A.M. I never slept that late.

On the bedside table next to the radio stood a tall glass full of crimson liquid. From the glass protruded a stalk of celery.

Leaning against the glass was a folded piece of paper.

I hitched myself up in bed and reached for the paper. I unfolded it. It read:

> *Brady, dear:*
>
> *Try city hall. They record marriage licenses.*
> *It was lovely.*
>
> *Gloria.*

I rolled over and sank my face into the pillow beside me. Gloria's smell. Her perfume, her sweat, her sex. It certainly hadn't been a dream.

I picked up the Bloody Mary she had made for me. Gloria made excellent Bloodys. She stirred in about a tablespoon of horseradish and several generous shakes of Tabasco and Worcestershire and the juice of an entire lime. She seasoned it with celery salt and fresh ground pepper. I stirred it with the celery stalk and drank it down fast. It was thick, like half-congealed blood, tangy and hot. I could almost feel it burn away the demons. The ice pick in my head began to melt away.

After I finished Gloria's Bloody Mary, I stumbled into the bathroom. The mirror was still steamed over and a big bath towel was spread over the rack. I touched it. It was damp. With my forefinger I wrote *Brady & Gloria* on the misted mirror. Then I wiped it clear with the palm of my hand. I climbed into the shower. I made it as hot as I could bear it, and I stood under it for a long time. Then I turned off the hot water and quivered under the frigid for a count of thirty.

By the time I had toweled dry and slipped into jeans and a sweatshirt, I felt nearly human.

Before she left, Gloria had brewed coffee. I poured a big mugful and took it to the table by the glass sliders. The two storm fronts, as predicted, had collided somewhere over my apartment. I could barely see the ocean through the thick mixture of rain and snow that angled down from a low sooty sky and splatted against the glass. I could hear the low moan of the wind trying to squeeze around the edges of the sliders. Three inches of slush covered the balcony outside the sliding doors. In the night it had snowed. Now it was in the process of changing over to rain. Later it would change back. Typical February nor'easter. Inland it would be all snow.

I sipped coffee and smoked cigarettes and tried to sort out the assault of negative emotions I was feeling. Betrayal was one of them. Betrayal by that treacherous groundhog, who had promised springtime, not more endless winter. Betrayal by Gloria. She had arisen early, jotted me a note, and slipped away without waking me up. She had deprived me of the delicious pleasure of waking up with her beside me. It made me feel vaguely used.

I smiled to myself. I had done the same thing more than once, and had never understood why it upset women. In one way or another, the important women in my life usually managed to find a way to make me see things their way.

And I was forced to admit that I felt lonely. My apartment, usually a haven, seemed silent, cold, dreary. I knew that if Gloria hadn't been there and then left, I wouldn't miss her.

I went to the kitchen and dumped a can of Hormel corned beef hash into a skillet. I let it brown on the bottom, turned it over with a spatula, pushed it into a pile, and fried three eggs. I slid the hash onto a plate and the eggs on top of the hash, and took the whole mess to the table. I ate and watched it storm and tried to decide whether I should spend some of this miserable Saturday at the office.

The decision was easy. Who the hell worked on Saturday?

CLIENT PRIVILEGE 105

I slid Wagner's *Gotterdämmerung* into the tape deck and turned up the volume, counterpoint to the howl of the storm. Then I sat at my fly-tying desk. I tied a batch of weighted Pheasant Tail nymphs. It was finicky work on little sixteen and eighteen hooks. It demanded my full attention, as I knew it would. It reminded me of all the nymphs I had broken off the previous summer in the jaws of large trout and in streamside brush, and of some of the trout I had caught, too, and those memories washed away the depression I was feeling. After all, New England and nor'easters and a deceitful ground-hog to the contrary notwithstanding, spring was less than six weeks away.

I had lived without Gloria for a decade. Nothing had changed.

In the middle of the afternoon I went to the phone and pecked out the Lavoie number. Mrs. Lavoie answered.

"This is Brady Coyne calling again, Mrs. Lavoie," I said.

"Yes?"

"The lawyer? Who dropped in yesterday?"

"I remember you, Mr. Coyne."

"I was just wondering if you'd changed your mind about giving me your daughter's address."

"No. No, we haven't. I thought we made it clear—"

"You did," I said quickly, "and I'm sorry to bother you. I just hope you understand that I intend Karen no harm, but it's extremely important that I talk with her. I was hoping you would help me."

I heard her sigh. "You'll probably find some way to find her. You law-yers . . ."

"I'm going to try," I said. "I wanted you to know that. I'd rather have your permission."

"You don't need our permission."

"No. You're right. Your approval, maybe. Your understanding. Your coop-eration."

She was silent for a long moment. "At first," she said finally, "I suspected you were a policeman, or a private detective, or something."

"No. I really am a lawyer."

"Then," she went on, "I looked you up in the phone book. I guess you're a lawyer, like you said."

"Yes."

"So then I got to wondering what you really wanted."

"I need to talk to your daughter, just as I said."

"My husband and I, we figure there's something strange going on. I mean, first that man—"

"What man?"

"Why can't you all just leave us alone?" This burst from her suddenly, harsh and desperate.

"Mrs. Lavoie—"

"I mean it. Please, Mr. Coyne."

I hesitated. "What man?"

"That television man."

"Wayne Churchill."

"Yes. Him."

"He was there?"

"Well, of course he was here. I assumed you knew that."

"No, I didn't."

"He was here, yes."

"When?"

"A couple days before . . ."

"Before he was killed," I said.

"Yes."

"What did he want?"

"I'm begging all of you to leave us alone. We don't want to talk about it."

"It's very important," I said.

I heard her sigh. "I don't know what he wanted. All I know is he came here and he and John—that's my husband, you remember—they went out. They were gone for about an hour. John didn't tell me what they talked about. I figured if he wanted me to know, he'd've told me. Then you called, asking about Karen. So I figure it can't just be coincidence. That reporter, then you. I don't know why all of a sudden everyone's interested in my daughter. We're quiet people. Just ordinary folks. We mind our own business. There's no reason why reporters and lawyers should want to talk to us. But I know that Churchill man was murdered. We don't want to be involved. We aren't involved. We just want to be left alone. Do I have to beg you, Mr. Coyne?"

"I just would like to talk to Karen."

"No, no, no. Please. No. Just let us be. We are quiet, simple people. We like it that way."

"I hear you, Mrs. Lavoie."

"You have no business interfering in our lives. None of you."

"Okay."

She paused. "Well, thank you, then. Does that mean you won't try to find Karen?"

"I can't promise you that."

"In the name of God—"

"Mrs. Lavoie," I said quickly, "did you tell the police about Churchill's visit?"

"Of course not. I told you. We don't like to be involved in things that don't concern us."

"But his conversation with your husband—"

"I don't know what they talked about. John didn't tell me, and I didn't ask."

"It could be relevant."

"I really don't see how."

"Please, Mrs. Lavoie. Your husband should talk to the police."

"My husband makes his own decisions, Mr. Coyne. I do appreciate your advice."

"Except—" I began. But she had hung up.

The storm assaulted the city all day Saturday, slush from the skies. I spent the rest of the afternoon tying flies. Gold-ribbed Hare's Ears, some tiny Pale Morning Dun emergers, a few Zug Bugs. Then I fashioned a dozen spent-wing Adams on eighteen and twenty hooks, which gave me a stiff neck. I heated up a can of Campbell's split-pea and ham soup for supper and sipped it from a mug. I watched a Charles Bronson movie on Channel 56. Then I switched over to *Saturday Night Live*, which turned out to be a taped rerun that I had already seen. I watched it anyway.

The wind was still howling late at night when I went to bed.

Sunday morning a brilliant winter sun blazed from a cloudless sky. The slush on my balcony had frozen solid. Little icicles had formed on the undersides of the railings, and they were dripping slowly, glittering in the sun like little gems as they fell. I slid open the doors and stepped outside. The air was thin and frigid. I thought of Phil, the Pennsylvania groundhog, curled snugly in his lair under the earth. That rascal had the right idea.

In the middle of the afternoon my phone rang. My pulse quickened for an instant. I thought it might be Gloria.

"Coyne," I said.

"It's Rodney Dennis, Mr. Coyne."

I sighed. "I've got nothing to say to you."

"I hoped you might've reconsidered my offer."

"I'm not interested in what you call your offer."

"Sir—"

"Furthermore," I said, "if your own lawyers haven't properly advised you, I will. One of my specialties is libel." This wasn't, of course, true. I doubted if Rodney Dennis knew that. "I suggest you be very discreet, just in case you were contemplating associating my name with Churchill."

"Please hear me out."

I lit a cigarette. "I'm listening."

"I was hoping we could work together. We both have reasons to want to see this case resolved. It's my impression that the police are dragging their feet. You're a suspect, Mr. Coyne. I've done a little investigating myself. I don't think you did it. But I think you know something about the case. If we could pool our resources—"

"I don't know anything, and if I did I'd share it with the police, not you. Can I make myself any clearer, Mr. Dennis?"

"If you could just tell me what Wayne said to you the night he died—"

"No."

"What have you got to hide?"

"I am about to hang up. Good evening, Mr. Dennis."

"Check the eleven o'clock news, Mr. Coyne."

I held the receiver away from my face. As it descended onto its cradle, I heard Rodney Dennis say, "Please, Mr. Coyne. You're making a big—"

I spent the rest of the day with the Sunday *Times*. I discovered that the Wayne Churchill murder was not news fit to print in New York. I tried to watch some golf on television. The golfers were wearing polo shirts in Palm Springs. The women in the galleries were uniformly young and beautiful. They wore shorts.

I had a peanut butter sandwich and an apple for supper. I wasn't very hungry. I thought of calling Gloria, but I didn't. I thought of Pops, on a yacht somewhere in the Gulf.

I spent the evening working the crossword. I left several blanks on it.

Before I went to bed, I turned on my television. I switched it to Channel 8. The lead story on the eleven o'clock evening news was the weather. The suburbs were still trying to push twelve inches of wet snow off their streets. There were many school cancellations. The list scrolled across the screen against a backdrop of pastoral snow scenes while Nat King Cole sang "Winter Wonderland."

When the reporter's face reappeared, he painted on a grim smile and said, "Now a message from Rodney Dennis, the Channel Eight station manager."

Rodney Dennis was gazing sternly into the camera lens. "Six days ago," he said, "one of the best television newsmen in the nation was brutally murdered. He was gunned down in his own home. You have seen Wayne Churchill on this station. You know he was a young man, a vigorous reporter, full of enthusiasm and energy. This is a tragedy for all of us who knew him— we here at Channel Eight, who worked with him, and you, whose homes you invited him to enter via your television sets."

Dennis turned his head, anticipating the shift of cameras. "In the time that has elapsed since Wayne's murder," he continued, "we at Channel Eight have done our best to keep you updated on the progress of the police investigation. We have reported faithfully to you all that we have learned. And that, as you know, has been very little. The police invesigators have refused to be interviewed. They tell us only that they are pursuing promising leads."

His mouth twisted into a sneer at the words *promising leads*.

The camera zoomed in close on Dennis's face. "We are not satisfied. We at Channel Eight do not intend to allow Wayne Churchill's murder to suffer the fate of too many homicide cases in this city. We will not let you or the police forget Wayne Churchill. I have therefore been authorized to announce that Channel Eight is offering a reward of five thousand dollars for information leading to the arrest and conviction of the person or persons responsible for the murder of Wayne Churchill. We will continue to pursue this case with the same vigor, the same relentless investigative energy that was the trademark of Wayne himself."

Dennis's face on the screen was replaced by a telephone number, which Dennis's voice read to us. When he returned, he said, "Naturally, we guarantee absolute anonymity. Operators are standing by at this number, and will be standing by twenty-four hours a day for as many days as it takes until Wayne Churchill's murderer is safely behind bars and cannot kill again."

The anchorman reappeared. "Thank you, Mr. Dennis," he said. "And in other news, a spokesman for—"

I snapped off my set. I'd heard enough news for one night.

Later I lay on my back staring up into the darkness of my bedroom and tried to understand Rodney Dennis's persistence in pursuing me. Was he on to Pops? It was possible. If Dennis knew about Churchill's rendezvous with me at Skeeter's, he might know more. Except if that were the case, he wouldn't need me as desperately as he seemed to.

Most likely, it was what Mickey Gillis had said. Wayne Churchill had bequeathed to Channel 8 the ultimate newsman's legacy: His murder was a blockbuster story. Dennis was doing his job. He was bloodhounding that story.

As I drifted off to sleep, however, the question continued to nag me. What *was* Rodney Dennis's agenda?

· FOURTEEN ·

I TRIED TO CALL POPS first thing Monday morning. Robert reminded me, with all the courtesy that comes of a Harvard education, that he had promised to have Judge Popowski call me as soon as he returned from his vacation. I was supposed to infer from this that Pops had not returned.

"So when do you expect him?"

"I believe he's due back sometime today, Mr. Coyne. If he checks in at the office, I will remind him to call you."

"Well, okay."

I hung up and swiveled around to look out of my office window. The new snow that draped the city buildings was still so white it looked fake. Smoke, smog, and automobile exhaust would fix that before the sun set. Still, even for an unreconstructed country boy, it looked pretty.

Julie came a-scratching at my door.

"Enter," I called without turning around.

"Brady, there are three men—"

"Have a seat, Julie."

I rotated around to face her. She was standing in front of my desk. "Go ahead. Have a seat," I said.

"It's those two policemen. There's a third guy with them."

"Please sit."

She shrugged and sat.

"You're a woman," I said. "Tell me. Why can't a woman be more like a man?"

She grinned. "That's from *My Fair Lady*."

"I need an answer."

"Your Hungarian lady again?"

"No," I said. "Forget it."

She reached over the desk and put her hand on top of mine. "Poor baby."

I took my hand away. "Christ," I mumbled. "Now this one patronizes me."

Julie tossed her head and stood up. "Well, these three are all men, so you should enjoy them. Ready?"

"Send in the clowns."

She left and returned a minute later, followed by Sylvestro, Finnigan, and a third man I hadn't seen before. He was tall and very thin with a squirrel face and close-cropped mouse-colored hair. Sylvestro wore the same brown topcoat. Finnigan was back in his black leather jacket with the fake fur collar. He was carrying a bulky briefcase.

"I see the police have been galvanized by Channel Eight's reward," I said.

Sylvestro gave me his shy smile. "Galvanized might be an exaggeration, Mr. Coyne. But we are grinding along in our own fashion."

"Well, come on in and have a seat."

I gestured toward the sitting area in the corner of my office. Sylvestro and Finnigan sat on the sofa. The other man took the soft chair beside them. They left the straight-backed wooden chair facing them for me.

I took the seat. "Did Julie offer you coffee?" I said.

Sylvestro nodded. "We declined. This," he said, jerking his head sideways at the thin man, "is District Attorney Alan Woodruff."

"Assistant D.A., actually," said Woodruff. His small, round mouth was full of protruding teeth that got in the way of the words as they came out. I wondered how his lisp affected juries. "There's only one D.A. There's about a hundred A.D.A.'s."

"Woody, here, prosecutes homicides," continued Sylvestro, as if Woodruff had not spoken. "He's on the Churchill thing."

It was a ploy I was familiar with. Ostensibly, the ADA's function at sessions such as this one was to make sure that the police followed the proper forms during their interrogation of a suspect, lest a procedural error result in inadmissable evidence at trial. The message, which Sylvestro and Finnigan knew a lawyer such as I would easily read, was this: I had become a suspect; they had the goods on me; they expected to take me to trial; they expected to win, barring a screwup with my rights; and this Woodruff, who would likely prosecute the case, would watch over today's proceedings and head off a screwup.

None of those things was necessarily true, I knew, and I supposed they knew that I knew it. Nevertheless, Woodruff's presence symbolized the fact that I had graduated from witness to suspect.

Woodruff, in other words, would serve as the cops' attorney.

I held my hand out to Woodruff. He frowned at it for an instant, then gripped it quickly.

"Now, then," said Sylvestro. He glanced at Finnigan, who nodded, opened up his briefcase, and produced a little Sony tape recorder. He placed it on the table between us and pressed a button. A tiny red light went on.

"Testing this thing," said Finnigan into the tiny microphone. "One, two, three." He turned it off, rewound it, and played it back. It sounded okay. He looked at Sylvestro and nodded.

"We'd like to record this, Mr. Coyne, if you don't mind," said Sylvestro.

"For my own protection," I said.

He smiled. "Sure. Right."

I shrugged. "I guess it's all right."

"Good. Appreciate it."

Finnigan flicked on the recorder. Sylvestro cleared his throat. "February the ninth, ah, nine-forty A.M. In the office of Brady L. Coyne." He peered up at me. "Mr. Coyne, before we ask you any questions, you should understand your rights."

"I'm not sure how far I'm willing to go with this," I said. "I do understand my rights."

"You have the right to remain silent."

"Yes. Right."

"Anything you say can be used against you in court."

"I know that."

"You have the right to have a lawyer for advice before we ask you any questions and to have him with you during questioning."

I nodded.

"Please reply verbally," said Sylvestro, nodding his chin at the recorder.

"I understand," I said.

Sylvestro smiled at me. "If you cannot afford a lawyer," he recited, "one will be appointed for you before any questioning, if you wish."

"Oh, I can afford one. I *am* one."

"If you decide to answer questions now without a lawyer present, you will still have the right to stop answering at any time until you talk to a lawyer."

"I very likely will take you up on that one."

"Do you understand what I have read to you?" said Sylvestro.

"Actually, you didn't read it. You recited it. You did a good job. And I understand perfectly."

Sylvestro smiled. "Thanks. Sorry about doing that. So are you willing to talk about this case?"

"You mean the Churchill case, I assume."

"Yes."

I shrugged and lit a cigarette. I should call Zerk, I thought. He'd ream me out if I talked to these cops without him. On the other hand, I had nothing to hide, and, after all, I *was* a lawyer. I thought I could handle it.

"Mr. Coyne?"

I nodded.

"Verbally, please."

"I'm willing to talk," I said after a minute. "I may take you up on stopping, though."

Sylvestro smiled. "Good. Thanks." He glanced at Woodruff, who was staring at the red eye of the tape recorder. Then he looked at Finnigan. Finnigan nodded his head once. Sylvestro turned to me.

"Okay, Mr. Coyne. Would you please repeat for us everything you did last Monday evening, beginning with the time you entered Skeeter's Infield."

"I want to ask you something, first," I said. "For the benefit of your tape recorder."

Sylvestro shrugged. "What?"

"Two reporters have called me. They indicated they knew I was involved in this thing." I frowned at him.

"Your question is . . . ?"

"How'd they hear that?"

"Not from me." Sylvestro turned to Finnigan, who arched his eyebrows and shrugged.

"Well," I said, "I don't appreciate it."

"We have told the media nothing except that we're working our asses off on this case, pursuing leads, loads of possibilities, blah, blah. It's hard to keep secrets, Mr. Coyne. Everybody wants a piece of this case. That's why we're here."

"Media pressure," I said.

He shrugged. "We'd be here anyway."

"Can we . . . ?" said Finnigan.

Sylvestro nodded. "Okay, Mr. Coyne. Would you mind telling us again about the night of the murder, now?"

"Sure," I said. And I did, telling it the same way I had the previous two times, but keeping the times straight. They didn't interrupt me. "And then I went to bed," I concluded.

"Why'd you say you were meeting Churchill?" said Finnigan.

"I didn't say. As you know."

"You're refusing to answer."

"Clever deduction."

"You citing the Fifth?"

"No. I don't happen to be concerned with self-incrimination right now."

"Incriminating somebody else," he said, leaning toward me.

"What's your next question?"

"Are you gonna be uncooperative here, Mr. Coyne?" said Finnigan.

"I am trying to cooperate as much as I can."

Woodruff was staring at me. I couldn't read his expression.

"Okay, then," said Finnigan. "So what was it you said you and Churchill argued about?"

"I didn't say that, either. I didn't even say we'd argued. We've already been over that."

"Protecting a client," said Finnigan.

"Protecting a client's confidentiality, which is his privilege when he retains a lawyer. It means something a little different."

Finnigan shrugged. "And how did you get from Skeeter's to Churchill's place on Beacon Street?"

"I didn't go there. I told you that. I went home."

"Did Churchill let you in?"

"I wasn't there."

"Did you go with him, or did you follow him?"

I sighed. "I didn't go there."

Woodruff's eyes darted back and forth from Finnigan to me during this exchange. Sylvestro was leaning back, staring beyond us to the window. I sensed he was listening carefully.

"Where do you keep your thirty-two, Mr. Coyne?" said Finnigan.

"I don't have a thirty-two. I do have a thirty-eight, which you have seen. I keep it in my safe."

"Why did you pick Skeeter's for your meeting?"

"Can't tell you."

"Who are you protecting?"

I shook my head. "This is getting nowhere, and I'm getting a little pissed. If you had something, you'd arrest me. So why don't you go get something, if you think you can, before you come in again to interrupt my work? I don't think I want to answer any more questions. If you keep insisting on asking them, I'm going to call my lawyer. It'll take him a while to get here."

"Mr. Coyne," said Finnigan, leaning toward me, "can we look through your files?"

"Are you kidding? Of course you can't."

Finnigan glanced at Woodruff. "I guess we'll have to get a warrant."

I took my wallet from my hip pocket and extracted a hundred dollar bill.

I laid it on the coffee table. "That says I know you can't get one. You guys want to cover it?"

None of them did. I left the bill on the table.

Sylvestro scratched the top of his scalp and leaned toward me, an apologetic smile on his face. "You've been very patient, Mr. Coyne."

I nodded. "It hasn't been easy."

"I hope you understand . . ."

I waved my hand. "Sure. You've gotta do your job."

He shrugged. "I want to ask you something else. You don't have to answer if you don't want to."

"I think we've pretty well established that already."

"Right. Okay. Now, what the papers haven't printed is this. See, Churchill was known to fool around with cocaine." He cocked his eyebrows at me.

I nodded and said nothing.

"That mean anything to you, Mr. Coyne?"

"No."

"You already knew that?"

"How would I know that?"

"You don't seem surprised."

"I'm not, particularly. What I hear, lots of people fool around with cocaine. I've heard that cops fool around with cocaine."

He smiled. "What about Churchill?"

"I don't know anything about him."

"Not even where he got his dope?"

"For the benefit of your machine, and for your record, no, I don't know where Wayne Churchill got his dope." I took a deep breath. "Look," I said. "Something's bothering me."

The three of them inched forward.

"Churchill was killed a week ago tonight, right?"

They nodded, almost in unison.

"And for a week you guys have made no progress on this case. Hounding me, whether you know it or not, is not progress. You think you got yourselves a suspect, I surmise. So you think you've done your job. But, see, I didn't kill the man. That means someone else did. And now a week has passed. Your killer could be in Hong Kong by now."

"That bothers you," said Finnigan.

"I should think it'd bother you."

"Don't underestimate us."

"I must say, it's hard not to."

"If you can help?" said Sylvestro.

It was delicate. I knew that Churchill had seduced Suzie Billings, the secretary in the Clerk Magistrate's office, into giving him a photocopy of the old application-for-complaint form that Karen Lavoie had filled in, the form that named Chester Y. Popowski as the respondent in an assault-with-intent complaint. The form also indicated that Karen had subsequently withdrawn the complaint, and no process had issued. If the cops had found that form, surely they would have had the sense to question Pops. Surely, then, they would see that Pops, not I, had a motive for murder. The motive was linked to an old relationship from the days when Pops was an ADA and Karen a clerk in the East Cambridge courthouse.

Surely . . .

Except Pops was a powerful judge. Power translated into influence. Old favors can be reciprocated on demand. Potential evidence can be mislaid. A discreet suggestion, the mention of a name, and Brady Coyne becomes a suspect.

I began to see the picture more clearly. I was all they had. Maybe they knew they'd get nowhere with me. If so, we were all playing out a charade and when the hubbub died down, when Channel 8 had milked the story dry, Churchill's death would remain unsolved, like most murders in Boston. Eventually they'd leave me alone.

Or maybe they really thought I did it. Maybe they thought that I sold cocaine to Churchill, or bought it from him. Maybe Pops had found a way to point a finger at me. My rational self doubted they'd ever arrest me, or if they did, that they'd ever get past a grand jury with probable cause. But the part of me that secreted acids into my stomach feared it, all the same.

And whether they arrested me or not, Chester Y. Popowski was free and clear and off on his new career as federal judge.

It pissed me off. And I didn't know what to do about it.

I wished there were a way of learning what had happened to that photocopy of Karen Lavoie's application for complaint. It seemed to be the only concrete link in this case.

"Mr. Coyne?" said Sylvestro.

"Nothing," I said. "I was just sitting here marveling at your collective incompetence. But you've probably done that yourselves."

Sylvestro smiled tolerantly. Finnigan's smile conveyed something else. Woodruff studied the tape recorder.

"Anyway," I said, "this being the end of this interrogation, I have work to do."

"I still got a question," said Finnigan.

I looked at him and shook my head.

"Who are you protecting?"

"Mr. Finnigan," I said, "you are a slow learner."

"Fuck it," said Finnigan. He reached forward and turned off the recorder. "Let's get out of here."

Less than an hour after the three lawmen left my office, Julie buzzed me. When I answered the phone, she said, "Your friend, that Suzie, is on line one."

I didn't bother correcting her. Technically, Suzie was my client. But I hadn't let Julie in on that yet. So I said, "Thanks," and stabbed the blinking button on the console.

"Hello, Suzie," I said.

"Oh, Jesus, Mr. Coyne." Her voice was soft, but I detected the sharp edge of hysteria in it.

"What's the matter, Suzie? What's happened?"

"The—there were some policemen. They came to my apartment yesterday."

"They found the photocopy?"

She sniffed and cleared her throat. "God. I can't seem to get control here. I'm sorry. No. I mean, I don't know. They didn't say anything about that photocopy. But they were asking me all kinds of things about Wayne."

"What kinds of things?"

"About our—you know, our relationship. Did I know he had other girl-friends, was I jealous, what I was doing the night he got killed—"

"Did they read you your rights?"

She hesitated. "No. Is that bad?"

"No. It's good. It means you're probably not a suspect."

"But they seemed to know a lot, Mr. Coyne. That I had a key to his condo. That we—we slept together. They asked about coke."

"What about it?"

"Did I know Wayne did coke."

"What'd you tell them?"

"I said I knew that."

"Did they ask if you did?"

"No. But they asked if I knew where he got it. The same question you asked me. I told them no." She sighed deeply. "I'm kinda scared. I mean, I already was scared. But this is different. I mean, now I'm *really* scared."

"Okay," I said. "Take it easy." I started to tell her that if the police came by again, she should call me and I would join her. Then I thought how that would look to Sylvestro and Finnigan if I, of all people, were her lawyer.

It would look damned suspicious, is how it would look.

"Suzie," I said, "I'm going to give you the number of an excellent lawyer. A better lawyer than me at this sort of thing. Call him, tell him I told you to retain him. Tell him everything you've told me, and anything else you can think of about Churchill. He will advise you to say nothing more to the police unless he's with you. Do as he advises."

She hesitated. "I don't know, Mr. Coyne. It was hard enough telling all this to you. I don't know how I'll feel about going through it all over again."

"Trust me, Suzie," I said. "Do it this way." I gave her Zerk's name and phone number and made her repeat them to me. "Promise me, now."

"Okay. I promise." Her voice was small but controlled.

"Good."

"Something funny," she said.

"What's funny?"

"Those policemen. They asked me about Rodney Dennis."

"The television guy?"

"You know him?"

"No. Not really. I know who he is. What did they ask about him?"

"Well," she said slowly, "nothing, really. Did I know him, had I met him, did Wayne talk about him. Stuff like that."

"What's funny about that? The police always ask about other people."

"Well, for one thing, he was the only one. I would've maybe expected them to ask about Gretchen or some of Wayne's other girlfriends, but they didn't. And the other thing . . ." Her voice trailed away.

"Suzie?"

"Hm? Oh, I was just thinking. Sorry."

"What was the other thing?"

"About Rodney Dennis. Right. The other thing was, they mentioned him right in the middle of all those questions about coke, Mr. Coyne. I mean, I told them what I knew, which was that Wayne had mentioned Mr. Dennis. He was Wayne's boss. But that was all I knew. Don't you think that was kinda funny?"

"Yes," I said. I thought it was even funnier that the police hadn't mentioned the name Coyne to her. "It's funny, Suzie. But don't worry about it. Just give Mr. Garrett a call."

· FIFTEEN ·

AFTER I HUNG UP WITH SUZIE, I waited for the length of time it took me to drink one cup of coffee and smoke two cigarettes. Then I called Zerk's office in North Cambridge.

"Xerxes Garrett, Attorney," answered one of his secretaries. He had two, a white one and a black one. Zerk liked to say that he ran an equal opportunity office, and he wouldn't discriminate on account of race, sex, religion, country of origin, income, or golf handicap, whether it came to hiring office help or taking on clients.

He said this pointedly. Zerk did a great deal of *pro bono* work. My clientele was, as it happened, all white, mostly WASP, generally wealthy. Not that I turned needy folks away. They just didn't tend to seek me out.

"It's Brady Coyne, Mary," I said. Mary was an Irish lady from South Boston with six school-age kids and an alcoholic husband she hadn't seen in four years. "I need to talk to Mr. Garrett."

"Well, do ye, now, Mr. Coyne?"

"That I do, Mary."

"This bein' business or pleasure?"

"It's business, Mary. Honest."

"Well, you just hold tight, Mr. Coyne, and I'll see if I can get him for ye."

A minute later Zerk came on the line. "Yo, bossman."

"We've got to talk."

"Whoa," he said. "Not even a 'how are the wife and kids'?"

"You haven't got a wife and kids. Whereas I have a problem."

"Client who can't foot the bill?"

"No. I'm serious. I've got a bunch of cops who think I killed somebody."

"Yeah, I suppose that might qualify as a problem. Need a lawyer, huh?"

"I think it's time I retained counsel."

"Good thinking. You know what they say?"

"Yes. In fact, you learned it from me. One of the several golden nuggets of wisdom I have given you. The attorney who defends himself has a fool for a lawyer. I think I've already proved myself a fool. Can we meet?"

"Lemme look." A minute later he said, "I'm in court all day. Why don't you come by at five this afternoon."

"Five it is."

"Meanwhile, as if I had to tell you, don't talk to anybody."

"Sure. I know that. Another thing. I referred a client of mine to you."

"I've already got a shitload of clients."

"This one's name is Suzanne Billings. She's young and beautiful and blond and she may be a suspect in a murder case."

I heard him chuckle. "The same murder case?"

"Yeah."

"She's probably better off with me than you for a lawyer, then."

"That's what I figured."

After I hung up with Zerk I walked out of my office.

"Be gone about an hour," I told Julie.

"Hey, don't worry about it," she said. "I'll mind the store."

"I wasn't worried."

"You wouldn't be," she said.

I took the elevator down to the parking garage and strode over to my reserved slot. Here and there on the concrete floor large puddles of melted snow had spread under parked vehicles.

My little BMW seemed to hunker self-consciously among the larger and shinier models that surrounded it. I had bought my first Beemer shortly after Gloria and I were divorced, which was before I had any awareness that a BMW made some sort of statement to other people. I liked it because it was small, maneuverable, and dependable, and because it came with a terrific stereo system. I did not seriously consider getting a Jag or Mercedes or Volvo wagon. Those cars, it seemed to me, inevitably did make a statement.

In five years I put 120,000 miles on my first Beemer. It took me to trout streams from the Catskills to the Cumberland Valley to Nova Scotia and to most trouty waters in between. It zipped through city streets and slipped into undersize parking slots. It never let me down. When I finally, and reluctantly, realized it was time to turn it in, I was faced with a dilemma.

During the time I had been driving it, my car had somehow become a driving machine.

An *ultimate* driving machine, no less.

And I, by virtue of driving that machine, had become some kind of superannuated yuppie.

I seriously considered getting a Dodge. I don't like easy labels. A bachelor lawyer driving a BMW—that was too easy.

But I realized that a Dodge, too, would make a statement. As would a Volkswagen, a Ford Escort, or a Ferrari. In the end I said a pox on all of 'em and got myself another little white BMW with an even better stereo system.

This one was five years old now, and pushing 110,000 miles. There were a couple dings on the door panels, and a rust spot the size of a quarter had appeared on the hood. It was about time to turn it in. I supposed I'd get another driving machine.

I nosed it out of the garage and cut across to Storrow Drive. I got behind a van with a bumper sticker that read MAKE WAR, NOT LOVE . . . IT'S SAFER. A true slogan for our times.

It was when I was crossing the Tobin Bridge that I first noticed the dark blue sedan two cars behind me and realized that it had registered somewhere in my brain back in Copley Square. I wondered if Sylvestro or Finnigan was driving, and decided that they would have assigned an underling the deadly boring task of tailing me.

Then I thought maybe it was some newshound from Channel 8, sniffing out the story he thought he had.

Whoever he was, he was either not very good at it, or else he had been instructed to take no pains to disguise his intentions. I figured it was probably the former.

As I hooked onto Route 93 where it was elevated high above the city, my first impulse was to try to lose the guy in the blue sedan. I figured it wouldn't be hard in my driving machine.

Then a better idea occurred to me.

So I kept the needle on fifty and the blue sedan in my rearview mirror all the way to the turnoff to Medford Square. I parked in the lot behind the big brick and concrete building. Medford City Hall looked like a big, solid high school, vintage 1950, when they were still making schools that looked like schools rather than California office parks. The blue sedan didn't follow me into the lot. When I walked around to the front door, I spotted it cruising slowly past.

I figured if he was a cop, he'd radio for someone else to go in after I left, flash his badge, and demand to know what I'd been doing in there, so the guy in the car could continue to follow me.

If it was a reporter, he'd surely want to know what I was doing at Medford City Hall.

Either one was okay with me.

The City Clerk's office was in Room 103 on the first floor. I walked in and propped my elbows on the counter until a woman at a desk looked up and spotted me. "Help you?" she said without getting up.

"I want to check a marriage license that was issued here," I said.

"Date?"

"I'm not exactly sure. Between 1970 and 1975, maybe. Is that close enough?"

"I'll need one of the names . . . ?"

I grinned. "Sure. Karen Lavoie. I want to know who old Karen ended up marrying."

She smiled and nodded, as if this were a common request. She got up and came to the counter. She wore thick glasses. Behind them were two large blue eyes, one of which wandered off to study the ceiling while the other peered at me. I focused my smile on the one that seemed to be doing most of the work.

She slid a scrap of paper and a pencil to me. "Write down the name on this and I'll look it up."

I printed Karen Lavoie's name on the paper. She picked it up and disappeared around a corner into what I assumed was a room full of records. After what seemed like several minutes she returned with a thick square ledger. She heaved it up on the counter and turned it around for me. It was already opened to the right page.

"There you go," she said.

She remained standing there, one of her eyes watching me, as I studied the license. It included the place of the wedding (St. Agnes Catholic Church), the person who performed the ceremony (the Rev. Matthew O'Donnell), all other pertinent names, and the date. I said to the clerk, "Can I have another piece of paper, please?"

She gave me one and the pencil, too. I printed "Peter Roland Gorwacz" on the paper. I was delighted it wasn't Smith. I gave the pencil back to the woman.

"She married Pete Gorwacz," I said to the clerk. "Son of a gun."

She smiled at me in her walleyed way.

"Thank you very much for your help," I added.

She just shrugged. It was her job.

I paused at the foot of the steps outside City Hall to light a cigarette. The blue sedan was nowhere to be seen. It didn't matter. My tail knew where I'd been. If he was any good, he'd find out what I had been doing there. I strolled around back to the parking lot. I slid into my car and took the scrap of paper out of my shirt pocket. Peter Roland Gorwacz. A helluva name. I figured it would be an easy name to track down. I figured I'd be able to find Karen Lavoie Gorwacz, wherever she was.

I also figured either the cops or Channel Eight would do the same. Sooner or later, it would lead them to Chester Y. Popowski.

When I walked into my office, Julie looked up at me with that tight little grimace on her lips and that hooded look in her eyes that said, "So nice you could drop in."

I hung up my coat and went to her. I stood before her desk like a contrite schoolboy who has been nailed by his principal for playing hooky. "Hi," I said.

"Oh," she said, flashing a big phony smile of greeting. "How wonderful."

"I have returned."

"For how long?"

"For the whole entire rest of the day."

"Why?"

"Because I work here."

"You do?"

"Well, actually, I may leave a little early. Barring court appearances and whatnot, of course."

"Of course."

"Had lunch?" I said.

"Oh, sure. I had nothing else to do. Just closed up shop, hopped a cab, and had the daily catch at Jimmy's. Coupla martinis." She sighed. "How the hell could I have lunch?"

"I dunno. Sorry. Hey. Let's celebrate. How about a big fat Italian sub with lots of hot peppers, extra cheese?"

"Celebrate? What's to celebrate?"

I shrugged elaborately. "I don't know. Another beautiful winter's day? The benign hibernation of Punxsutawney Phil? The fact that in a month I can go trout fishing if I'm willing to freeze my assets?"

"My," she said, her head cocked to one side, smiling for the first time since I had walked in, showing me that big dimple in her cheek. "Aren't we chipper this afternoon."

"I've had a productive morning."

"Me too," she said pointedly.

"So what about the sub?"

"With a Pepsi Cola?"

"Absolutely."

She tilted her head at me. "Do I have to run out for it?"

"No. I will run out for it."

"Go," she said. "And quickly, before you change your mind."

I went. I was back twenty minutes later. We spread out the waxed paper on my desk and leaned over it while we ripped chunks out of the big sub rolls. Oil dribbled off our chins. Pieces of pickle and hot pepper and chopped onion and tomato spattered down on the paper.

We ate without talking. When we were done, Julie wiped her mouth with a paper napkin, belched delicately behind her hand, and said, "Okay. Peace offering accepted." She sipped from her can of Pepsi.

"Thank you."

"Wanna talk shop?"

I shrugged. "Do I have to?"

"It's unavoidable."

"Okay. Shoot."

She rattled off a list of clients and lawyers who had called, or who I should call. She reminded me of a conference with a client scheduled for Tuesday, two appointments with lawyers on Wednesday, and a Bar Association luncheon on Friday.

There had also been, she added, a call from Mickey Gillis. And yet another from Rodney Dennis.

After Julie left I lit a cigarette. I had to be careful. Since Channel Eight had decided to offer a reward, the media competition for the Churchill story would have escalated.

Dennis's call I would not return. I owed him nothing. But I had to call Mickey. She was a good friend. She was a better reporter, though, than she was a friend, I reminded myself.

I stubbed out my cigarette and called her.

"Mickey Gillis," she said.

"It's Brady."

"Oh, hi. Hang on a minute."

Before I could say okay I had been clicked off. I pictured her there in her cluttered office with a phone on each ear pecking at her word processer and riffling through endless stacks of odd-shaped scraps of paper and somehow paying full attention to all of it. I didn't know how she did it, but she did.

It was five or six minutes before she came back on the line. "Boy," she sighed. "Guy telling me he saw this state senator in a gay bar down off Boylston Street. Told me he thought it was my kind of story. I asked the guy his name. He wouldn't tell me. Asked him what he was doing there. He giggled. I told him it wasn't my kind of story, even if it was a story. Which it isn't. He giggled some more. Finally I told him to fuck off, and he kinda gagged. What a job this is."

"Yeah, but you're so good at it."

"I am, ain't I?"

"That you are, Mickey."

"Reason I called."

"The Churchill thing, huh? Mickey, please don't ask me questions."

"Why Brady Coyne, you big shit. What do you think I am?"

"Sorry, Mickey."

"Are we becoming paranoid?"

"Why does everybody accuse me of being paranoid?"

I heard her raspy laugh. "I won't ask you any questions, sweetheart. I thought you might like to know what I've found out. Still interested?"

"Sure."

"Just a few names that might help you. Current and/or recent girlfriends. Turns out old Wayne was quite the cocksmith. Got a pencil?"

I fished one out of my desk drawer and slid a pad of paper toward me. "Yes."

"Okay. First, Gretchen Warde. Spelled with an *e* on the end. Chick who found the body. Assistant producer over at Channel Eight, where Churchill worked. God knows she had a motive to snuff the guy."

"Jealousy, right?"

"Right. The man was juggling three of them at the same time. None was supposed to know about any of the others. Each had a key to his condo. Each had been promised they would soon be permitted to move in and keep house."

"So all three would've had the same motive."

"Sure. They're all prime suspects, for obvious reasons, though what I hear, the cops've got another hot one. Right?"

"Right," I said. "Me."

"Anyway," she said, "this Gretchen Warde claims she called the cops within five minutes of arriving, and the M.E. placed the time of death at least an hour earlier."

"Like about what time?"

"Somewhere between ten-thirty and eleven. The girl says she got there a little before midnight."

"If so, she's clear, then."

"Assuming her story holds up."

"Okay. Who are the others?"

"One named Megan Keeley. Owns a boutique on Newbury Street."

"Good-looker, I bet."

"Oh, yeah. Seems to be the kind Churchill specialized in. She says she's covered for the entire night. She claims she was playing Churchill the same way he was playing her, and has a boyfriend to back her up. I betcha the cops are grilling the two of them. Third name—"

"Suzie Billings," I said.

Mickey, for once, was silent for an instant. "Hey, I'm impressed."

"Don't be. It was an accident."

"I get most of my good stuff by accident, too."

"Tell me about Suzie Billings."

"Secretary in the Clerk Magistrate's office at the East Cambridge courthouse. Kinda ditzy, what I hear. Probably the best-looker of the three, actually."

"And she's got a story, too, huh?"

"My sources are a little vague on that, Brady. None of 'em is exactly clear. This Billings broad's got the same motive as the other two. More dubious alibi, I hear, though I don't know what it is. But evidently they don't see her as the type."

"There's a type?"

"You know what I mean."

"They think I'm the type and she isn't?"

"Hey," she said. "I just work here. You want this stuff or don't you?"

"I do."

"Then don't get pissed at the messenger."

I sighed. "I'm sorry, Mickey. It's getting downright irritating, that's all."

"So maybe you and I should go get drunk."

"Yeah. Being suspected of murder is one helluva good reason to go get drunk." I remembered Friday night with Gloria. "In fact, I already tried it."

"Did it work?"

"For a little while."

"Yeah, that's the thing about getting drunk."

"You got anything else, Mickey?"

"You probably heard, Rod Dennis over at Channel Eight's offering a reward."

"I heard that, yes."

"I'd really love to scoop the bastards."

"Mickey, if I could help you, I would."

"You hear the cops're looking for a drug angle?"

"Yes, I heard that."

"How? It's not in the papers."

"I've got sources, too, Mickey."

"Mmm. I bet."

"What about the drugs?"

"Hey, Coyne. You're the one with the sources. This a one-way street here?"

"It has to be for now, Mickey. I hope you'll continue to fill me in."

"Oh, sure. In memory of Granny Hill and the back seat of that old Volkswagen of yours. Anyhow, that's all I got for now. I still got my feelers out."

"Keep 'em out, please."

"I will. Have I earned a dinner? At least a drink?"

"Both, I think. Soon, okay?"

"I'll have to accept that."

· SIXTEEN ·

IT WAS A LITTLE BEFORE FOUR-THIRTY. It would take half an hour to wend through the commuter traffic to Zerk's office in North Cambridge. I went to my office door and poked my head out.

"Hang out the Gone Fishin' sign," I said to Julie. "I'm about to depart, and you might as well too."

She opened her mouth to protest, but I held up my hand. "I've got a meeting with Zerk at five."

"Those policemen, huh?"

I nodded.

"Okay," she said, shrugging. She switched off her word processer and tugged on its dust cover. "It'll give me a chance to get some shopping done."

I went back into my office, hefted the big Boston white pages out of the drawer, and plopped it onto my desk. I looked up Gorwacz. There was a Gorwacz, Michael R., listed for Medford. Peter Roland's parents, I guessed. Gorwacz, Peter R., had a number in Somerville. There was also a listing for Gorwacz, K. L., on Seventh Street in Cambridge. That was it for the Gorwacz clan. Not a household name in Greater Boston.

It took very little pondering for me to figure out that Karen Gorwacz, née Lavoie, was either separated or divorced from Peter Roland.

I copied down the Seventh Street address and phone number of K. L. Gorwacz into my little breast-pocket notebook. Then I retrieved my coat and went down to my car.

Commuter traffic clogged Copley Square, as I had anticipated. I shoved a Sibelius tape into the deck and turned up the volume and inched my way onto Commonwealth Ave. heading toward Mass. Ave. and the Harvard Bridge across the Charles. I kept glancing into my rearview mirror to see if the dark blue sedan had pulled into the traffic behind me, but it was impossible to tell. There were dozens of dark blue sedans back there. Any one of them might be my tail. I hoped so. Eventually I would lead him to Karen Lavoie Gorwacz.

Of course, the clever rascal could have changed cars on me.

Zerk's office is on Massachusetts Avenue in North Cambridge. It's in an old refurbished colonial next to a funeral home set close to the street behind a neatly trimmed hedge, which presently lay buried beneath a mound of the weekend's snow, already stained with dog pee. Zerk had the entire first floor for his suite of offices—one for each of his secretaries, one for himself, and a large conference room.

The upstairs of his building was shared by an accountant and an architect.

Mary was at the receptionist's desk when I got there almost on the dot of five. She was a big, solid woman with a hard face and a soft smile. I could easily imagine her whacking her kids around and then hugging them to her considerable bosom.

She greeted me with her gap-toothed grin and told me to go on in, Mr. Garrett was waiting for me.

Zerk was at his desk when I pushed open his door. His gray chalk-striped suit jacket hung from a coatrack in the corner. His vest was unbuttoned. His ecru button-down Oxford shirt was loose at the collar. His cuffs were rolled halfway up his thick, ropy forearms, and the knot in his green paisley tie had been pulled loose. He had his feet up on his desk, and he was tilting back in his chair. His dark brow was furrowed as he spoke softly into the telephone that was tucked against his shoulder. He raised his eyebrows when he saw me. A quick grin showed in his dark face. He beckoned me in with a jerk of his head.

I took the chair in front of his desk. His office had once been a living room. There was a fireplace in the corner into which Zerk had had a wood-burning stove installed. It glowed warmly on this chill February afternoon. A nice homey touch.

Keeping the phone snugged in the crook of his neck, he bent to the bottom drawer of his desk and came up with a bottle of Jack Daniel's and two glasses. He poured a couple fingers into each and shoved one toward me.

I lit a cigarette and sipped. In a minute Zerk hung up. He reached across the desk and we shook hands.

"Troubles, huh, bossman?" His handsome face crinkled with concern.

I nodded. "Troubles, indeed."

He grinned. "I expect you're gonna tell 'em to me."

"I'd like to."

He sat back and laced his hands behind his head. "Go for it, then," he said.

So I did. I told him how exactly one week earlier Judge Chester Y. Popowski, my client, had persuaded me to meet a mystery man at Skeeter's, and how the mystery man had intimated that he intended to blackmail the judge over some matter concerning a woman named Karen Lavoie, who Pops had admitted having a brief affair with seventeen years earlier, and who, I learned, although Pops had omitted this part, had filed a complaint against him and then dropped it. I told Zerk that the next day a Boston homicide detective and a state policeman appeared in my office to query me about Wayne Churchill the television newsman, who had been murdered and who was the selfsame man I had met with at Skeeter's shortly before his death. I told Zerk that I had answered some questions inaccurately. Others I refused to answer at all.

I told him that Mickey Gillis and Rodney Dennis had learned that the police were questioning me, too. That someone had leaked the fact that I was a suspect.

I told him the cops had been back twice to interrogate me. On their second visit, they simply rehashed the first interrogation. The third time they came, they had recited my Miranda rights for me. They had taped the interview. And they had brought an assistant district attorney along with them. For purposes of intimidation, I assumed.

I told him a cop or else a reporter in a blue sedan was following me around.

"You answered their questions," he said, interrupting.

I shrugged. "Just those unrelated to Pops."

"Just those," he said, "that might incriminate you."

"They can't incriminate me. I didn't do anything."

"After I told you not to."

"Actually, by the time you told me not to it was too late."

"You didn't know better." He rolled his eyes.

"I knew better."

"Real dumb."

"I know. I thought I could handle it. I *am* a lawyer."

"Shee-it!" he blurted. "They tell you you've got a right to counsel. You're a lawyer, you know how important that is. I even already told you this, not really thinking I needed to. Thinking I was insulting your intelligence by even mentioning it. And you go ahead and talk anyway."

"I admitted it was dumb. I don't think I did any harm."

"You're one stubborn honkie."

"I know."

He sighed. "Glad we agree. So, what else?"

"That's about it," I said. "I'm reluctantly assembling the evidence. I think Pops did it. He had a motive. He had opportunity. He even had a patsy."

"You."

"Yeah. Me."

"He sure as hell did."

"I know. If he planned it that way, it's damn clever. Elegant, even."

"And you can't say a damn thing about him on account of client privilege," said Zerk.

I spread my hands and lit another cigarette. "That's about it. You're the only one I can talk to about it."

"Because of client privilege," he said. "You being my client."

"Yes."

He leaned back in his chair and laced his fingers behind his neck. He gazed up at the ceiling for a moment, then looked at me. "You just filling me in, or are you looking for advice?"

I shrugged. "I'm not sure. Both, I guess."

"Well, first off, next time those cops come by, don't for crissake talk to 'em until I get there."

"Right," I said. "Though I haven't told them anything so far. At least nothing incriminating. Hell. There *is* nothing incriminating."

"You haven't helped yourself by what you've told them. Answering some questions, refusing to answer others. You'd've been better off saying nothing."

"I've got nothing to hide."

"Wrong. You've got the judge to hide. Looks to them like you're hiding plenty. You haven't exactly allayed their suspicions."

"Can't help it. The point is, I'm innocent."

Zerk grinned. "Boy, lawyers can be as dumb as anybody when they get in a spot like this. Since when did innocent mean anything?"

I nodded. "I know. You're right. That's why I'm worried."

"You should be worried."

"This makes me feel much better."

He smiled quickly. "Did you ask the judge to release you from your obligation?"

"I hinted. He didn't bite. I can't ask."

"You're right about that." He frowned. "Worse comes to worse, you can violate privilege." He fixed me with a stare.

"Nope. Just can't do it."

"Didn't figure you would. Had to ask. Still, I am obliged to remind you of your other sacred obligation."

"To the law, you mean."

He nodded. "You're an officer of the court, Counselor. That imposes some pretty damn important responsibilities, too."

I nodded miserably. "I know. I'm conflicted, believe me. The thing is, right now all I could say about Pops was that I think he did it. I mean, in my mind, I know he did it. Because it just fits together. But I don't have anything you could call evidence. Just my theory. Am I obliged to share that with the police?"

"If he weren't your client, would you?"

I shrugged. "I suppose I would, yes. I sure as hell don't like the idea of his getting away with this, any more than I'm particularly fond of finding myself a murder suspect."

"Then you've got what we thoughtful types call a moral dilemma."

"You're telling me."

"You probably already knew that, huh?"

"Hell, Zerk. My whole practice is based on the sanctity of the attorney-client relationship. You know as well as I do that I'm not a hot-shot lawyer like you. I'm a decent negotiator, I know my limits, and I take good care of my clients. I pay attention to them. I listen to them. I can nod sympathetically with the best of them. They like to talk to me. They know I can keep my mouth shut. I'm discreet. Discretion is about the only thing I'm really good at. Most of my clients, that's mainly what they pay me for. Discretion. And client privilege is the taproot of discretion. So right now I'm stuck with protecting Pops. Even if he murdered a man. Even if I end up accused of it. But," I added after a moment, "it burns my nether cheeks, I don't mind telling you, and I wouldn't mind if the cops glommed on to his tail instead of mine."

"In the name of justice," said Zerk.

"In the name of keeping my ass out of prison, mainly."

"What'd you do if you actually did come up with hard evidence against Hizzoner?"

"A murder weapon or something," I said.

He nodded.

"Why, hell, I'd come to you, Zerk. And I'd ask you what to do." I shook my head. "I'd be even more conflicted than I am right now. Which is conflicted enough."

He sloshed some more Jack Daniel's into our glasses. "Right now, not much I can do for you unless they interrogate you again. Or arrest you. Aside from delivering facile homilies."

"I know. I just wanted you to know the story and be prepared."

"If they're harassing you, I might be able to do something about that."

"I think they've got a tail on me."

"Can't do much about that."

"Wouldn't want you to. For all I care, they can follow me everywhere. Somebody's been following me. Either the cops or the media. Either one is okay with me. If they learn something, that's none of my affair. Matter of fact, I've tracked down Karen Lavoie and I'm planning on paying her a visit this evening. They'll probably follow me there." I shrugged.

Zerk studied me for a minute. "You said you might be willing to listen to a little advice."

I nodded. "I'll always listen."

"It's good advice," he said.

"I know what you're going to say."

"I'm gonna say it anyway. Here it is. Cease and desist. Stop your damn sleuthing. Stay away from this Karen. Stop pokin' around. From what you've told me, the cops've got nothing on you except a couple of circumstances. Suspicious-lookin', maybe. But if they had more they'd've arrested you by now. They're not gonna come up with anything more. Unless you do something stupid. Cool it, bossman, and it'll all go away."

"Except for one thing," I said.

"What's that?"

"In a couple weeks Pops' nomination will be approved by the Judiciary Committee. Then he gets the okay from the Senate. Then he gets sworn in. See, it's not just my innocence that's bothering me. It's his guilt. I don't want that son of a bitch made federal judge. I don't want him to get away with this."

Zerk shook his head back and forth sadly. "It's not your job to make that decision."

"But I'm the only one who knows."

"Look," he said. "In the first place, you don't know. You suspect. Just the same way the cops suspect you."

"Difference is, he's got a motive. I know he's got a motive, and I know what it is. Churchill was trying to blackmail him because he did something worse than just have an extramarital affair with Karen Lavoie. Hell, she filed charges against him. Christ, he—"

Zerk reached across his desk and put his hand on my arm. "Leave it be, Brady. Go back, do your job, let the cops do theirs."

I drained my glass and set it onto his desk with a sigh. "Thanks for the good advice. You're a helluva lawyer, if I do say so. I trained you well."

"That," he said, "happens to be true. All of it. Your friend called me."

"Suzie?"

He nodded. "She's pretty scared."

"I know."

"Think she did it?"

I shrugged. "She didn't seem the type."

Zerk rolled his eyes. "There you go again."

· SEVENTEEN ·

I LEFT ZERK'S OFFICE around six. I headed down Mass. Ave. toward the Square. If a cop or a reporter was on my tail, I couldn't spot him.

After a lengthy search, I found a parking slot on Brattle Street that seemed to be legal. I walked about a mile back toward the Square until I came to one of those new restaurants that seem to keep springing up around Harvard Square. This one, like most of the others, featured high beamed ceilings, with lots of shiny wood and brick and glass and chrome. Ferns hung in pots from the beams. I wondered idly who kept them all watered, and if they had to climb around on stepladders to do it. Men and women in business garb were gathered 'round the bar in the corner. It was too early for most of them to eat, apparently, so I had no trouble getting a table.

I wondered if they drove rusty five-year-old driving machines. Newer ones, probably.

I wondered where the Harvard kids hung out these days.

The menu featured salads and a variety of sandwiches, most of which, by any other name, were hamburgers. Hamburgers with sprouts and guacamole, hamburgers with Brie and bacon, hamburgers, for heaven's sake, with Newburg sauce.

My waitress, who told me she had a BA in fine arts from Smith and couldn't find a job that took full advantage of her skill at identifying slide projections of old paintings, agreed to persuade the chef to cook me a burger with a slab of cheddar, although nothing so plebeian was listed on the menu. She also pointed to the place on the menu where plain black coffee was listed among the exotic blends and mixes.

I lingered over my second cup of coffee, and it was a little after seven-thirty when I found a parking slot around the corner from Seventh Street, which was practically in the shadow of the East Cambridge courthouse. In all those years, Karen Lavoie Gorwacz had not gone far.

The street was poorly lit and deserted, except for an old man who was being tugged along from snowbank to trash can by a large leashed dog of complicated ancestry.

Still no sign of my tail. I wondered whether I had inadvertently managed to lose him, or if he was still stuck in traffic back in Copley Square, or if he was more skilled than I had originally given him credit for.

I found the number the phone book had indicated as K. L. Gorwacz's and rang the bell. In a moment I heard footsteps hollowly descend an inside stairway, and then the door opened. I recognized the Lavoies' grandson from the pictures I had seen on their television, although he was a year or two older than their most recent portrait. He was wearing black jeans and a black T-shirt that advertised a Def Leppard concert at the Worcester Centrum.

"Hi," he said. "Help you?"

"I'm looking for your mother."

"Sure. Hang on."

He turned and yelled back up the stairs. "Ma. Some guy for you."

"Who is it?" called a woman's voice.

The boy turned to me. "Who're you?"

"Brady Coyne. I'm a lawyer."

"A lawyer named Brady Coyne," he yelled up the stairs.

"Well, let him in."

He pulled the door all the way open and stood aside. I entered a tiny foyer at the foot of a long flight of stairs, the entire length of which was illuminated by two bare bulbs, one at the top and one at the bottom of the stairs. I held my hand to the boy.

"Paul Gorwacz," he said, gripping my hand firmly. He was nearly as tall as I, and painfully thin, with wavy black hair down around his shoulders and an active case of acne. He was nurturing a fuzzy black mustache that looked more like a smudge of soot than hair on his upper lip.

I followed him up the stairs, which opened into a living-dining-kitchen area. The faint aroma of boiled cabbage lingered in the air.

Karen Lavoie Gorwacz was seated at the kitchen table, which was littered with envelopes and scattered papers. They looked like bills and unanswered correspondence. She appeared considerably older than her wedding picture, which made sense since she had been married about seventeen years earlier. Deep frown lines were etched between her eyes. Her dark tousled hair was lightly streaked with gray. She wore glasses, and a pencil protruded from behind her ear. A coffee mug and an ashtray and a pocket calculator sat among the papers on the table in front of her.

The sink was stacked with dirty dishes. Newspapers littered the floor of the living room area.

Paul wandered in among the newspapers and flicked on a small tabletop television. Karen slouched back in her chair and looked at me over the top of her glasses. "I guess I was expecting you," she said.

I stood across the table from her uncertainly. I had unbuttoned my coat but had not taken it off. "You were?"

She nodded. "My father told me you'd probably try to talk to me. He told me not to."

"And?"

She shrugged. "Sit down, if you want. Coffee?"

"Sure. Thanks."

I draped my coat over the back of a chair and sat at the table. She rose from her seat with a sigh. She was wearing a shapeless sweatshirt and baggy blue jeans. She was not as slim as she had looked in her wedding picture. She went to the stove and turned on the gas under an old-fashioned aluminum coffeepot.

She came back and resumed her seat. She took off her glasses and lit a cigarette. "I probably shouldn't've let you in," she said after exhaling a long plume of smoke, "but I'm sick of doing what my daddy tells me all the time, you know?"

I nodded.

She peered at me with her eyebrows arched. "Well?"

"Well what?"

"Well, you gonna tell me what you want from me?"

I nodded. "Yes," I said. I glanced over my shoulder at Paul, who was sprawled on the floor behind me watching the TV.

"Paul," said Karen, "you go into your room and do your homework."

"For crissake . . ." he muttered. But he got up, flicked off the set, and disappeared behind a door. He closed it with more vigor than was necessary, and in a moment the loud, insistent beat of rock music vibrated from his room.

Karen looked at me and shrugged. "Kids," she said. "Hard enough with both parents to boss 'em around. Paul's a good boy, though. He and I've gotten close since . . ."

Since his father left, I thought. I nodded and smiled.

"He goes to school, keeps to himself," she said. "Got a good job at the sandwich shop. Rindge and Latin's not a bad school if you steer clear of the bad element, which, thank God, Paul's got sense enough to do. I'd like him to go to college, but, tell you the truth, I'll be happy if he graduates, maybe goes into the navy or something." She stopped and smiled. "That's probably not why you're here, huh? To hear about my kid?"

I shook my head. "No." I paused. I wasn't sure how to approach it with her. I sensed if I started wrong I'd learn nothing.

"You once worked in the courthouse," I said.

She stared at me for a moment and then stood up and went to the stove. She poured some coffee into a mug. "Cream and sugar?" she said.

"Black, please."

She put the mug in front of me and sat down again.

"What were you saying?"

"I mentioned that you used to work over at the courthouse."

Fetching my coffee had given her a minute to think about it. She watched me through narrowed eyes. "Yes. I once did. It was a long time ago."

"You knew Judge Popowski?"

"He wasn't a judge then."

"But you knew him."

She shrugged. "I suppose. He was an A.D.A. You got to know all the A.D.A.s."

I sensed I had started wrong. I took a deep breath. "Look," I said. "Let me level with you. I'm Judge Popowski's lawyer. He's been nominated for a federal seat—"

"Good for him," she said. The vertical creases between her eyes deepened.

"You don't like him."

She shrugged and said nothing.

"You had a relationship with him," I blurted. "I have to know about it."

"Like hell you do," she said quietly. "Like bloody hell you do."

"Somebody thinks they can blackmail the judge. Your name is involved."

"Thought," she said.

"Huh?"

She laughed sarcastically. "Somebody thought they could blackmail him. That somebody's dead now. Right?"

I nodded. "So you know about Wayne Churchill."

"Yeah, I heard about him. Sure. It's been all over the TV. He called me up, wanted to come over to talk to me." She gazed steadily at me.

"Did he?"

"Come over? Hell, no, he didn't come over. He called on the telephone. I told him not to bother coming over, I wouldn't let him in. My father told me he might be around. Told me not to let him in. Told me this Churchill wanted to make trouble for us, wanted to snoop around in our lives."

"Mrs. Gorwacz—"

"Hell," she said, "you might as well call me Karen, you want to poke around in my life."

"Karen, then. What did Churchill want, did he say?"

"Oh, he said, all right. A slick talker, he was. Wanted the same as you, I suppose. Wanted to know all about me and Chester. And I told him just what I'm gonna tell you."

"Which is?"

"Nothin'. It's my goddam life, such as it is, and what's done is done and it's none of anybody's business." She stood up abruptly and went to Paul's door. She banged on it and yelled, "Turn that damn thing down, will you? We can hardly hear ourselves think out here."

She came back and sat down. "He's jealous. Hates for me to bring men home. Not that I hardly ever do. Not much time for men." She looked beyond my shoulder and smiled. "Men don't seem to have much time for me, either."

The thumping bass sounds from Paul's room suddenly ended. His door opened. Paul had on his coat. "I'm going out," he announced.

"Where to?" said Karen.

"Out."

"You come here."

Paul glowered for an instant, then went to his mother. She reached up her arm and he bent obediently to kiss her cheek. "I won't be late," he said.

"You behave yourself."

He glanced at me and rolled his eyes. "Sure, Ma. I always do."

She patted his arm and he left.

After the downstairs door slammed shut, Karen looked at me and smiled thinly. "It's hard to know how much rope to give them."

"I know," I said. "I've got two boys of my own." I didn't tell her that Gloria had done most of their upbringing.

"He's a good kid. I've got to trust him."

I nodded and sipped my coffee. "When did Churchill call you, Karen?"

"The Saturday before he got killed," she said promptly. "He called in the afternoon. Paul was off working at the sandwich shop. I was trying to catch up on stuff, just like I was tonight. I can't seem to ever get caught up. I was polite to him. But he kept prodding and pushing and finally I told him I was going to hang up on him. My father told me I shouldn't even talk on the phone to him. He says I shouldn't trust men. He says I'm too naive, that I should know what men are after. But I don't see it that way. I figure I'm grown up, I can take care of myself if I have to. Daddy doesn't agree. I don't know. Maybe he's right. He was very emphatic about me not talking to that Churchill man. I mean, I did talk to him on the phone. But I didn't tell him anything, and I told him not to come over, that I wouldn't let him in if he did. I wouldn't've, either. Anyway, it was some shock when I saw on the TV that he'd been murdered. I hear they've got a suspect. Probably a woman, I figure. I've seen him on TV. He was a good-looking man. Good-looking men are nothing but trouble."

"You didn't tell him anything?"

"Nope. And I'm not gonna tell you anything, either." She peered at me, frowning. "Mr. Coyne, if you'd called me on the phone, I wouldn't have let you come over. I don't like him telling me what to do, but I know he's right. My father, that is. He said not to talk to you."

"But you did let me in."

She smiled softly. "That's my mother. She says you've got to be polite, show your breeding. She'd say let the man in but don't say anything to him. My mother and father don't always agree with each other, but they agree on that. Don't share private business with strangers. I think they're right."

I paused to sip my coffee. Then I smiled at Karen Lavoie Gorwacz in an effort to soften what I was going to say. I figured she wouldn't answer, but I had nothing to lose by asking. "You filed a complaint against Chester Popowski shortly before you left your job at the courthouse," I said quietly.

She stared at me for a minute, then let her breath out with a big whoosh. "Does the whole world know about that?"

"Churchill did. I do. Then you withdrew the complaint. Is that what Churchill had to blackmail the judge with?"

She narrowed her eyes. "Ask your friend the judge."

"I'm asking you, Karen."

"He won't tell you, will he?" She nodded, acknowledging that she had asked a rhetorical question. "Well, neither will I. It's over and done with. Look, Mr. Coyne. Please. Whatever happened seventeen years ago is just ancient history. I got married, had a nice son, nice husband, too, for a while. Then we split and I ended up with this life and I've gotta do the best I can with it. My daddy's right about that. Dredging up the past just makes for misery. I don't need any more misery. So I'm gonna tell you what I told that Wayne Churchill, what I shoulda told you when you came knocking at my door. Please go and leave me alone."

"Karen," I said gently, "the police may try to ask you the same question I'm asking you."

"Please, Mr. Coyne. Don't threaten me. It gets my back up."

"It's not a threat. I'm just telling you it may happen."

"They can question me if they want. I know my rights. I don't have to say anything if I don't want to."

"I'm afraid it's not that simple."

"You are trying to threaten me. Listen. A person's got a right to their own privacy, I know that much. Me and Chester Popowski and anybody else. I just shouldn't even have let you in here tonight. I was only trying to be polite, like my mother taught me, instead of being suspicious like my father. But since I did make the mistake of letting you into my house, you might as well tell the cops and your judge and television reporters and anybody else who's interested. Karen isn't telling anybody about her life. And nobody's gonna change my mind about that. I'm sorry that Churchill man got killed, and I know there's a big reward for catching whoever did it. But it's got nothing to do with me."

"Really," I said, "you should tell the police you talked to him. It might help them find who killed him."

She shrugged. "I doubt it. Anyway, that's their problem."

"No, it's everybody's problem. You ought to tell the police."

"Well," she said, "I'm not going to."

I sat back and smiled at her. "Okay. Fair enough. I hope I haven't upset you."

She shrugged. "Not any more than I'm already upset."

I took a business card from my wallet and put it by her elbow. "In case you change your mind," I said.

She glanced down at it. "I'm not gonna change my mind."

"Well, just in case."

I got up and shouldered on my coat. She rose and came around the table. She followed me down the steep stairs to the front door. In the foyer I turned and held my hand to her. "Thank you for being hospitable," I said.

She took my hand and nodded. "I learned that from my mother."

I smiled. "I know. I was there."

I walked out. Through the open door she said, "Please, Mr. Coyne. Just leave me alone, okay?"

· EIGHTEEN ·

I GOT BACK TO MY APARTMENT a little after nine. I had given up on the blue sedan. I decided I had probably imagined being followed to Medford in the morning. Wishful thinking. Neither the police nor the media was going to allow me to help them that easily.

The light on my answering machine was blinking. I pressed the button, heard it whirr and click, and then a man's voice. "Mr. Coyne, this is Rodney Dennis. It's, ah, let's see, five-thirty Monday afternoon. Left a message at your office but you didn't get it, I guess. Hoping you had a chance to think over what I suggested yesterday. Give me a call, huh?"

He left two numbers, his office and his home.

I let the machine rewind, erasing his message.

I wished Rodney Dennis or some intrepid reporter would latch onto Karen. Or the police. Either one. They'd get her to talk, whether she wanted to or not. She'd put them onto Pops.

I undressed my way into my bedroom and slipped into a ratty old sweat-suit, aptly named. I decided I should try to remember to send it through a washing machine sometime.

I sloshed a little Jack Daniel's into a glass and took it to the telephone. After a brief, losing battle with my self-respect, I dialed the old homestead in Wellesley. Joey answered.

"H'lo?"

"Hi, son."

"Oh, hi, Pop. What's happening?"

"Not much." Like hell. "You?"

"Ahh." A verbal shrug.

"School?"

"Fine. Okay."

"Well, what're you doing?"

"Now? Trying to read *Crime and Punishment.* All these Russian names . . ."

Crime and Punishment. A book for our times. "Mom around?"

"Nope. She's out."

"Expect her back soon?"

"Dunno. She didn't tell me. Should I have her call you?"

"Sure. If she feels like it. Tell her it's nothing important."

"Okay. Whatever."

"Well, get back to your homework."

"Yup. See you."

"Bye, son."

I hung up with Joey and sat at the table overlooking my view of the harbor. It's not much to see on a cloudy February night. Various shades of darkness, with an occasional ship's light a-blinking, some afterglow of the city lights. But it soothes me, and staring out at it helps me muster perspective on worldly preoccupations.

Like being suspected of a murder I didn't commit. And like what I recognized as an unhealthy reattachment to my former wife, after ten years of relative serenity.

The former preoccupation seemed easier to manage than the latter. I would simply heed Zerk's advice. Forget the Churchill killing, ignore my suspicions of Judge Chester Popowski, go about my business, and trust the cops to go about theirs. I figured I had overreacted, which was typical of me. I tended to jump into things with both feet instead of sticking my toe in first.

I tried to figure out if I had learned anything from Karen Lavoie Gorwacz. It was impossible, since I didn't know whether she had lied to me. Either way, she was at the center of whatever secret Wayne Churchill had uncovered about Pops. I had already known that. If she had told me the truth, Churchill called her on the phone, tried to pump her. She told him nothing. She had probably overreacted to him, though, confirming whatever assumptions he had made after seeing the complaint she had filed against Pops seventeen years earlier. It had apparently been enough for him to threaten Pops—which was enough for Pops to kill him.

Rodney Dennis's intuition was on target. There was a blockbuster story there. The only problem was that I wasn't part of that story.

I finished my drink, took my glass to the sink, rinsed it out and put it away. I wandered around my empty apartment, trying to see it as Gloria had seen it.

Okay, it was not real neat.

Actually, it was kind of messy.

Truth to tell, it was a disaster. Clothes, shoes, books, empty cardboard boxes, and unopened junk mail remained wherever I happened to drop them. Nobody would believe, from looking, that I could ever find anything I was looking for.

Gloria probably interpreted it as my unreadiness to live on my own. She would deduce, feeling fully vindicated, that I needed a woman's touch, someone to pick up after me the way she had for all those years, someone to see that my ties matched my suits, my shirts were pressed, my diet was balanced, my bills were paid. She would not know by looking around my apartment that I could manage all those things very well for myself, thank you. She would not know that I liked it that way, preferred it to the compulsive orderliness of our Wellesley home, where I always had to remember to wipe my feet and put the magazines back in the rack with the titles facing up and double-check the locks on the doors before bed each night.

Until Gloria had spent the night with me on Friday, I hardly ever noticed the slovenly disarray in which I lived. Oh, it was a mess. But it was an orderly mess, in its own way. It was comfortable. It was home.

Now she had me noticing it. I wondered if I'd ever see it right again.

I fiddled with the television and found nothing. I picked up the current issue of *Field & Stream* and read everything except the deer-hunting articles.

The phone rang. I flinched at it, then forced myself to let it jangle three times. If I answered it too quickly, Gloria would think I was poised for her call.

"Coyne," I said.

"Mr. Coyne, Rodney Dennis here."

"I still have nothing to say to you, Mr. Dennis."

"Well, listen, Mr. Coyne—"

"Please stop calling me. I'm going to hang up now."

Which I did.

At eleven I turned on the news. Channel 8. The lead story was the Churchill murder. As it turned out, a non-story. The reporter said that there were no new leads in the case and repeated the reward offer. Rodney Dennis did not appear.

The suburbs had dug out from the storm. Another was due in later in the week. A policeman had been wounded in a shootout at Downtown Crossing. A prominent Wayland physician had been killed in a freak skiing accident at Killington over the weekend. A child abuse case had come to trial. Sabers were rattling again in the Middle East.

Uplifting stuff, all of it.

The only good news was a Celtics victory over Portland, and even that was marred by an ankle injury to Kevin McHale. When the news was over I watched Johnny Carson's monologue. He told a few good jokes about television evangelists.

Gloria didn't return my call.

It wasn't as if I had anything particular to tell her. I just wanted to say hi.

Hell, I missed her.

I turned off the TV. I loaded the coffee machine for the morning. I brushed my teeth.

Midnight. She still hadn't called.

Either she was staying out very late, or she was staying out all night.

Or else she didn't care enough to call me back.

The hell with her.

I went to bed.

I was knotting my tie at around seven-thirty the next morning when the phone rang.

"This is Jack Sylvestro."

It took me a minute for the name to register. I had expected it to be Gloria. "What can I do for you?" I said to the cop.

"I'm down here in the lobby of your building. Mind if I come up?"

"No, that's fine, I guess."

In the three minutes it took him to ride the elevator up to the sixth floor I considered and rejected the notion of calling Zerk. I'd find out what Sylvestro wanted first.

He rapped lightly on the door and I opened it. The homicide detective was even more rumpled than usual. A shiny gray stubble showed on his cheeks and chin. Dark rings bagged under his eyes.

"You look like you could use some coffee," I said.

He nodded and sighed. "That would be great. Black."

I went to the machine and poured a mug for him. He slouched at the table overlooking the ocean, still burrowed in his shapeless brown topcoat. The morning had dawned cloudless and bright. Whitecaps flecked the blue harbor, and gulls were being swept sideways by the wind. Sylvestro squinted out at the scene. "Nice view," he said, sipping.

I sat down with him. "What's up, Lieutenant?"

He ran the palm of his hand over his face. "Wonder if you'd mind humoring a confused old flatfoot."

"Isn't that what I've been doing for the past week?"

One side of his mouth smiled briefly. "Yeah, I guess. You've been patient with our bumbling around, I'll give you that. Don't know as I'd've put up with it all." He took another sip from his mug, then set it onto the table and leaned forward on his forearms. "I want you to come for a little ride with me."

"Where?"

"I'd rather not say."

"You are stretching the limits of my good humor, Lieutenant."

He nodded. "I know."

"Do you intend to arrest me?"

He shook his head. "No. I don't intend to. Nothing like that. Look, Mr. Coyne. I know you think we've been harassing you. I know you think we're incompetent and shortsighted. Maybe we're guilty of harassment, I don't know. I guess it's what cops do. But we're not incompetent. The fact that we haven't told you everything we know about the Churchill case doesn't mean we haven't been working on it. For that matter, you haven't told us everything you know, either. Anyway, no, I'm not arresting you. I need about an hour of your time. You'll see why."

I lit my first cigarette of the day and stared at him. "Where's your sidekick?"

"Finnigan? Finnigan doesn't approve of what I'm doing. So he decided not to come."

"I think I should call my lawyer."

Sylvestro shrugged. "You don't need him. But go ahead."

I got up and went to the kitchen phone. Sylvestro continued to stare out at the ocean. I called Zerk's home number. His answering machine informed me he was not home and invited me to leave a message after the beep. I declined the invitation, disconnected, and tried his office. A machine answered there, too.

After the office machine beeped, I said to it, "Zerk, it's Brady. I'm off on a scavenger hunt with Detective Sylvestro, the homicide cop. I will answer no questions. I will not incriminate myself. I assume you'd advise me not to go. So thanks for the implicit advice. I'll let you know what it's all about as soon as I know."

When I hung up, Sylvestro stood. "Thanks," he said. "Ready?"

There was a Boston police cruiser parked in front of my building with a uniformed cop behind the wheel. Sylvestro and I got into the back. "No lights, no siren," said Sylvestro to the driver, who grunted in reply.

He steered onto the Expressway, weaving proficiently through the early rush-hour traffic, and then exited onto Storrow Drive, paralleling the frozen Charles. After we crossed the river, we took a right onto Mt. Auburn Street, heading toward Harvard Square. Twenty minutes after we left my apartment building on the waterfront, we pulled up in front of the main entrance to the Mt. Auburn Hospital.

Sylvestro opened the door and got out, then leaned in. "This is it, Mr. Coyne. Come on."

I slid out of the car. "What's this all about?" I said. I felt that somehow I had been bamboozled.

"Be patient with me," he said. "You'll see. Follow me."

Sylvestro flashed his shield at the visitor's desk and then led me to a bank of elevators. We shared the ride with a pair of young interns who were discussing the anatomy of a nurse of their acquaintance.

We got out of the elevator, turned left, and found ourselves in a waiting room. Its only occupant was a bald man with a black mustache. He stood up when he saw us. Sylvestro went to him and they spoke briefly in low voices. Then they came to where I was standing.

"Mr. Coyne, this is Detective Orvitz of the Cambridge police," said Sylvestro.

Orvitz nodded but did not offer his hand, so I didn't either.

"She's awake," said Orvitz to Sylvestro. "Wanna take him in?"

I looked from one cop to the other. "Just a minute," I said. "I'm not sure I want anything to do with this."

Sylvestro put his hand on my shoulder. "Come on, Mr. Coyne. It'll only take a minute."

I shrugged. "I came this far."

He led me down a corridor to a small private room. A figure lay on the bed. It was a woman, judging by the tangled mass of dark hair on the pillow. Her face was turned away from us. The back of her head was bandaged. She was either sleeping or staring out the window at the blank brick wall across the air shaft. She was not attached to any tubes or wires, so I guessed her condition was not considered critical.

"Mrs. Gorwacz," said Sylvestro softly.

She turned her head slowly. When I saw her face, I whispered, "Jesus!"

Karen Lavoie Gorwacz looked like she had gone ten rounds with Marvin Hagler. Her left eye was the dark, shiny red of an unripe plum and swollen to a narrow slit. A deep gash on her cheek had been crudely stitched. Encrusted scabs of dried blood showed in her nostrils. Her bottom lip was split and puffy.

Sylvestro went to her bedside and touched her hand. "How are you feeling?" he said.

She stared from him to me with her one functional eye but did not answer.

"Karen," continued Sylvestro kindly, "are you ready to tell us who did this to you?"

She turned her head away from him.

Sylvestro gestured for me to come stand beside him. I did.

He touched her arm. "Karen, please," he said.

She rotated her head to look at us.

"Do you know this man?"

She stared at me, then gave a tiny nod. The corners of her mouth twitched with the pain of moving her head.

"Is he the one who hit you?"

She looked at me for a long time. I saw tears well up in her good eye. Slowly they spilled out and coursed down her cheek. Her swollen eye was crying too. She reached up to her face with her hand and touched her wet cheeks with her fingertips. Her hand, I noticed, trembled.

Then she shifted her gaze to Sylvestro. Slowly, imperceptibly, she shook her head. Her puffed and cracked lips whispered, "No."

He nodded. "Okay. Good. Now, tell us who. Please."

She turned her face away from him.

Sylvestro looked at me and shrugged. "She won't say. She's very frightened. We've tried to get her to tell us. She gets this wild, panicky look and then she cries."

I gripped his arm above the elbow. "We've got to talk," I said.

He peered at me for a moment, then nodded. "Okay. Come on."

I started to leave, then went over to the bed. I touched Karen's shoulder. She looked up at me for a moment, then closed her eyes. "Please," she said softly.

I squeezed her shoulder gently, then removed my hand. "You must tell these men who did this to you."

She shook her head without opening her eyes. I hesitated for a moment, then turned and walked out of the room. Sylvestro followed me.

I controlled myself until we were in the waiting room. Then I grabbed a handful of Sylvestro's brown topcoat. "That was a stupid, unprofessional trick," I hissed at him. "I don't believe—"

"Come on," he said. "Let's sit down."

"You sit down. I'm too mad."

Sylvestro sat and I paced. "You were trying to set me up," I muttered. "You thought I was the one who beat up that poor woman. You wanted to see how she'd react to seeing me. It was a cheap trick." I stopped and stared down at him. "Did it occur to you that if she had identified me, it would probably not be admissible in court? Huh? Did you think of that?"

Sylvestro smiled and waved his hand. "Come on, Mr. Coyne. Have a seat."

I took a deep breath, then sat beside him. Orvitz, two seats away, had been watching us with what looked like amusement.

"You're right," said Sylvestro. "If she said you were the one who beat her up, we'd be screwed. Hell, I'd be the main one who got screwed. But listen. If she had identified you, Mr. Coyne, I would have been as surprised as you, believe me."

"Well, then—"

He held up a hand. "Hear me out. I'll admit that for a while you were a suspect on the Churchill thing. Problem is, I couldn't for the life of me figure out why you'd kill him. That bothered me. It didn't particularly bother Finnigan, but it bothered me. I've been studying you over the past week, Mr. Coyne. I've done some research. You're a highly respected lawyer. Very ethical, from all I can learn. You've been in a number of tight situations, and you've handled yourself admirably. You killed a man once. That, too, was admirable, under those circumstances. I have concluded that you didn't kill Churchill." He paused. "I have also concluded that you know who did."

He stopped and stared at me, eyebrows arched.

I shrugged.

He nodded. "I know. You can't say anything. Look. You went and visited this woman last night. Why? I'd like to know. Nothing wrong with a divorced man visiting a divorced woman. Except she gets beat up. I mean, this Karen, she's connected to you, and you're connected to Churchill, so maybe she's connected to Churchill, too, see? So far, at least, we've come up blank. But, okay, I figure one way of seeing it is, it's the lady, this Karen"—he jerked his head backward in the direction of her hospital room—"who killed Churchill. This Churchill was quite a womanizer. Oldest story in the world, handsome young guy gets it on with a lonely, horny divorcee, then dumps her for something younger and sexier, so she goes to his pad to confront him, ends up pumping a couple thirty-two slugs into him. Oldest story in the world. Except, of course, that doesn't explain who beat the shit outta her."

I was shaking my head and smiling.

"Ahh," grumbled Sylvestro, "it's a fucked-up case. I can't get a handle on it. Last night around midnight I got a call from Detective Orvitz here. Said this woman had been brought by ambulance to the hospital. Her son came home and found her half conscious on the living room floor. The boy said a lawyer name of Coyne must have done it, that you were with her when he left. For good measure, Orvitz found your business card on her kitchen table. He knew about the Churchill case from the state cops. Recognized your name."

"I don't beat up women," I said.

He nodded. "No, I don't suppose you do. Still, you gotta admit you're a helluva suspect here."

I nodded.

"Let's suppose you didn't do it. She's okay when you leave. She's alone. The kid's off somewhere. I figure someone was waiting outside for you to leave, then went in. Someone she'd let in. Someone she knew, just like Churchill let his killer in. Same guy. Who knew both of them."

"Karen let me in," I said. "She didn't know me."

Sylvestro shrugged. "I figure this. I figure old Karen in there did have a thing going with Churchill. She's got a boyfriend somewhere, right? Jealous type. Found out about it. Whacked Churchill, then beat up Karen for good measure."

I arched my eyebrows. "Gorwacz? Her ex-husband?"

"Maybe," said Sylvestro. "That's most logical. We're working on that one." He cocked an eyebrow at me. "Fact is, Mr. Coyne, you were there last night. You could've done it. Hell, you could be the jealous lover."

"Come on."

"Why not?" Sylvestro smiled. "Finnigan liked it." He shrugged. "Ah, hell. I didn't really think it was you. Wouldn't've brought you here this way if I did. Anyway, Orvitz was all for rousting you last night. I persuaded him to let me handle it. So, yeah, it was a cheap, tawdry trick. I wouldn't have tried it if I thought you did it. What I wanted was, I wanted you to see what we're dealing with. Because I know damn well you're protecting somebody. And whoever it is you're protecting doesn't just shoot bullets into television news reporters. He also likes to beat the shit out of women. Because I'm convinced —and I'll bet you are, too—that whoever killed Churchill is also the one who did this to Mrs. Gorwacz. And the poor woman is too scared to tell us who it is."

I shook my head. "I'm sorry. I can't say anything."

"Did you see her face, Mr. Coyne?"

I nodded.

"Did you see the fear in her eyes?"

I sighed heavily. "Yes. I saw it."

Sylvestro gripped my sleeve. "Then how in the name of God can you refuse to let us bring in this animal?"

"I think you know."

"Client privilege, right?"

I nodded.

He leaned back and scowled at me. "What if he had killed her? He could have. He came damn close to it. She's got a minor concussion. They think it's minor. Two cracked ribs, three busted teeth. Stitches on her cheek, some more in her scalp. Supposing he'd killed that girl? Then what would you say about client privilege?"

"You think this is easy for me?"

He shrugged.

"It's not," I said. "Believe me, it's not easy." I looked at him for a long minute. "What would I say about protecting my client? I guess I'd say that, like most principles, this one is important enough to preserve even when it doesn't seem to work. It's the main ethic of my profession. Without it, nothing works. Sometimes cops arrest the wrong man. He goes to trial. He gets convicted. He goes to prison. Sometimes innocent men are even executed. That doesn't stop you guys from arresting somebody else. That's what you do. That's the ethic of your profession. Arrest people who you think are guilty and then pass them along the line to the next step in the process. The principles are okay. The system just breaks down sometimes."

"Sure. Law school stuff. Sounds nice in the classroom." He shook his head back and forth. "You know a murderer and a woman-beater. You could see justice done. It's your fucking obligation as a lawyer, as an officer of the court. And you refuse."

"Catching him is your job," I said. "That's the system."

"Yeah," he said after a minute, "that's the system, all right. That's why cops get blamed when crimes go unsolved. The goddam system. Lawyers."

"Lawyers have their place. So do cops. They're different places. You know that."

He shrugged. We sat in silence for a few minutes. Finally, he said, "Well, Mr. Coyne, for what it's worth, I'd respect you a whole helluva lot more if you'd tell us who this monster is."

"And I," I said, "I'd respect me a whole helluva lot less."

He shook his head slowly. "I just figured, once you saw her face . . ."

"You put it on the line, bringing me here, didn't you?" I put my hand on his shoulder. "You're really a softie, aren't you?"

He looked up at me and smiled sadly. "Ah, fuck it."

"I can't do it," I said quietly.

He sighed. "Well, then. We might as well get out of here."

The police cruiser was waiting outside the hospital. We drove back to my apartment without talking. The rush-hour traffic was heavy, and it took nearly an hour. Sylvestro stared out the side window the whole way, as if he thought his silence would punish me.

When we arrived in front of my apartment building I opened the door and got out. I leaned back in.

"I got a question," I said.

He shrugged. "Go ahead."

"You been following me?"

"Huh?"

"Tailing me. You know . . ."

He smiled. "Why the hell would I do that?"

"I just thought, if you suspected me of . . ."

"Shit," he said. "If we'd been tailing you, we probably would've seen who beat the crap out of Karen Lavoie last night, huh?"

I nodded. "Well, good luck," I said to Sylvestro. "I hope you catch him."

"Think, Mr. Coyne. Think about that girl's face."

"I'm not likely to forget it," I said.

· NINETEEN ·

AND INDEED I DIDN'T FORGET Karen Lavoie Gorwacz's bruised and broken face. It looked at me all morning. Those tormented wet eyes accused me of sins I hadn't committed. Every time I saw Julie, with her clear skin and fine cheekbones and big Irish green eyes, I imagined her the victim of a beating such as Karen had endured. I pictured Gloria with her eyes slitted and her nose twisted and bleeding. I thought of my friend Sylvie Szabo with her delicate Hungarian features smashed, her fine pointed chin crushed, her jaw shattered, her teeth broken.

Pops.

I remembered the time back in New Haven when he had beaten that bully's face into a bloody pulp, and his sudden rage. But that was different. That was self-righteous rage, the rage generated by a rigid concept of justice. I tried to imagine Pops in a similar manic tower of rage punching in the face of Karen Lavoie, and I failed. It simply didn't fit the man I knew, my old friend from law school, that genuinely virtuous, if flawed, man, the esteemed judge.

Then I remembered. Pops was in Florida.

So Pops couldn't have done it. And if Pops hadn't beaten up Karen Lavoie, he probably hadn't killed Churchill, either. Which meant that I didn't know a thing about either assault.

It brought the principle of client privilege back into focus. Protecting the confidentiality of clients *did* make sense. In this case, the simple good sense it made was that my client was guilty of nothing. Had I shared my suspicions with the police, I would have been guilty of a great deal.

Sylvestro said he didn't suspect me. And now I knew that Pops was innocent. I was left with curiosity. That and the picture of Karen's face.

At noon I called Zerk and told him what had happened.

"I tried to call you back. Tell you not to go. You shoulda told me where you were going."

"I didn't know."

"Well, you're an idiot for going. That's my first observation."

"You have another observation?"

"That Sylvestro is one stupid cop. That's my second observation." He paused and chuckled. "I suppose you and him balance each other out. You're an idiot and he's stupid. But, shit, if it actually was you who had done it, he'd've fucked up his whole investigation."

"Yeah, well he didn't really think I did it. He just wanted me to get a good look at her. He's actually quite a guy, that Sylvestro. I saw tears in his eyes when he talked about that woman's face. He wasn't being a cop then. He was just being a human being. He knew what he was doing, the risk. But he thought it would prick my conscience. He wanted me to violate privilege. But, of course, I couldn't do that."

"This is highly principled of you. Admirable, in fact."

"I know," I said. "It sounds sanctimonious as hell, doesn't it?" I hesitated, then chuckled. "Here's the thing, Zerk. Pops is in Florida. So he didn't beat up Karen Lavoie. I figure he didn't kill Churchill, either."

Zerk hesitated. "The one don't necessarily prove the other."

"Well, it seems to."

"Makes it a helluva lot easier to stick by your principles, though."

"Yes," I said. "Principles are great when they're not complicated by other principles."

Around four-thirty in the afternoon Julie buzzed me. "It's Judge Popowski."

"I got it," I told her. I pressed a button on the console and said, "Pops, you're back."

"Yep. Got in yesterday afternoon. Didn't get your message until this morning, though. Been busy as hell, trying to climb through all this stuff on my desk, or I would've called earlier. Jesus, you should see the docket . . ."

Yesterday afternoon! Karen Lavoie was beaten up last night. Pops could have—

"Brady? You there?"

"I'm here, Pops. Sorry. I was distracted."

"Well, I got this message you called. What's up?"

"We've got to talk, Pops."

"I told you, I don't really need my hand held. The nomination'll be approved if Teddy's got his votes in line. That's how it works."

"Not about that."

"Oh," he said. "You're still on that other thing. Nothing changed while I was gone, huh?"

"Yes, that other thing. It doesn't go away. Some things have changed."

"So tell me."

"I want you to buy me dinner tonight."

"Brady, for crissake, I can't just—"

"Listen," I said. "This is my call this time. I'm not going to let you put me off. We've got to talk."

I heard him sigh. "Yeah," he said. "I guess we've got to get it over with. Clear the air."

"Right. Clear the air."

"You know your job, Brady."

"I'm your lawyer. I know that."

"Okay. Look. I need a couple hours. Suppose you meet me around seven."

"Fine. Where?"

"I don't know. Why don't you come by the courthouse. Meet me down in the lobby. We'll figure out where to go."

"You're not planning to stiff me, Pops?"

He laughed. "Why would I do that?"

"Because you're paying."

I parked in the municipal garage around the corner from the courthouse. I locked up and walked over. The lobby was deserted except for the policeman who watched me go through the metal detector. My car keys set the thing off, so I had to go back, empty my pockets, and do it again. The cop seemed bored by the whole process. I guess I didn't look suspicious. I found that a little disappointing. I retrieved my keys, change, and Zippo, and found an uncomfortable wooden bench from which I could watch the bank of elevators.

After fifteen minutes I wanted a cigarette. The cop, for lack of anything better to do, was leaning against the wall watching me from under the pulled-down beak of his cap. NO SMOKING signs were everywhere. I stifled the urge.

At seven-twenty the elevator dinged softly and the door slid open. Pops stepped out and looked around. He spotted me and raised his hand. I stood up. He came over and we shook hands. "You want fancy or simple?" he said.

"Fancy."

He grinned. "That's what I figured. I made reservations. Got your car with you?"

"Yes."

"Good. You can drive."

He said good night to the cop and we went outside. It was cold, and we both turned up the collars of our topcoats. Pops wore no hat. His magnificent shock of silver hair glistened in the streetlights.

We strolled over to the parking garage without talking. I didn't want to confront him until we were seated across from each other. I wanted to be able to study his face.

The garage was an empty concrete cavern, dimly lit. Our footsteps echoed as we walked up the ramp to the second level, where I had left my car. Odd shadows angled from the great pillars that supported the structure. The floor was damp. Here and there melting snow dripped from the ceiling.

We found my car. Pops waited by the passenger door while I went around to the driver's side. I fumbled for my keys. Then something made me hesitate. It was a soft click, and what occurred next happened in a split second, but in my brain it took a long time.

There was that click, a recognized sound. The unlatching of a car door, my brain decided. Not the way a person would normally get out of a car. This sound was cautious and careful. Muffled. Secretive. This was a sound that did not want to be heard.

Someone had been sitting in a car, I figured. We had seen no one drive in, nor had we noticed anyone walk in ahead of us. So whoever was opening his car door had been sitting there, waiting.

Waiting for what?

For us, said my brain. For me or Pops. Or both of us.

But why?

I heard the scrape of a foot on the concrete floor.

"Pops!" I yelled. "Watch it!"

I dropped to my knees beside my car.

The sudden explosion of the gunshot crashed and reverberated through the garage. Then immediately there were two more. I heard the ping and whine of ricocheting slugs. Then came the rapidly diminishing sound of running feet. I jumped up to try to see. But I saw nothing.

Then I was aware of a dark and awful silence in that dank empty concrete building.

"Pops," I called softly. "Hey. You okay?"

There was a frightening moment when I heard nothing except the distant murmur of traffic from outside the garage. Then I heard Pops mutter, "Oh, shit."

"Are you all right?"

"I ripped the knee on my goddam pants. I whacked my elbow. Otherwise, yeah, I'm okay."

I went around to his side of my car. Pops was standing up brushing off his pants. I touched his shoulder. "You sure you're okay?"

He hunched his shoulders into his topcoat. "Yeah, I'm sure. I'm better than your car."

He pointed to a groove on the door panel beside him where one of the bullets had creased it.

"Close," I said.

"Too damn close. Let's get the hell out of here. I could use a drink."

I went around and got in and reached over to unlock his door. He slid in beside me. "In a minute this is going to hit me," he said. "Somebody tried to kill me. Some son of a bitch tried to shoot me, for crissake."

"Who'd want to kill you?"

He tried to grin. It looked sickly. "I suppose," he said slowly, "it could be lots of people. Guys get sent up, they like to blame somebody. A judge is as good as anybody." He shrugged. "They sit around in Walpole for five or six years, dreaming of how they're gonna get their revenge. It keeps them going. It's their dream. Their anger and hatred fuels it. It could be lots of people." He shivered. "It's hitting me," he said. "Whew!"

I lit a cigarette. "I'm having an insight," I said.

He nodded. "Something to do with how precious life is. And how transitory. Right?"

"Not exactly," I said. "You didn't kill Wayne Churchill after all, did you?"

"Me?" He laughed quickly. "Hell, no. You got it mixed up. Somebody just tried to kill me. I didn't kill anybody." He turned on the seat to look at me. "Is that what you've been thinking? You thought I killed that Churchill?"

"Yeah, actually. That's what I've been thinking, Pops."

He shook his head slowly, smiling.

"And you didn't beat up Karen Lavoie either, then, did you?"

"Karen?" He frowned at me.

"Somebody did," I said. "I figure the same guy wanted to kill you, too."

"Why?" he said softly. "I don't get it."

"Me neither," I said. "But you're going to tell me all about Karen Lavoie, including all the stuff you left out the first time, and then maybe between us we'll figure it out."

He stared at me for a minute, then nodded. "Okay," he said. "I'll tell you all about it. But let's get a drink first, okay?"

"Hell, no," I said. "The first thing we do is call the cops. There's a crazy person running around out there trying to shoot people."

He put his hand on my arm. "No," he said softly.

"No?"

"No cops."

"Are you nuts?"

"Think about it, Brady."

"You're worried about the publicity. Your appointment and all."

He sighed. "Damn right I am. And me being here with you, and your being a suspect in the Churchill thing. If the papers ever latched onto this story . . ."

"No harm, no foul, huh?"

"Something like that."

"What about my car?"

"Hell, I'll pay for the repair, if that's what's bothering you."

"It's ruined, Pops."

He laughed. "You want me to buy you a new one?"

"I accept."

I started up the car, paid the parking fee, and pulled out of the garage.

"Where to?" I said to Pops.

"Locke-Ober's. I made a reservation. You said you wanted fancy. And gimme one of those things, will you?"

"What?"

"A cigarette."

"You don't smoke," I said.

"I once did," he said, as I handed him my pack of Winstons. "In Nam I smoked. Two packs of Camels a day. I loved to smoke. I figured I was going to die anyway, it would be really dumb to deprive myself of something that might be bad for my health."

He used the cigarette lighter on the dashboard, dragged, and exhaled with a great sigh of satisfaction. "I quit when I got on the plane that flew me out. Literally. I had a cigarette going when I walked up the ramp. Flicked it away as I stepped in. It was the last time I smoked. Before now. I still dream about cigarettes sometimes. I guess there's something about being reminded of one's mortality. I swear, if one of those slugs had hit me just now, my dying thought would've been regret that I had quit smoking only to have an assassin kill me."

I headed across the river in the thin traffic. Pops really did seem shaken by the experience. He almost had me convinced that he hadn't murdered Wayne Churchill or beaten up Karen Lavoie.

I turned my poor battered little car over to the attendant outside Locke-Ober's, and we walked up the little alley to the restaurant.

The maître d' greeted Pops effusively, calling him "Your Honor." When Pops introduced me to him, he bowed and murmured, "A pleasure, sir," with the faint hint of an eastern Mediterranean accent. Charming as hell.

Our table was waiting upstairs. One waiter left menus and a wine list, a second poured water into the crystal on the table, a third took our drink orders, and a fourth left a basket of steaming breads and rolls for us. In a moment, the third returned with our drinks—Jack Daniel's on the rocks for me, Dewar's and soda for Pops.

I lit a cigarette and held the pack to him. He shook his head. "One was great. If I have another I won't like myself."

"You are a paragon of self-control, Pops."

"Yes," he said, nodding and smiling. "Self-control is one of my main virtues. Want to know about the others?"

"I want to know about Karen Lavoie," I said.

He nodded. "Right. I know. I should've told you before."

"Of course you should. Why didn't you?"

He shrugged. "Embarrassment, I guess. Plus the fact that it was all so long ago and so irrelevant that I never thought anything would come of it. Even when I got that little note in the mail, and that phone call. It's not like I actually did anything so terribly wrong, Brady. Certainly nothing that would disqualify me from a federal seat. But, yeah, I guess that was it. Embarrassment. Plus, well, maybe I didn't completely trust you."

"Are you serious?"

He tilted up his glass and looked at me over the rim. "It wasn't really you I didn't trust. Hell, you're about the most discreet man I know," he said slowly. "Still, things have ways of slipping out. Maybe you'd inadvertently say something to Julie, or leave something in writing for the wrong eyes, or if there were police—"

"Julie's at least as discreet as me," I said. I leaned over the table toward Pops. "I suppose it doesn't matter why you didn't tell me before. But now I've got to know."

"Maybe I will have another cigarette. Just one more."

I slid the pack across the table to him and then passed him my Zippo. He lit up and looked at me through the smoke. "It was a long time ago," he said. "I'd been a Middlesex County assistant D.A. at East Cambridge for a couple years. The D.A. liked me. I was older than most of the other A.D.A.s, and he gave me good cases. I got into homicides very quickly. High visibility stuff. The papers liked me, too. Lots of convictions. I was a Vietnam vet, Yale Law School, turned down all the big Wall Street firms to prosecute bad guys in Beantown for about the same money a junior high school math teacher makes. I was good copy. The governor had already promised me a District Court seat, first one that came open. I wanted it bad."

He stared at me for a moment. "I remember all that, Pops," I said. "Don't forget, I was already your lawyer then. We were law school chums."

"Just setting the scene," he said. "Marilee and I had been married for five years. Phyllis had just been born. I'm trying to be objective here. I was a dashing fellow. I got lots of attention. Invited to lots of social functions. Marilee couldn't always go with me. There were always ladies eager to be seen with me. But I behaved myself."

"A paragon," I said.

He shrugged and smiled. "Yeah, well, not exactly. There was this young secretary . . ."

"Karen."

"Yes. Karen."

Our waiter appeared. "Another round of drinks," said Pops. "We're not ready to order." He turned to me and paused until the waiter moved away. "Karen," he said. "She was attractive. Very young, very naive. A pretty girl. Oh, she wasn't spectacular. Not even the prettiest girl to give me the eye, it wasn't that. But there was a—a vulnerability about her, an innocence, and—hope you don't consider this boasting, Brady, I'm just trying to reconstruct it for you—she clearly worshiped me. She had these dark, serious eyes. They were always focused on me, it seemed. Somehow, from this girl, it was wonderfully flattering. I couldn't help being aware of her, the way she watched me."

"So you—"

"So I ignored her. For a very long time. Until one night. I was working late. I often worked late. Not many of the others did. Or if they did, they took it home with them. It was very stressful work. Way too much to handle, really. None of us ever felt fully prepared. But most of the A.D.A.s survived by getting the hell out of the courthouse as soon as they could. They did a lot of drinking after work. They lugged briefcases with them. I never did that. I always made a point to leave my work in the office. I was considered a drudge by my colleagues. They figured I was angling for something more, out to make a name for myself. True, of course. But that's not why I hung around. I just didn't want to bring my work home. I felt I owed Marilee and the baby my attention when I was there. Anyway, on this particular night I was at my desk as usual. It was seven-thirty or eight o'clock. I was in my shirt sleeves, my shoes off, my feet up on my desk. I was reading law. Old cases. Looking for precedents. And Karen came in. She had a cup of tea for me. I was beat. I'd had no supper. She put the tea on my desk and sat across from me while I sipped it, just looking at me and smiling. We didn't say much. After a few minutes she got up from her seat and came around behind me and began to massage my neck and shoulders. I should have told her not to. But it felt good. I was tired and hungry and my back and neck ached. She had strong hands. So I closed my eyes and went with it. She was standing close behind me and I could smell her scent. Musky, it was. Somehow, very sexual. Sometimes I smell that scent even nowadays, and it brings Karen back to me. She worked her hands on my neck and around to my face. She sort of urged my head back against her stomach. I could feel her warmth, the softness of her. It was very intimate. Her fingers worked on my jaw and cheeks and temples and eyes and my scalp and I'll be damned if I didn't get aroused."

I shook my head slowly. "So you—"

"So I nothing. After a while she stopped, smiled at me, and left. I'll bet neither of us said a half-dozen words the whole time. Just 'Hi' when she came in and 'thank you' when she gave me the tea. 'Long day,' and 'you look tired.' Stuff like that. Anyhow, I thought about her constantly after that. Made a point to hang around late the next night. Hoping she'd return. But she didn't. Nor the night after that. But the third night she did. She came into my office, closed the door behind her, locked it, and turned to look at me. She smoothed her skirt on her hips, staring at me, her mouth open a little, licking her lips with her little pink tongue, like it was something she'd seen in a movie, practiced in front of a mirror. Damnedest, sexiest gesture I've ever seen. She came over to me, and pushed my chair back from my desk. She stood in front of me, close, so I could smell that scent. She reached down and undid my necktie, then she began to unbutton my shirt. I wanted to grab her hands, tell her to stop. But I couldn't make myself. Brady, Jesus, it was like I was bewitched. I swear to God, this girl seemed so shy and innocent and unspoiled, and there she was, kneeling in front of me, undressing me, doing these things to me. I couldn't resist her."

"If you're asking me to condemn you, Pops, forget it."

"I don't need your condemnation, Brady. I'm perfectly capable of condemning myself. Which I proceeded to do. I avoided her for a week. Started leaving the office at four-thirty or five like everyone else. Figured, okay, I'd bring my work home. But I couldn't get Karen out of my mind. So—well, you can figure out the rest."

I nodded.

"I gave in to it. It made my work and my family and my impending appointment seem insignificant. I lived for those evenings in my office. We never went anywhere, never did anything except—you know. We never even talked much. I knew very little about her. Just that she lived at home with her parents, I knew that. She had a boyfriend who wanted to marry her. I sensed that she'd had a rigid upbringing. That she was very inhibited. Except with me. She asked nothing of me. Making love, she did it all, really. I rationalized that I'd been seduced, it wasn't my fault. That whatever happened with Karen didn't diminish my love for Marilee and the little one. Karen was separate, unconnected to any other part of my life. She didn't make me a worse prosecutor or husband or father. Nobody was hurt. It was just a nice, sweet thing, with its own separate little niche in my life." He smiled sourly at me. "The same old story, huh?"

"It's kind of a cliché, Pops, yes."

"A cliché. Well, yeah, it was. Of course. But it didn't seem like it at the time. It seemed unique. I felt I was special. Blessed by this marvelous girl. Listen, I was a lucky guy. I survived Nam. Zipped though Yale Law. Married the woman I wanted to marry, had a healthy baby, was taking the career ladder three rungs at a time. I just figured this was part of being a special man. I deserved it, somehow. I was young and strong and invulnerable. Then Karen told me she was pregnant. And that didn't fit in with any of the rest of it. That wasn't supposed to happen. Somebody screwed up the fairy tale."

Pops paused and looked around the room. Almost instantly our waiter appeared. "Gentlemen?" he said.

Pops ordered a lamb chop. I had the swordfish. We both asked for the Bibb lettuce with the dill dressing.

After the waiter left, Pops said, "She was different, then, the night she told me she was pregnant. She was hard. I sensed it instantly. She felt I owed her. She wanted me to marry her. I refused. Point-blank. I told her to forget it. I'd never leave Marilee. I told her I didn't even believe her. And if she was pregnant, how was I to know it was mine? She had a boyfriend. It could've been his. I expected her to cry and carry on, or threaten. But she didn't. She just walked out. That unnerved me. It didn't fit."

"I know what happened next," I said.

Pops nodded. "I stayed late the next night. I figured she'd be back. And she was. Told me she'd filed an application for complaint with the Clerk Magistrate. I felt like someone had slugged me in the solar plexus, Brady. It literally knocked the wind out of me. She was going to charge me with rape. Whether she could've made it stick or not was irrelevant. I was ruined. I asked her what she wanted me to do. She said marry her. I pleaded with her. She said, no, she'd thought it over. She'd even told her parents. And I had to marry her. I told her it wouldn't work, we could never have a marriage on that basis. And she got a sly look, and I realized that she had another agenda.

Finally it came out. She had a price. This sweet, seductive little nineteen-year-old girl had a price."

"Ten grand," I said.

He nodded. "Yes. Wayne Churchill's price. Ten thousand dollars. Firm. It was as if she was selling a car. That was her price. Hell, back then ten grand was more than half a year's salary. It was a lot of money. But I agreed. I came up with it. I had some back pay from the army, I borrowed against the equity in the house, I sneaked some out of our joint account, I sold off some stocks, and I came up with ten thousand dollars. And I felt like I was getting a bargain."

Our salads arrived. We began to munch them. "Her part of the deal was to withdraw the complaint, quit her job, and never contact me again. Which she did. She was gone two weeks later. I checked upstairs and the complaint was filed away. Buried, as far as I could tell, forever. I heard later that Karen had gotten married within a month. It was assumed that's why she quit. And until a week ago, that's the last I heard of Karen Lavoie. Until I got that note in the mail."

"So why the hell didn't you tell me all this right then?"

"Embarrassment, plain and simple. I didn't want you to think badly of me." He shrugged. "I should have told you. I know. And I suppose I shouldn't have been so cocky. Karen could have told someone. But there was no proof. I would have denied it all. The word of an eminent judge against hers? I really wasn't worried."

"Wayne Churchill came up with that old complaint," I said.

Pops cocked his head at me. Then he nodded slowly. "I thought of that. Couldn't figure out how. They're supposed to destroy those old records. He must've been a hell of an investigator. Did he get Karen to talk?"

"No, I don't think so. He had a girlfriend in the Clerk Magistrate's office. Another one of the secretaries there—a woman named Helen, I met her—has been there since before Karen left. The office gossip, I gather. She might've mentioned something about you and Karen to Churchill's girl-friend."

"Nobody knew about us, Brady."

"Don't kid yourself, Pops. I bet everybody knew. You can't keep that sort of thing a secret in an office. Anyhow, and I'm just guessing here, I figure Helen told Suzie Billings, and she mentioned it to Churchill. How he learned about that complaint I don't know. Helen again, maybe. But it wasn't destroyed, and Suzie dug it out for him, made a copy. Churchill also talked to Karen's father. I don't know what he got out of him. He also tried to talk to Karen. She told me she refused to see him."

Pops shook his head slowly. "That Churchill, you've got to give him credit."

I nodded. "He was a good investigator, for sure. Anyway, I think Wayne Churchill had the story pretty well pieced together. He wanted confirmation from you. He probably had enough without it, but he'd been burned on stories before. So he felt he needed something out of you. Not direct confirmation necessarily. I doubt if he expected a tearful confession out of you. He probably was just looking for some behavior that would assure him he had the story right. That's why he mentioned that figure to me. Ten grand. He wasn't actually blackmailing you. He just wanted you to know that he knew what had happened."

Pops grinned. "It would've been a helluva story, wouldn't it?"

"Yes. Except Churchill got killed before he could write it."

"I didn't do it, Brady. Believe me, that never occurred to me. I don't think that way. Oh, I was prepared to lie. I even lied to you. I would have brazened it out if I had to. I don't know what it would've done to my appointment. Probably ruined it. Not so much what I did. But the publicity. That complaint. I would've had to ask Teddy to withdraw my name. But I never would've admitted it. For Marilee's sake, I couldn't. And when I heard that Churchill was killed, I figured there was a God after all, that the golden boy here still had a little more luck going for him."

"Even when you knew that I was a suspect."

"God help me, Brady, I'm sorry. I just knew that you didn't do it, and I figured you'd work your way out of it."

I wiped my mouth with my napkin and sat back in my chair. "You want to know what I know?"

He nodded cautiously. "Yes."

"Karen Lavoie married a guy named Peter Roland Gorwacz. They had a son. He's sixteen or seventeen now." I arched my eyebrows and smiled at him.

Pops stared at me. "You think—?"

"Yeah, I think. I think the kid was yours. The timing fits."

"Oh, man," said Pops, shaking his head. "I figured she'd get an abortion, if she really was pregnant. I just assumed that's what she did. It never occurred to me . . ."

"I've met her parents," I said. "I would judge them to be simple folks, good Catholics, who raised their daughter that way. *Roe v. Wade* was brand-new law back then. These people would never tolerate abortion, Supreme Court or not. Nor would Karen. I figure she married her high school sweetie quickly by telling him she was pregnant with his kid. So your secret was her secret, too. She had as much reason to keep it quiet as you did."

"So it had to've been that secretary who told Churchill."

"I don't know. Maybe it was Karen. She's divorced now. Maybe her husband found out. Maybe she told him. Maybe she doesn't care who knows about the paternity of her boy anymore. The husband could've told Churchill. Hell, Paul, the son, he could've, too. I just don't know."

"My kid," whispered Pops. "Jesus!"

"I don't know this. It's a guess."

He stared at me for a long moment. "Then," he said slowly, "who do you guess killed Churchill?"

I shrugged. "My best guess is still you, my friend."

He smiled at me, shaking his head. "You are a tough son of a bitch, Coyne, know that?"

I shrugged. "You could have set up that little demonstration back there in the parking garage. Make me think, hey, if someone's trying to shoot Pops, it must be the same guy who shot Churchill. Right?"

He rolled his eyes. "Look," he said. "I didn't do it, okay? Listen. I know the law. You know I do. Suppose I told you I did it. Gave you all the gory details. What could you do?"

I spread my hands. "I'd be in a helluva tough spot, Pops. What could I do? In the final analysis, absolutely nothing. I'm your lawyer. I got no choice."

"Exactly. I know you. You wouldn't peep a word. You know the ethic. And you're an ethical man. Besides which, nothing I told you would be admissible. Knowing this, both of us, if I had killed Wayne Churchill, it would be in my best interest to tell you everything. Ironic but true. Lay it all out for you. Every detail. The more I told you the safer I'd be. So I'd have nothing to gain, and everything to lose, by not telling you. Agreed?"

I nodded. "Agreed." I hesitated. "Except for one thing."

He frowned. "What?"

"I know you, Pops. You're a decent human being. Even if you killed a man, you're still a decent person. You care what people think of you. You'd be embarrassed to tell me you killed Wayne Churchill, just as you were too embarrassed to tell me about Karen. It's human nature to lie. To friends, to wives, to lawyers. For all I know, that's what's happening right now."

He stared at me for a minute. Finally he said, "Christ, Brady. I'm not like that. I'm not the kind of guy who goes around killing people."

I shrugged. "You're not the kind of guy who diddles with ninteteen-year-old secretaries, either."

· TWENTY ·

WEDNESDAY. Nine days since Wayne Churchill had been murdered. I spent the morning in a conference room at the Suffolk County courthouse negotiating, and then persuading the wealthy Anne Covington to accept, a fat settlement from the dentist who had, in the process of performing a root canal, permanently severed one of her facial nerves. As a result, Mrs. Covington's new smile looked like a death rictus.

Anne Covington rarely smiled, anyway. And before her surgery her smile had frightened small children and household pets. The new version could almost have been considered an improvement, something my adversary Carl Dalton, the dentist's attorney, had the good sense to imply without stating. There was no telling how significant a judge might find that information, as we both knew. A trial would have been a crapshoot. We both considered the out-of-court settlement a victory, which Carl and I celebrated at Marie's in Kenmore Square over linguini with clam sauce and a bottle of something musty and red.

I did Julie's bidding for the rest of the afternoon. I left the office a little after six, strode across the square and bought a bedraggled bunch of carnations from the Puerto Rican lady on the corner, and took them back to my car. By the time I got to Mt. Auburn Hospital it was nearly seven.

All the seats in the waiting room were taken. One of them was occupied by Detective Orvitz of the Cambridge police, who nodded to me when I walked in as if he had been expecting me. I jerked my head in the direction of Karen Lavoie Gorwacz's private room and raised my eyebrows. He got up and came to me.

"The family's in there with her," he said.

"Her parents?"

"Yes. And her son."

"I better wait."

He nodded. "This is a social visit?" he said, cocking his head inquiringly.

"You suspect the criminal has returned to the scene of his crime?"

"You never know, Mr. Coyne."

I shrugged. Orvitz returned to his seat. I picked up a copy of *Today's Health* from a table and scanned an article on colon cancer while leaning against the wall. Uplifting stuff.

After about twenty minutes they came out. Mr. and Mrs. Lavoie looked grim. Paul, Karen's son, looked angry. When he saw me he stopped for an instant, whispered something to his grandmother, then came to me.

"Hi, Paul," I said, holding out my hand to him.

He hesitated for an instant, and then took a hard backhanded swipe at my hand.

"Hey!" I said.

"You son of a bitch," he said. "You dirty prick."

He grabbed the front of my coat with his left hand and drew back his right fist. I tried to twist away from him. Detective Orvitz was suddenly there, hugging both of Paul's arms against his sides.

"Easy, there, pal," said the cop.

"He's the guy," said Paul. "He's the one that beat up my mother."

"Your mother says no."

"She's afraid," said the boy. "She's afraid he'll do it again."

Orvitz moved in front of Paul, so that he was standing between us. "Now, don't try something that'll get you in trouble, son."

Paul glowered at me over Orvitz's shoulder. "I'm gonna get that bastard," he said.

"No you're not," said Orvitz softly.

Like a hockey player rescued by a referee from a fight before his manhood was actually tested, Paul gave me one final look that was intended to frighten me and then went back to his grandparents, who had been watching the scene with matching frowns on their faces.

"You okay?" said Orvitz to me.

"Fine," I said. "Thanks."

"I expect you could've handled the kid. But we don't want a scene."

"No, we don't. Think it's okay if I go in and see her now?"

"You brought her flowers. You ought to deliver them." He paused. "I'll be right here," he added, which, translated, meant "Don't start beating on her again."

As I walked past Mr. and Mrs. Lavoie, I said hello to them. They nodded to me and said nothing.

Karen's bed had been cranked up so that she could sit. Her hair had been brushed and she was wearing a pale blue robe over a lace-trimmed nightgown. The bruises on her face had darkened and spread so that the entire left side of it was a uniform purple. The swelling had increased. She looked considerably worse than the previous morning when I had first seen her.

I held out the carnations. "Hi, Karen," I said.

Her swollen lips tried to smile. It came out one-sided. "Hi," she croaked. "Pretty," she added, referring to the carnations. "You can stick 'em in that vase."

A large cut-glass vase perched on the windowsill beside her bed. It contained a spectacular bunch of pink roses. I went over and jammed the carnations in with the roses, then returned to Karen's bedside. A pair of straight-backed chairs had been drawn alongside. I sat in one of them.

"How are you feeling?"

"Oh, boy," she said. Pain pinched her face, and her voice was hoarse. "Like an elephant stepped on me."

"Your family. How are they taking it?"

"Scared. They're frightened. They think someone wants to kill me." Her smile worked only on one side of her face. It looked cynical.

"Hard to blame them."

She looked at me through her one good eye, then shrugged.

"Have you told the police yet who did it?"

She turned her head away from me.

"Karen," I said, touching her arm. "Was it Pops? Did the judge do this?"

Slowly her head rotated back. She stared at me for a long moment. Then the tears came. "Please go away," she said.

"I know all about the two of you," I persisted. "Pops told me. I know about Paul. I know that Wayne Churchill found out. Whoever did this to you is probably the same one who killed Churchill, you know. You've got to let the police do their job."

She was shaking her head back and forth. "I told them you didn't do it, Mr. Coyne. So please. Just mind your own business."

"Karen—"

"Go away. Leave me alone."

I looked at her for a moment, then shrugged. I stood up. She was looking toward the vase of flowers, away from me. "Well, good-bye, then," I said. "I hope you feel better."

I started for the door.

"Mr. Coyne," she whispered.

I turned.

"Thank you for the flowers."

I smiled and nodded. Then I left.

The crowd in the waiting room had thinned out. Orvitz was still in his seat. Mrs. Lavoie was sitting beside him, staring blankly at a magazine that was spread open on her lap. Her husband and Paul were not there.

She looked up at me with her eyebrows upraised. I nodded to her. She got up and went into Karen's room.

I went into the corridor to the elevator and pushed the button. The elevator was on the third floor. It was moving down. It would have to complete its trip down before it came back up. It would be a while. I leaned my back against the wall to wait.

A minute or two later, Mrs. Lavoie approached me. Her head was bowed. She held a handkerchief in her hand. She stood beside me and looked up at the lights.

"I already poked the button," I said.

She turned to look at me. Her eyes were red and her cheeks glistened with tears. She had not been crying when I had seen her in the waiting room.

"Are you all right?"

She nodded and looked away.

"I hope you know," I persisted, "I didn't do this to Karen."

The handkerchief went to her eyes. "Oh, I know that," she said with a sort of short choking laugh.

"It must be very difficult for you and Paul and your husband," I plowed on, feeling awkward but abhorring a conversational vacuum.

She glanced at me, then looked up at the elevator lights.

"I don't understand why Karen won't tell the police who did this to her," I said.

"I'm sure you don't, Mr. Coyne," she said, still studying the lights.

The lights indicated that the elevator had begun to ascend. We watched them blink their way up to our floor. The elevator stopped with a muffled clunk and the doors slid open. Mrs. Lavoie and I stepped aside to allow two doctors to get off. Then she and I got in. I jabbed the button for the lobby.

"Where's your husband?" I said to Mrs. Lavoie as we rode down.

"He took Paul home. The policeman suggested it'd be better if he didn't stay there after . . ."

"He's upset. It's understandable."

"We didn't want a scene anyway. John drove Paul back to our house. He's staying with us while Karen's—until she can go home." She looked up at me and tried to smile. "It was nice of you to come visit her."

I shrugged.

"We—my husband and I—I hope you don't think we've been rude to you."

"No. I understand. Your privacy is important. It's just—"

"I know. I appreciate your point of view. I hope you can appreciate ours."

I nodded. "Sure."

We came to a stop and the doors slid open. We walked out into the lobby. Mrs. Lavoie touched my arm. "Mr. Coyne, you don't happen to know where there's a pay phone?"

I shook my head. "You can ask over at the desk. Look, do you need a ride?"

"I can call a taxi."

"I'd be happy to give you a ride."

"Thank you anyway. I can get a cab."

"Really," I said. "It'd be no problem."

She cocked her head to the side, hesitated, then nodded. "If it wouldn't be out of your way."

"Not at all," I said.

We walked out of the hospital and headed for the parking lot. "This is very nice of you," she said.

"I'm a nice guy," I smiled.

"Yes," she said. "Yes, I think you probably are."

We found my car. I unlocked the passenger door and opened it for her. After she got in, I went around and got behind the wheel. I pulled onto Mt. Auburn Street and turned right, heading for the Square. Mrs. Lavoie sat rigidly erect beside me, gazing fixedly straight ahead.

"Mrs. Lavoie," I said after a minute, "I want you to know that I know about Karen."

She continued to stare out the windshield. "It's really not any of your business," she said softly.

"Well, perhaps. Except a man was killed, and I thought—I think—it's related to what happened to Karen. Karen and Judge Popowski."

I watched her as I said this. She didn't flinch.

"You know about her and the judge, don't you?" I persisted.

"We know," she whispered.

"I felt I had to find out," I went on gently. "And I believe that this is related to what happened to Karen the other night."

I glanced at her when she didn't reply. She was nodding.

"Do you believe that also?"

The handkerchief materialized in her hand. She dabbed at her eyes with it.

"I'm sorry," I said. "I know you're upset."

We drove in silence for a while. I negotiated the complexity of traffic lights, loops, and one-way streets in Harvard Square and headed west on Mass. Ave.

"Mrs. Lavoie," I said, "did Karen tell you who beat her?"

She said nothing. From the corner of my eye I saw the handkerchief flutter at her face.

"Was it the judge? Was it Chester Popowski?"

"No." Her voice was a whisper, but at the same time emphatic.

"Then—?"

"Mr. Coyne," she said quietly, "please."

I shrugged.

There are at least a dozen stoplights on Massachusetts Avenue between Harvard Square and Route 16. Every one of them was red when I got to it. I cracked my window and lit a cigarette. Mrs. Lavoie continued to stare straight ahead. Her fingers alternately stroked and strangled the handkerchief she was holding in her lap.

I turned onto Route 16 heading for Medford. "I don't know what to do," she said.

"There's a vicious criminal out there."

"I know that."

"He's killed a man. He almost killed your daughter."

"You don't think I know that, too?"

"Then why—"

"Do you think it's been easy all these years? Trying to keep a family together, seeing my little girl . . ."

Her voice trailed away. The handkerchief dabbed at her eyes again.

"Wouldn't it be better to get it off your chest?" I said carefully. "Wouldn't you feel better?"

"It's not that simple, Mr. Coyne. I wish it was, but it isn't."

"But for Karen's sake . . ."

"It's not that simple," she repeated. "I told you. You just couldn't understand."

"You know, don't you? Karen told you just now, when you went in to say good-bye to her after I was in there, didn't she?"

"She told me." Her tone had changed. Her voice was flat, devoid of affect.

"You must tell me," I said.

"I already knew," she whispered. "I didn't want to know, but I knew."

"My God," I said.

Because then I knew too.

· TWENTY-ONE ·

I N THE MIDDLE OF THE MORNING on Friday, Julie cracked open my office door and stuck her head in. "That policeman is here."

"Just one?"

"Yes. Lieutenant Sylvestro."

"Send him in, please."

Her head disappeared for a moment. Then she pushed the door open all the way. She held it while Sylvestro shambled in. I stood up and went around my desk. We shook hands in the middle of the room.

"You made an appointment this time," I said.

He smiled. "This one's a little different from the others."

I returned his smile and gestured toward the sofa. "Have a seat," I said to him. "You look beat."

"Tough couple days," he said with a sigh.

"Coffee?"

"Yeah. Good."

"I'll get it," said Julie from the doorway.

Sylvestro sat on the sofa. I took the chair across from him. He looked at me out of his hound dog eyes. "Wanted to thank you," he said.

I shrugged.

"Also to apologize."

"Not necessary."

"It wasn't just Finnigan, you know. It was me, too. We both thought we had a live one. That's just the way we played it."

"Good cop, bad cop," I said. "It's okay. I know how it works."

"Not that business of luring you to the hospital. That was just me. Finnigan was against it."

I smiled. "It turned out to be a good trick."

"Anyhow . . ." He waved his hand in the air.

"All's well that ends well, huh?"

"If you call this ending well. We solved the crimes. That doesn't always mean a happy ending."

Julie came in with our coffee. She placed the two mugs on the table between Sylvestro and me. He looked up at her and smiled mournfully, which was the only way he knew how. "Thanks," he said to her.

"Anything else?" she said.

"This is great, thanks," I said.

After she left, latching the door behind her, Sylvestro said, "How did you figure it out?"

"Mrs. Lavoie told me."

"Come on. She'd never do that."

"Oh, not in so many words. She couldn't have done that. But she made it pretty clear. I think she wanted me to know. Did you get evidence?"

"He confessed everything. Gave us the weapon. He seemed greatly relieved."

"What about Karen?"

"She won't have to testify, I don't think. I doubt it goes to trial."

"He was the one who shot at the judge in the parking garage, too?"

Sylvestro sipped his coffee and nodded. "He was on a mission. Had been all his life, I guess. When you called me the other night, after you drove Mrs. Lavoie home, I knew you were right. It all fit. You gotta feel for her."

I smiled. "Poor woman. Here I was, feeling sorry for myself, with my own hypothetical version of a moral dilemma, and she'd been living with a real one for all of her married life. How can you be both a good mother and a loyal wife in that circumstance?" I shook my head.

"You go to church, you practice denial, and you suffer horribly," said Sylvestro. "All that Catholic guilt shit. One way or another, none of us escapes it."

"He'd been beating Karen all her life, huh?"

"Both of them. His daughter and his wife." Sylvestro stuck his forefinger under his collar at the back of his neck and carved it around to his throat. "You should've heard him. He felt no guilt whatsoever. The poor benighted bastard's absolutely convinced he's God's messenger on earth. No guilt for him. He still thinks he's the perfect father and husband."

"He must've been out of his tree when Karen told him she was knocked up by the judge."

"He beat the crap out of her then, of course. Then he made her strike the deal with the judge. The main thing for him was to keep it quiet. Of course, she had to have the baby. Fortunately, or at least that's how he saw it, this Gorwacz was waiting in the wings. He married her. And everything was fine, until Karen finally told her husband where Paul really came from. Gorwacz left her. Poor bastard couldn't handle that. And Karen told Paul, too, though evidently the boy took it all right. Nothing would've happened, probably, if Wayne Churchill hadn't latched onto the story and tracked down the Lavoies."

"He had to protect the family's secret."

Sylvestro nodded. "At whatever cost. So he followed Churchill to Skeeter's that night. And when he came out, he followed him home. Went to the door. Churchill let him in, naturally. Figured he was gonna get his story. But John killed him. Figured that was it. End of the story."

"Until I showed up," I said.

"Yeah. Then he figured he had to eliminate you, too. Protecting his daughter, his family's good name and all."

"He drives a blue sedan, doesn't he?"

"Yes. He admitted he was following you around, waiting for the right time to get you. He's crazy, of course. But cautious. He saw you go to Karen's that night. When you left he went in and beat her up, like he'd done so many times before. After all, she had disobeyed him, letting you in. When he told us this, he looked at us with these innocent eyes, as if anybody would've done the same thing. Anyway, he kept following you. When you parked in the garage over there by the courthouse, he figured it was a good opportunity. But when you came out with the judge, he decided the judge was the target of choice. After all, he was the one who had caused everything."

"So he shot at Pops."

"And, fortunately, missed."

I drained my mug. "So what's going to happen to John Lavoie?"

Sylvestro made an inverted smile. "The D.A. wants to go for second-degree murder. Lavoie's got a public defender. They entered a plea of not guilty. They're holding him in lieu of bond. I figure he'll go for insanity, they'll bargain it down to manslaughter or something." He shrugged.

"He'll never survive prison."

"I don't know," said Sylvestro. "This is the kind of guy who survives it pretty well."

The following Tuesday I met Pops at the College Club on Commonwealth Avenue, one of the several private clubs of which he was a member. I descended the few steps, hung my coat, and entered the dining room. It was early. Pops was seated in the corner. All the other tables were empty. I joined him. He was sipping from a glass.

"What're you drinking?" I said.

He grimaced. "Poland Spring. I gotta be back on the bench at two."

A waitress came over. I ordered a Bloody Mary. Figured I'd get some vitamins.

Pops leaned across the table to me. "I talked to Teddy yesterday."

"Oh?"

He nodded. "Asked him to withdraw my name."

"I don't—"

Pops waved his hand at me. "I'm not asking for your advice, now, Counselor. I've thought it through. It's not just the publicity. That'll probably happen anyway. All of this'll get out, one way or the other. Channel Eight's still poking and probing at the whole Churchill thing. And it's not that the Senate's likely to vote me down. Push comes to shove, they'd probably approve me. That's what Teddy told me. He said he had the votes."

"Then . . . ?"

"Several things. All this, Karen and all, it puts the Senator on the spot. He didn't say so. Didn't have to. I'm supposed to know that. It's how it works. You want to play the game, you play by the rules." He paused to sip from his glass of spring water. He cleared his throat. "Then, of course, there's Marilee and the girls."

"You haven't told them?"

He smiled. "Of course I told them. Everything that's happened, it's made me realize I've been waiting to tell them all the time. See, it isn't just that I'd rather they heard it from me, the way it really was, without distortion, than read about it in the tabloids. It's the—the damn guilt, the pretense. The honorable judge. Shit. Talking to you at Locke-Ober's, it felt damn good, Brady. A catharsis. After I talked to you that night, I knew I had to tell Marilee."

"How'd she take it?"

He shook his head slowly. "That's another thing. I didn't give her credit. I figured she'd go bananas. See, all this time I was thinking that she thought I was Mr. Perfection, that the slightest chink in my shiny armor would devastate her. Oh, she was upset. She cried. Said she always trusted me. But, bottom line, she forgave me. Said I was just a man. Everybody's entitled to mistakes. Said she loved me, and that's what counted, and she didn't intend to stop loving me, even if she could. Which she said she couldn't." He smiled. "The girls didn't even blink an eye. I don't know, Brady. Kids nowadays, they see so much, nothing fazes them. We better order."

We wrote our luncheon orders on a slip of paper with pencils provided expressly for the purpose. Our waitress immediately came over and took them from the corner of the table. She paused and said to me, "The pencil, sir?"

I had stuck it into my jacket pocket. I retrieved it and handed it to her. "Sorry," I said. "I didn't intend to steal it."

"It's not a felony," she said, her tone suggesting that it was at least a misdemeanor.

When she left, I said, "I've been feeling bad, Pops."

He smiled. "Yeah. Me too."

"I really thought you did it. I believed you killed Churchill."

"I knew that all the time. It was logical. My own damn fault for not telling you everything."

"Even if you had, I think I still would've thought you did it."

"Hey, look—"

"No, listen," I said. "You've always been a kind of hero to me."

"Ah, shit, Coyne."

"No, really. Even back at Yale. You were this guy, older, been through the war, so damn upright. I mean, none of the rest of us had the same handle on things as you did. Right and wrong. You not only knew the difference but you lived it. And when you became an assistant D.A., and then a judge, and, Jesus, asking me to be your lawyer—well, it was flattering as hell for me. You've got to understand."

"Forget it, Brady, for crissake. This is embarrassing."

"Tough. Hear me out. What happened was, when you told me about your affair with Karen, I was able to rationalize it. It didn't matter to me, because, well, I guess I don't have a very clear morality on such things. But when it began to look like you'd killed Churchill it just knocked the props out from under me. It skewed everything."

"Well," he said, "I didn't kill him."

I nodded. "I know. The point is, I believed you did. I saw you differently, and I don't know if I can go back to seeing you the old way. Something changed. I mean, I thought I knew you. Then I learned I didn't."

He stared at me for a minute. "Same thing happened to me," he said finally, his voice soft and sad. "You mistrusting me, I mean. It's kind of like what Marilee must be feeling about me. You can forgive. But still, nothing's ever the same."

"I want to be your friend."

He nodded. "Sure. We're friends."

"I'll be happy to continue to represent you. But if—"

He held up both hands and grinned. "Christ, Coyne. Nothing ever stays the same. Don't even think about it."

* * *

Gloria was seated sideways on a barstool sipping what looked like a gin and tonic. It was her favorite summer drink, and she was rushing the season by a couple months. Skeeter was down the other end pouring draft beer from a spigot. *Wheel of Fortune* played on the oversize television. The boys down the end were exchanging obscene suggestions on the subject of the blond woman who turned over the letters.

I thought of initiating our little charade with her. "Excuse me, miss. I know we've never met. But I can't help thinking. Would you come to bed with me?" And Gloria would fling her arms around my neck and kiss me wetly on the mouth.

But I detected a rigidity in her back and a subtle tension along the curve of her cheek and neck that warned me off. Gloria wasn't always in the mood for games.

I straddled the empty stool beside her. "Hi," I said.

"Hi." She touched the side of my head and leaned over to kiss me. She brushed my cheek quickly in a way that prevented me from kissing her. Then she straightened away from me. "How've you been?"

"Good. Fine. Has Skeeter offered you his special?"

"He calls it a Don Buddin. Says it'll make you keep dropping things. The active ingredients are vodka and port wine."

"Think I'll stick to Jack Daniel's."

"What happened to that Rebel Yell you were drinking?"

"That was just a phase. I'm back to the tried-and-true. Good old Blackjack."

She sipped her drink. I lit a cigarette. After a minute or so Skeeter came over. "Hey, Mr. Coyne," he said. "How do you like the Sox this year?"

"With that big horse in the bullpen, I think we've got a shot."

"I agree, I agree. Listen. Try a Don Buddin. You remember him."

"A poor shortstop. No, let me have my usual."

He brought me my drink. I raised it to Gloria and we touched glasses. "To your career," I said.

"And yours."

We sipped. "Anything new on the photography front?"

"Even getting shot down by *Life* turns out to be a good thing. Nothing really exciting. But I'm getting a few calls. Word seems to be getting around."

"You're off and running, then," I said. "That's great."

"What about you, Brady? What've you been up to?"

I shrugged. "Nothing much. Been fishing a couple times. Doc Adams and I are going to Connecticut on Sunday."

"You and your trout."

"You eaten?" I said.

She nodded.

We fell silent. I stared down at the top of the bar. From the corner of my eye I watched Gloria's hands on her glass. She was rubbing the condensation on the side with the pad of her forefinger, stroking it in little soft circles. It reminded me . . .

"So what's up?" she said suddenly.

I looked up at her. "What do you mean?"

"You wanted me to meet you. Here I am. What's on your mind?"

I smiled. "Oh, you know . . ."

Her returning smile was weak. "Oh, Brady."

I shrugged. "There was that night—you remember, the storm, you made me the Bloody Mary—"

Her eyes slid down from my face and looked into her glass. She poked at the lime wedge with her forefinger. Then she lifted her finger and touched it to her tongue. "Yeah," she said finally, still looking down. "I thought it was something like that."

"I've felt, I don't know . . ." I smiled.

She raised her eyes. "Nothing has changed, Brady."

I studied her face for a moment. Then I nodded and smiled. "You're wrong," I said. "Everything has changed. It just hasn't changed in the right direction."

We had another round. Gloria talked about Billy and Joey and her plan to repaper the downstairs of the Wellesley house. I got her to laugh when I told her about my client who wanted to alter his will to have his head sent to a cryonics outfit in California when he died. He said it was a lot cheaper than having them freeze the whole body.

When we were done we went out into the balmy April evening. She thrust her arm through mine and we strolled to the lot where she had parked her car. I stood beside her while she unlocked it and slid in. She shut the door and rolled down the window. I leaned down and kissed her on the corner of her mouth. She said, "Keep in touch." Then she started up the engine, waved quickly, and pulled away from the curb.

I watched her drive away. Then I began walking back to my apartment. I sniffed the air. It was ripe and rich with decay and rebirth, even in the city. April. Tomorrow, I decided, we'd hang out the GONE FISHIN' sign.